THE SECRETS OF TREASONFIELD HOUSE

J. C. Briggs

SAPERE
BOOKS

THE SECRETS OF TREASONFIELD HOUSE

Published by Sapere Books.

24 Trafalgar Road, Ilkley, LS29 8HH,
United Kingdom

saperebooks.com

ISBN: 978-0-85495-649-4

Only a story gathered from the hills,
And the wind crying of forgotten days…
'A Preface for a Tale I Have Never Told' by Geoffrey Bache
Smith, killed in action December 1916

PART ONE: 1952

1

Westmorland, England

Marie Beaumont watched the child skipping about the ruins, followed by a puppy, a small, gambolling creature. They looked so innocent, absorbed in their game of what looked like a version of Grandmother's Footsteps, the child sneaking a look at the dog before skipping ahead, then stopping suddenly and freezing. The dog followed, danced round the immobile figure, and barked for attention, not understanding why the little boy covered his face. Then the child was off again, scampering away, leaping over the fallen masonry, his high giggle piercing the heavy silence. A smiling woman appeared with another dog on a lead, and the boy and the puppy ran to her. She heard their laughing voices fade as they walked away, but she didn't move. A happy mother and child, she thought, unburdened by dark memories. Unlike her childhood. No one had come to her smiling with such love. She lit a cigarette and continued to look at the ruins, now just a collection of stones, a few crumbling walls mostly concealed by the ivy, nettles and weeds that had grown over it throughout the long years.

Treasonfield House had burnt down in 1930, long after she had left Hawthorn Park. Aunt Giselle had written to inform Marie of her husband Matthew's accidental death in the fire. She remembered the house from her childhood, still standing, but empty and boarded up then. It had belonged to her uncle's grandfather. Marie was told to stay away. 'It is dangerous,' Aunt Giselle said. 'It is nothing to do with you.' And her lips folded in a tight line, her eyes narrowing in warning. Marie was too frightened of her to disobey. She had never known who had lived there; even Mrs Todd, the housekeeper at Hawthorn Park would not be drawn. 'Tenants,' she had said. 'Foreigners, like your — well, never mind that — they left before the war. Nowt to say about them.' Marie knew by instinct that Mrs Todd didn't like Aunt Giselle. She had wondered if Mrs Todd didn't like her, either, because she was foreign. Not that she really knew what that meant. She only knew in her childish way that she didn't belong.

Mrs Todd repeated the warning, too. 'Have your head knocked off if you go pokin' about there.' But from time to time, she went that way on her bicycle, looking down at the abandoned house. It was so silent and mysterious. Wild nature was beginning to take over, ivy creeping round the windows and the door. Weeds sprouted on the roof and out of the chimney pots; willowherb and buddleia made their home on the terrace, spilling from the time-encrusted urns and from the broken pavement; nettles colonised the flowerbeds and the woods cast a shadow over the place. In the trees, there was an old cottage, also boarded up. Marie had never dared go too near the house or the cottage, which looked as though a witch might live there.

She hadn't thought about the place in years. She had never intended to come back. She wrote to Aunt Giselle from time to time, but life had happened. She lived in London, worked as a translator, married, had children — two. Teenagers now, at home with their father, where she longed to be.

She thought about her uncle. Not a man you could get close to. Not really an uncle, in any case — only by marriage. Aunt Giselle had written, but Marie had not gone to the funeral. Her aunt had made it clear that it would be very quiet. There was no need for Marie to come all the way from London. Marie was relieved. She had not been happy at Hawthorn Park, where Aunt Giselle had lived after her marriage. Marie had been six years old when she had arrived, but she had known somehow that she wasn't wanted, that her aunt had taken her in out of duty. Marie's father — Aunt Giselle's only brother — had died at the end of the war, and Marie had no one else. Her mother was dead, too — she had died when Marie was born. Aunt Giselle had nothing to say about Marie's mother. She didn't want to talk about the war. 'A lot of people died. That's what war does. I do not wish to live in the past.' And her mouth would harden into that tight line, her eyes cold and remote.

Hawthorn Park was a house of secrets, too, like the desolate Treasonfield. Aunt Giselle and Uncle Matthew were always polite, but distant, even with each other — as if they were strangers. Marie thought about them now, Aunt Giselle with her silvery blonde hair and pale blue eyes, very thin and severe about the mouth, Uncle, tall, too, but stooping and awkward because of his leg. She thought of the little boy skipping through the ruined house. Her uncle had been a child at Treasonfield. Impossible to imagine him as a carefree, skipping boy. He had lost a leg in the war. There were other injuries, too. She remembered his thin face, creased with pain, and the white scar against the brown skin, but he walked a good deal — nearly always alone. War left invisible wounds. She knew that. It scarred minds and hearts.

There were rarely any visitors to Hawthorn Park. Marie remembered the Pelhams coming occasionally on their way to somewhere else — Major and Mrs Pelham had known Uncle in the war. They only stayed for lunch, to which Marie was not invited. She ate in the kitchen while Mrs Todd bustled about with plates and dishes. And there was Uncle Ned who came, too. She had liked him. He was kind to her. He laughed a lot.

She remembered hearing Uncle laugh with him as they went out to take their long walks, their heads close together, deep in conversation. She remembered Aunt Giselle's narrowed eyes as she watched them disappear into the woods.

Marie had heard them talking on the terrace one night. Uncle said, 'I made a mistake.' And Uncle Ned said, 'We've all made mistakes. The trick is learnin' to live with them.'

In the silence that followed, Marie heard the chink of glasses. Then her uncle said, 'It's damn near impossible. It might have been different if we'd had a child, but that wasn't to be. She didn't — doesn't... I've suggested that we live apart.'

'She told me, but she won't. You brought her here. She has nowhere else. She can't go back to —'

'I know, I know, but somewhere in England — London, perhaps. I'd support her financially.'

'Well, you can try, but honestly, my lad, I don't think so. She's a determined woman. She had to be in the war.'

'Ruthless, Claire said.'

'She had a hard time.'

There had been no laughter that night. Marie had wondered who Claire was, but she knew better than to ask Aunt Giselle.

Aunt Giselle had stayed. It was true that she had an iron will, as Marie knew very well. When she'd wanted rid of Marie, that was it. At the age of eleven, Marie was to go to school in London. She never went back to Hawthorn Park. Why, she had wondered, why was she not wanted? What had she done? But the childish feelings faded. At school, there were rules, and it was quite clear what would happen if you disobeyed, though she was nervous at first. She had obeyed the rules at Hawthorn Park, but still she had been punished and sent away. Gradually, she came to feel secure. She was good at languages — she knew French, of course, and German came easily to her. Aunt

Giselle came to see her once a term, but their meetings were stiff. Marie knew that her aunt was doing her duty. She only wanted to know if Marie were working hard and behaving well. She always was. Aunt Giselle would nod as if satisfied and Marie would be kissed coldly on both cheeks. Marie was always relieved when the meetings were over.

Uncle Ned came to the school sometimes to take her out to tea, and he took her a few times to see Major and Mrs Pelham, but the connections with them were so tenuous that they didn't last and by the time she was eighteen and ready to spend a year in France, she had not seen them for two years. Uncle Ned stayed in touch and wrote to her, but he didn't come to her wedding, and the relationship dwindled to cards at Christmas, though he never forgot her birthday. Somehow, time went on; she married Geoffrey and was happy, her children came, and she never had time to see Uncle Ned. She thought now that perhaps she just wanted to forget Hawthorn Park and her unhappy life there.

But she was back and on her way to Hawthorn Park, where her aunt was ill. The solicitor had written to say that it was likely that her aunt would die, and he thought that as a beneficiary of the will and the only relative, Marie ought to come. Her aunt had asked to see her.

She shivered in a sudden gust of wind. It was time to go and find out what Aunt Giselle wanted after all these years.

2

There was a man in a dark suit standing on the front steps and looking towards her as Marie drove up. The solicitor, she presumed. Did that mean she was too late? She sat for a moment, feeling her heart beating too fast as her breath caught in her throat. What did she feel? Relief, and then shame for that. Not sorrow, but something that made her hand tremble as she fumbled for the handbrake. The old fear. And a new one. What did Aunt Giselle want of her? Did she have something to tell about Marie's father or her uncle? So many things Marie did not know. She didn't want to know. She took a deep breath, scooped up her handbag and opened the car door.

Looking up, she saw that the man was stocky and grey-haired. She swung out her legs and stood up to see a brown hand reaching out to her, a lined face, and a pair of twinkling grey eyes which seemed familiar.

'Marie,' he said, shaking her hand. A firm, warm grip.

'Uncle Ned! Oh, I am glad to see you.'

'It's been a long time, Marie, since I took you to dinner before you went to France.'

'It is. I'm sorry that I've been such a poor correspondent — you were always kind to me.'

'I understand. Life gets in the way — you've been happy, though? Your husband? Your children? They are well?'

'They are very well, and happy, too. I didn't want to come back. Is she here?'

'She's gone, I'm afraid. Yesterday. The solicitor sent for me a week ago. I was your uncle's executor. There are papers — a lot of them.'

'Oh, apparently, she wanted to see me —'

'It's a shock, I know, but come in. There's tea. Mrs Punch has set it in the drawing room.'

Everything was the same in the oak-panelled hall, the stone flags on the floor, the faded Persian carpet, the brassware by the hearth, the stone fireplace and mantel, intricately carved with garlands, above which were the two pairs of stags' horns and the pewter plates. There were the two oak chairs on which no one ever sat, the grandfather clock, the light pouring through the stained-glass window at the top of the first flight of stairs, behind which was tucked the little nook where the telephone was hidden. She looked up, half expecting to see Aunt Giselle coming down in her severe blue dress, her silvery blonde hair drawn back, her pale eyes looking coldly down at the child sitting on the window seat. Marie remembered always being at a loss, never knowing what to do with herself, waiting to be instructed.

Giselle was gone, but the clock ticked on. Time, inexorable and indifferent to human life. However, Marie felt her absence, she who had been the dominating presence in the house, her swift tapping feet heard on the stairs, coming from the library or from the kitchen downstairs, her voice authoritative and determined, giving orders to Mrs Todd, or the housemaid, Punch. Punch, she thought, the maid, who had been in awe of Aunt Giselle — perhaps she was housekeeper now. Mrs Todd must be dead — she would be too old to run this house now anyway. She had been devoted to Uncle and had treated Marie with a sort of rough kindness, but Marie doubted that Mrs Todd had missed her when she went. And Mr Todd. They'd both be in their seventies now. She remembered Uncle and Mr Todd often together about the grounds. Mr Todd had been kind to her, looked as if he felt sorry for her, but he had not answered her questions about Treasonfield either.

The drawing room was the same, too. She remembered the plasterwork frieze with the odd little faces among the vines — faces which had seemed to look at her accusingly. The pictures were still there, the one above the mantel depicting a ruined house in the moonlight with hills behind. She'd often wondered what lay behind the great oak door. Secrets, she thought now, secrets behind every door. Today the terrace doors were open, light curtains moving in the breeze as if someone had just left the room. Ned Turner stood waiting for her. When she was seated on the familiar chintz-covered sofa, he sat by the oak gate-legged table where Giselle had used to preside. She recognised the silver teapot. Aunt Giselle had always insisted on a formal afternoon tea — little sandwiches and cakes, fine china, cups you could see through if you held them up. Marie had seen nothing like them before, nor the silver sugar bowl with silver tongs to pluck out your piece of sugar, nor the silver cream jug.

As Ned filled her cup, she remembered how frightened she had been of touching anything. The only homes she had known were shabby apartments in back streets in Nyon and Geneva. They had never stayed anywhere for long. Her father was always shabby, too, smoking and drinking and starting at every footstep on the stair. He never mentioned her mother, but various women came and went. They were sometimes kind, sometimes not. She remembered Giselle coming sometimes. She gave Marie's father money. She paid hardly any attention to Marie. Marie had never belonged anywhere until she had met Geoffrey and had her own children.

'Sugar and milk?' Ned asked.

'Just milk, thank you.'

They sipped their tea for a few moments, then Ned said, 'I'm sorry you were too late.'

'I hadn't heard from her for months — a Christmas card. Duty, I suppose. She had no feelings for me.' And then she surprised herself. 'I don't think she had feelings for anyone, really. How did she die? She wasn't so old.'

'Fifty-seven. Cancer, I'm afraid. She was much younger than I am. I'm seventy-two now.'

'When did you come?'

'A few days ago. She wanted to give me my instructions and some papers.'

'Why did she want me to come? She didn't want me at Uncle's funeral. She never wanted me here at all.'

'I think she wanted to see you. She talked about the past, about her brother and his death.'

'I never knew what happened to him. He never came back one night. I was only six; a neighbour found me and wrote to Aunt, and then I was sent here — sent like a parcel. What happened to him?'

'He was shot, trying to escape arrest — he'd deserted from the Swiss Army.'

She looked at Ned, shocked. 'That's why he was always frightened. A coward, I suppose.'

'Not necessarily. They were conscripts, badly paid and badly treated. Someone must have betrayed him.'

'Who? Giselle? She never seemed to like him.'

'I don't believe that. Life was complicated in Geneva. The Germans were everywhere, and there were Swiss people who sided with them. It was often hard to say who was on which side. Giselle protected her brother and you as best she could, but she was involved in politics and put herself in danger, too, and then things happened that caused her to leave Geneva.'

'What things?'

'It's a long story, Marie. I knew most of it before I came back this time, but there are some things I didn't know, which explain why things went so badly wrong for Giselle and your uncle.'

'And for me. I could never understand her, or Uncle. His death was an accident, she said, the fire at Treasonfield, and she never mentioned him again. I know Uncle was a child there, but there was always some mystery about it. No one lived there. No one went there. Why was he there? What happened at Treasonfield?'

'Mrs Punch will give us supper and then I'll tell you everything.'

3

Marie went upstairs after they had tea. Uncle Ned said he wanted a walk and a smoke. He needed to think, and walking was the best thing he knew to get the brain in gear.

On the landing, Marie paused outside Giselle's bedroom, thinking about that severe face frowning at her, her tongue clicking impatiently, her brusque, 'Go out and play, for goodness' sake. I'm busy.'

What was wrong with me? What had I done? I was a child, she thought. A harmless, homeless child, her niece. Surely, that should have meant something. 'She had a hard time,' Uncle Ned had said that time when she was eavesdropping. What had happened to Giselle that had made her — ruthless, uncle had said. No, Claire had said that. Who was Claire? She had heard the name only once.

She had never been in Giselle's bedroom, which was always kept locked. She tried the door now, pushed and went in. The curtains were closed and there was the scent of lilies already decaying. The coffin was on trestles, its lid leaning against the chest of drawers. Would the dead face tell her anything?

The silver hair was drawn back from the face, which looked as though it were carved in ivory. The chin and nose were sharper than before. Giselle had not been exactly beautiful but fascinating in her remoteness and elegance. Her dress was unadorned dark blue, the kind she had often worn which had always given her that impression of severity. She was as austere in death as in life, and as unreadable. The colourless lips were folded, and the ice-blue eyes closed for eternity, not that they ever gave anything away. The face told her nothing about the self-contained woman who had lived here for almost thirty years, and who had kept her secrets. She had suffered and had been in danger, her marriage had been unhappy, and that was all Marie knew about her. Now she was gone, her secrets contained behind this ivory mask. Who was Giselle Favre?

Ned puffed on his pipe as he prowled the gardens of Hawthorn Park. How much to tell Marie? Everything, he supposed. It was always the best way. Secrets ate away at people's lives, those who kept them and those who told them. Marie would be shattered, but then she had been hurt already. Thank the Lord, she'd made a good marriage, and her children were happy. Perhaps they'd escape the legacy of Treasonfield and the war. The Great War — not the last one. Marie's children would have been too young to take part in that. Seven years since it had ended. He'd played a part — a desk job. Secret stuff, of course. He'd been too old to go tearing about France again. Not that he'd wanted to. It had been good to use his brain, to be a part of the victory over Hitler. Good Lord, it had been appalling to realise that they'd have to go to war again against the same enemy, but the second war had had its beginning in the first. Those who had watched the rise of Hitler had known that.

Ned thought about Treasonfield and the dark night in February 1918 when he had first gone there, sent on intelligence business by his old friend, Guy Pelham, who had been working at British Army General Headquarters in France. Major in the Intelligence Branch. Whispers of treason in high places. Whispers about a German spring offensive. Whispers of defeat. What a time it had been. Everything uncertain. Everything hush-hush, which was why he had arrived with a lorry in the dead of night to a house, hidden in the woods in remote Westmorland, in the parish of Middlethorp. He remembered the room in which the dead man had been found — an English gentleman's study. Oak-panelled with an arched fireplace. A massive leather-topped desk, of course, with a silver inkstand. Decanters on a highly polished oak table by the window. Ironic, really. The man hadn't been English at all, and certainly not a gentleman, unlike Sir Roland Riviere, who had lived at Hawthorn Park where Giselle now lay dead, leaving him to carry the burden of her last secrets.

Treasonfield. Just a ruin now, but that was where it had all begun on that winter's night. Ned thought it had ended on the night of the fire. He had thought it was sunset from a distance when he saw the red glow, but as he came closer, he had seen the flames tearing at the sky and the smoke billowing. He had stood stock-still, horrified at the sound of explosions, momentarily taken back to France — a bomb? Bombs? And then he had careered down the slope, blundering through the trees, stumbling along the gravelled drive, seeing the great tongues of flame coming from windows and doors, realising that the explosions were breaking glass and that Treasonfield was collapsing before his eyes. The sound of cracking timbers and falling stone was sickening. Mr Todd came running. They could do nothing but watch. But they thought it was all right — the house was empty. Except it wasn't, and they were too late.

They'd had to wait through days of rain until the firemen declared it safe to search. Ned had been astonished by Giselle's composure. Her husband was dead, and she hadn't seemed surprised.

'It had better be an accident,' she said.

He could scarcely believe his ears. 'You think it wasn't? Had something happened?'

'How do I know? He did not confide in me.'

'What was he doing at Treasonfield? He loathed the place.'

Giselle's expression was cold. 'If he wasn't in the graveyard, he was there. In that room. Blaming himself, trying to work out what he could have done differently.'

'That man was dead, and that wasn't his fault. The man was a traitor — we had to do something — it was our —'

She interrupted impatiently. 'Duty. I know that. It was about her. It was I who saved her, but that didn't matter because I was alive, and she was dead — she was just a girl —' She took a deep breath. 'I do not wish to speak of it. An accident. Very — unfortunate.'

Ned watched Giselle go upstairs, straight-backed and implacable. However, he accepted it. What was the point of raking everything up? A brave man's life to be picked over, his reputation to be tarnished.

As he thought about Treasonfield and the ruin it was now, Ned wondered. Had he known then what he knew now, would he have acted differently? Could he have prevented the fire? He had no idea. He only knew that the war's long shadow had affected his friend so that he believed he had nothing to live for.

His pipe had gone out, but he stood for a few moments more looking at the high fells where the sky was turning dark grey. The wind swooped down, rocking the treetops. Treasonfield over there through the woods. He saw the house as it was then in his mind's eye, the dead man shot through the mouth, the gun on the floor beside him. Treasonfield, France, Flanders, Geneva, London. Treasonfield again.

Ned turned away and walked slowly back to the house, revolving many memories. Marie would be waiting, and he had a story to tell. Some of it he knew first-hand, most of it from Claire and Matthew. And the last chapter from Giselle. But where to begin? France, he supposed, and a chance meeting between two young men at war.

PART TWO: 1918

4

Gouzeaucourt, France

It was as if they were alone. He had no idea how long it had been, but it seemed a long while, as if they were out of time, removed to some infinity. There was silence, too. Impossible that these two men should meet here where there were hundreds of thousands of men converging on a line which might determine the outcome of the war, the line from Ypres in the north to the south, beyond Verdun to the Swiss border, where the French army was gathered. And there couldn't be silence here. There was always something: the thudding of the guns somewhere; the distant crump of a shell; the whoosh of a rocket; the buzz of an aircraft, someone on a spying sortie; even the rumble of a faraway train — the sound of the Germans moving transport up to their front line.

But in a sudden silence, Matthew Riviere saw him. The smoke from the Mills grenades they'd chucked into the dugout cleared for a moment. Impossible, but he was there. In the misty moonlight — but there had been no moon on that night of the raid. The light of a star shell, then. He couldn't remember now, but Stephen was there. It was his face under his helmet all awry, his hand holding his pistol, his blue-eyed gaze fixed on Matthew. Stephen Lang knew Matthew and Matthew knew him. And that was impossible, too. Stephen's helmet was a German helmet, and he had leapt from the German outpost that they had attacked.

And then the searing pain in his arm. The tearing of his lungs. A sudden shock of light or fire. The blast of an explosion. The smell of earth and sulphur, the smell of hell. After that, nothing until the Advanced Dressing Station where he shifted between consciousness and unconsciousness, hardly aware of where he was, not knowing if he were dreaming a face that seemed to appear and dissolve into smoke, or if the voices he heard were real or in the dream. Someone nearby was crying out, indistinct words of terror and pain, but he didn't know that voice.

If he did wake from his morphine-induced sleep, he felt the crashing pain in his head and arm and remembered only that he had seen Stephen, and that could not possibly be true.

Had he seen a ghost there among the dead faces, the skulls, the skeleton hands pointing to the sky, the wire and the mud, the smoke, and the silence? Had he seen a dead man, like the ones he sometimes saw — still upright, unmarked as if carved in wax, but dead of shock? Or had he imagined a living man who was like Stephen?

5

Ytres, France

Claire Mallory shot to her feet, banged down her cup of Bovril, dragged on her coat, and ran out of the hut, jamming on her cap. She'd heard the commandant's whistle, and that meant casualties.

Things had been relatively quiet recently at Casualty Clearing Station 21; the clearing stations had been moved back from the old front line; base hospitals had been emptied of all but the most serious cases; many who had hoped for a Blighty wound which would have sent them home were held back. They were needed when they were well enough. All leave was cancelled. There was a palpable tension in the air, from the outposts of the front line and the field-ambulance dugouts to the brigade and divisional headquarters, the General Headquarters in Montreuil-sur-Mer, and the hospitals in the big towns. It was as if everyone were holding a collective breath, holding themselves still in readiness for what they knew was coming. There was to be a spring offensive by the Germans, but where and when no one knew. There were rumours, of course, which added to the tension.

The airmen made perilous forays behind the German lines, braving the anti-aircraft shells to bring back reports that the Germans were strengthening their front line, building trenches and gun positions. Transport was on the move over there. Troops were being moved from the Eastern Front. Supply dumps were being constructed, new roads, bridges, camps, hospital tents. Germany was clearly on the defensive or preparing for an attack in March. Maybe sooner. Maybe later. Reports came in from captured prisoners, but they were contradictory; one prisoner was certain that the attack was to be made from his sector, while another was sure that the push would come from his unit, which would be at the head of the assault. The German Command made certain that each soldier believed that his sector would start the offensive.

Where? That was the anxious question. Up behind Arras or down at La Fere, where the Fifth Army was adjacent to the French lines? Such junctions were always a weak point. Or further south, where the French army were expecting the offensive at Verdun? The Flesquières Salient opposite Cambrai, maybe, or south of Gouzeaucourt where General Byng's Third Army met the Fifth, another vulnerable point in the line of defence. The Somme? Dread name. St Quentin? Wherever it came, it would mean trains going to the base hospitals at Amiens or Abbeville from the casualty clearing stations and long ambulance convoys ferrying the wounded from the trains as they had back in November 1917.

The Germans had retreated behind the Hindenburg Line by the end of 1917, leaving destruction in their wake. Railways and bridges smashed, roads mined and cratered, fields and orchards flooded, livestock stolen, trees cut down, buildings booby-trapped and wells poisoned, castles stripped and blown up, villages and their churches dynamited, houses burned, the population scattered or taken prisoner. A world vanished. Scorched earth, smoke and flames were all that was left. A mutilated and monstrous landscape. No Man's Land, indeed. Nothing left to aid the enemy.

The winter which followed was one of the harshest ever known, though the iron grip on the land was a relief from the rain and mud of 1917. But even in quiet times, there were always casualties. The shelling was infrequent but still dangerous, and the guns still roared and flashed. By February there were casualties from machine-gun fire across the front line where the British infantrymen, sappers, and engineers heaved their picks and axes to shore up the old German trenches, rebuild fire steps and parapets, erect miles of barricades, wire the machine gun posts, mend gaps in the wire, establish depots and billets, repair roads, rebuild railway track, and transport ammunition — the Lewis guns, the trench mortars, and the hundreds of thousands of shells — to the ammunition dumps. Sometimes a dump was shelled, or a convoy of supplies or weapons. Horse lines were bombed from the air. Roads were blown up, leaving craters in the surface.

The Germans had maps. They knew where the roads were, and they knew what the British soldiers were doing along the front line where machine-gun fire answered the incautious sound of a wiring party. In one incident a platoon making its way up to the front had lost a quarter of its men, and there were casualties of night patrols and raiding parties. All along the line, patrols and raiding parties haunted No Man's Land, crawling on hands and knees in the dark, listening, ducking bullets, freezing to stillness in the light of a star shell, waiting for the signal to advance. Two soldiers had been killed and one lost a leg from a German booby trap — a delayed action mine. Impossible to tell the difference between a long delay fuse and an ordinary one without examining it closely.

The thaw was beginning; ice cracked underfoot in the trenches, water began to rise and duckboards to shift, then the rain came and filled the trenches and dugouts. The working parties crept through shell holes full of mud to secure strongpoints. An inadvertent noise brought the rattle of machine-gun fire, but that didn't yet mean that the attack had begun. The land wouldn't dry until April. The Americans would arrive in strength before then. Surely before April. March, maybe. Where, though? When?

Now on this bitter February night of sleet and rain, Claire felt a shock of alarm. Had it started? How many casualties?

The others on night duty were right behind Claire, huddling into their coats, skidding in the mud, reaching the ambulances — hoping the damned things would start — hearing the news, listening to the instructions. Their usual job was to drive to the dressing stations, pick up the wounded and bring them back to their casualty clearing station in the railway sidings at Ytres several miles behind the front line. At the CCS, the patients would be treated and sent back to the line if they recovered well enough, or they might be operated on and then evacuated by train to a base hospital at Amiens. If they were seriously incapacitated — amputees, or blinded, or gassed — they were sent on to Boulogne, from where they were shipped back to England if they would not recover in time for what was to come.

An ammunition dump had been shelled. Casualties then, Claire thought. Where? At Ruyaulcourt, north along the road to Hermies. Half an hour away — longer, of course, in winter, along the shelled and pitted road, but they were cranking the engines in minutes, the orderlies on board, then the drivers of this Red Cross ambulance convoy. Claire cursed the wretched crank, trying again, hefting the handle, scarcely breathing, waiting for the engine to start. She was last in the line. She heard the others start off and then the engine coughed, faltered a moment, stuttered to life, and she was in her seat, turning the wheel when the commandant put her hand on the door.

'Mallory, wait a minute. I need you to go to Hermies. Dressing station has a casualty which needs to be brought here. Been shot — possibly in the head. A couple of other casualties too, walking cases, I think. Some sort of raiding party.'

Claire watched as the rest of the convoy worked its way out of the railway sidings, leaving behind the CCS, the huts, the two canteens in marquees, the ruined village of Ytres. It followed the Canal du Nord towards Ruyaulcourt, about five miles away, bouncing in potholes, struggling on the swampy road through the ravaged landscape of devastated villages, tumbledown farms, crippled trees, and craters. Ahead, the sky was lit with flames from the explosions at the ammunition dump. Claire was sorry to see the convoy turn away — not that she wanted to go with them to what would be a scene of devastation. She could imagine the burns casualties. But still she felt the loneliness of the road ahead which led up to a ridge and, another five miles on, Hermies. Climbing, the engine groaned and wheezed, but she put her foot down hard and gripped the steering wheel more tightly. 'Please God,' she prayed, 'don't let me break down here.'

Here was a place of slaughter. Forty-five thousand men killed, wounded, or missing after the Battle of Cambrai at the end of last year. The tanks were supposed to be invincible, and they had broken through, but the German counterattack had prevailed. The casualties had been dreadful — so many burns and gas cases. The doctors had done what they could at the CCS, but many had died, and many had to be sent to the base hospitals at Amiens or Abbeville — it had been terrible seeing them off on the trains, knowing many would never come back.

The names repeated in Claire's head: Havrincourt, Ribécourt, Graincourt, Gouzeaucourt, Flesquières, and Hermies, where she remembered the cemetery with its malformed trees like skeletons in the dead land, the heaped soil and mud, the rows of plain wooden crosses and the hollow clang of the spade. The funerals were desolate occasions. So many plain deal coffins under their Union Jacks, the grey-faced chaplain who had seen too much, his words snatched away by the wind, vanishing into a distance where there was still the sound of guns. There were prayers which seemed hopeless in that wasteland of death and suffering, and the sound of 'The Last Post', so haunting and heartbreaking, making a hollow inside you, as if hope were gone from the world. Claire had thought about the thousands unburied, the corpses thick in field and wood, and she wondered what it was all for. Then she had to stop wondering, for the whistle went and she had her duty to do, which was so exhausting and terrifying at times that there was no time to think.

Claire could hardly see. Rain and sleet sliced straight into her face, or was it hail, or just stones churned up from the road? A windscreen would have been handy, but the ambulances didn't boast such luxuries. Their only protection was the red crosses on the canvas hoods and the sides of the vans. The drivers sat in their open cabs, exposed to the elements and hoping that a stray shell from either side wouldn't come crashing down on their heads. Damn! She felt the sting of a stone just below her eye.

There was a tin hat somewhere on the floor. She should have put it on. The drivers had to wear their caps for muster, or the commandant would have something to say — she who looked as if she slept standing upright, if she slept at all. Never a crease in her skirt. Her tie never askew as Claire's was now. Thank goodness it hadn't been noticed. Claire's skirt hadn't looked very smart, either, but her long blue coat covered the crumples. A skirt, though. All right on parade, but impractical in the field. But that was the Red Cross rule, and you had to pay for your uniform and kit, with no choice in what you wore. Trousers would have been much more sensible. They put on overalls to service the vans — a driver was responsible for the smooth running and maintenance of her ambulance, but sometimes you had to get the camp mechanic, and it wasn't always your fault if it didn't start. Freezing weather didn't help.

Water dripped from the canvas hood. Claire felt its icy slide down her collar. The steering wheel was wet, and her damp gloved hands slipped suddenly so that she nearly lost control and had to wrench the wheel straight. She stopped for a moment, feeling her heart thump. The immensity of the dark emptiness around her was nearly overwhelming. She put her foot on the accelerator again and felt the ambulance crawl forward. The road was going upwards. *Steady*, she thought to herself. She felt the wheels slipping, the gears grinding, but she was nearing the top of the ridge, and she hadn't been shelled or shot at — yet. To the right, she could see the dark shape of what must be the remains of Havrincourt Wood, which meant she would be descending in a minute or two. Somewhere over there, she thought, looking into the distance, an army was massing under the heavy sky. There were young men behind the enemy lines, too. There'd be new recruits, eighteen or so, perhaps, ready to maim, to kill, to die for their cause just as on this side, the same preparations were being made. Thousands of guns, hundreds of thousands, no, millions of shells. A star shell lit up the edge of a cloud mass. *A sign*, she thought, or a warning of some horror to come, and no one was heeding it.

The wheels slipped in the mud, and she was going downhill. She put her foot on the break gently and kept the ambulance in first gear. No madcap race to the bottom. That had happened before when she'd been surprised by a steep gradient and ended up in a ditch. She heard the boom of distant guns, the rumble of heavy traffic and the rattle of a train. She knew where she was and crawled down to the distant lights of the dressing station at Hermies to collect her patients.

6

Matthew Riviere forced himself to think logically. That would be better than imagining a ghost in the smoke. It would be better than thinking about his wound. He had been shot twice — by whom, he couldn't remember. The first shot had scraped his cheek — there'd been a lot of blood, but the bullet had whizzed past. His arm was bloody painful; he couldn't move it, though the doc here had got the bullet out. He knew where he was — the CCS at Ytres. He had been stretchered to the dressing station. Ambulance from there, he presumed. What he didn't know was how long recovery would take. He didn't want to go to Abbeville or Amiens. He wanted to go back on duty. And he wanted to know what had happened in the raid.

Go back to the beginning, he thought. *Put the events in order. Remember how it began, and then the raid itself might become clear.* The idea was to capture a German from behind the Flesquières Salient, which formed a bulge in the Hindenburg Line where they all knew the enemy was active. Time was getting on. Reports were contradictory. Everyone wanted to know when and where the attack would take place. The adjutant major came down from Battalion HQ with the colonel's message for Captain Matthew Riviere to the company's dugout behind the little rise beyond Gouzeaucourt.

A table with the map spread out. A bottle of whisky, two glasses. Matthew hung onto the details. Mud on a pair of boots. Clean breeches. Leather cross belting. Gleaming buttons. The major coming down the earth steps. Ammo boxes to sit on. Whisky poured. Candles in bottles. Shadows on the ceiling. Cigarette smoke curling to meet the shadows.

The smell of earth and sweat, petrol, smoke, and onions. He could smell it all now.

Matthew and the major had looked at the map. Below the rise which would give them some cover was a bit of brush and old tree stumps — safe enough if anything went awry, and beyond the rise where the Lewis gun would be, about one hundred and twenty yards away, was the German front line. Matthew's sentry had heard noises and a patrol in No Man's Land had heard voices. Something was up over there, he agreed.

'The weather?' he asked.

'Rain expected, so plenty of cloud cover. Should be all right. Trench mortars will hole the wire before you go. Wind's all right. Smoke bombs will cover you. A few minutes, that's all. Nab one if you can. We're desperate to know. GHQ thinks the thrust of the assault will be against the First and Third Armies, and if the Germans break through, you know what that means.'

'The Channel ports,' Matthew said, knowing that GHQ would fear for the supply of troops, ammunition, and food, all of which came through Calais, Dunkirk, and Boulogne. Fifty miles from the front.

'Byng thinks it might be us. So does the colonel. See what you can do, Captain Riviere. Pick a few good men.'

As if he'd pick any other kind, Matthew thought, but he didn't say anything. Neither the major nor the colonel, nor General Byng for that matter, would want to hear anything that sounded like doubt. And he didn't doubt the necessity of finding out about the German offensive. But the thing was, he didn't want to waste any of his good men. He wasn't at all sure. Beyond that rise the ground was a swamp with a bloody great shell hole in it, and if the wire wasn't holed — that happened

— or the raiding party came under fire, then they'd get nothing. And if they got through, the prisoners' evidence was always so contradictory. It might be some gibbering lad who knew nothing at all, and more than one of his own men might die for that.

'Something worrying you, Riviere?' asked the major, interrupting his thoughts.

Matthew looked at the pale, long-nosed face of the adjutant major. He made it sound so easy. 'No, sir, just getting the lie of the land.'

The major clinked glasses. 'Good man. Here's luck. The colonel will be delighted if you get one.'

Odd, Matthew thought now, distracted again. He couldn't remember the man's name or face, only an impression of a long nose and the black pencil moustache. Oh, and the uniform, clean and newly pressed. A looking-down-the-nose sort of chap.

Matthew asked for volunteers. Eight good men, one other officer, Lieutenant Cropper. All safe and sound, so Cropper had reported, or so Matthew thought. He thought Cropper had come to see him, but maybe he'd imagined that. He shook his head. It was as if his brain was filled with fog which cleared sometimes to show him the images he remembered. *So, stick to the order of things*, he thought. Dusk falling. Hot tea. Rum for the lads. Each man with a rifle and bayonet. Fifty rounds and two Mills grenades in their tunic pockets, the detonators checked. Smoke bombs to flush them out of the enemy dugout. Woollen caps — tin hats could make a noise. Hands and faces blackened with burnt cork. Revolvers for him and Cropper, tied to their lanyards.

Plenty of smoke from the trench mortars and smoke bombs from behind. On hands and knees up the incline. Noting the

Lewis gun. Hargreaves lying there. Good man. Wouldn't let them down. Slithering down the slope. Pretty good hole in the wire — enough to get through. Crawling across No Man's Land. Sixty yards, the map showed. In and out. Knife through butter, according to the major. Nice surprise for the Jerries in their hole. Nothing stirring opposite. Waiting. Listening. Freezing where they were as a Verey light went up from further behind the German line. Blowing the whistle. Rushing to the trench. Thick white smoke suddenly. A face. Stephen's face, more vivid than the adjutant major's, or Cropper's or even Hargreaves' by his Lewis gun. And then fire and pain.

What had happened to the German? That's what he had to find out. Of course, it couldn't have been Stephen. Yet how was it that Stephen's face looked out at him as clear as any photograph? And then he remembered the clear blue eyes. Stephen's eyes. And Stephen had known him. Lord, his head ached.

Was he dreaming? Sister looked at his restless face. She touched his bruised forehead. 'Temperature still too high,' she said. Not Trench Fever, thankfully, but fever, nonetheless. Infection? Pneumonia setting in? He'd have to be sent to a base hospital if that fever didn't abate.

Claire looked down at Matthew Riviere, asleep in his steel bed, and her heart turned over. She hadn't seen him for months. There were lines on his brow that had not been there before the war. The beloved face looked older but then so did she, and so did everyone else for that matter. Worn out, she thought, trying not to cough — she'd been coughing for days. It was a damned nuisance the way it came back, especially at night when she wanted to sleep. She was conscious, too, of her hair bundled under her cap, the cut on her cheek from that flying stone, and the grey pallor of her own face, which she had glimpsed briefly in the mirror as she had adjusted her tie. She had been careful, this time, to look as smart as she could in case Madam Commandant saw her and put her on fatigue duty. Sending someone to clean the lavatories was one of her favourites.

Matthew was frowning in his sleep. A restless sleep. He was in pain, perhaps, or dreaming of the front. His lips were moving and his eyelids were flickering as if he were about to wake, then his head shifted on the pillow and his eyes closed again. Sister had let Claire come in because she knew him and had brought him back from the dressing station.

The sight of him had shaken her to her heart's core. There had been three casualties from the raid. Two privates had been slightly injured. Only the officer was a serious case. He had been brought by stretcher to the ambulance, his head swathed in bandages, his face black, and his arm and shoulder strapped up. She hadn't known then. One of the orderlies came back with her. She couldn't drive and look after the patient at the same time. The medical officer at the dressing station said the orderly could find a lift back, and anyhow things had quietened down. They could spare him for a few hours.

Claire was glad to know that the orderly was there. The journey back from Hermies took place in even heavier rain, which beat down like lead shot on her canvas hood and forced her to crawl like a snail back up the ridge. Every judder and bounce, and every crash of the gears appalled her. The descent was worse than on the outward journey. She kept her foot on the brake and hoped she wouldn't stall or stick in a pothole or turn over in a ditch at the side of the road. It wasn't much comfort to think of the axe and shovel in the footwell. Digging oneself out on a night like this would be near-impossible.

It took nearly two hours to get back. The orderly looked cheerful enough, but then he'd been out of the rain and the patient hadn't made any noise. *Morphine*, Claire thought. Sometimes they screamed and shouted because of the pain. Some turned mad, some wept uncontrollably, but the orderly thought he'd had an easy ride this time, though he felt for the young woman whose exhausted face he saw in the light as she got out of her cab when they stopped at the entrance for stretcher cases.

Two orderlies came out for the stretcher, and it was then that the patient's arm slipped down to reveal something she recognised, but before Claire had a chance to look again, the patient was out of her hands. The ambulance had to be parked and she'd gone back to the hut. There was breakfast in the mess room, hot tea and bacon sandwiches, and she was glad of the warmth of the paraffin stoves. She was only sorry that she'd have to go out again to clean up the ambulance before she could snatch an hour or two in her bed. If there were no other calls later in the morning, she'd go and see him. It was Matthew's hand she had seen with the diagonal scar across the palm from the base of the thumb to the little finger, the scar and the hand that she knew as well as her own.

She remembered exactly when that had happened. She and Matthew and Stephen had been fishing. It was one of those occasions when Stephen and his mother were paying a visit from Switzerland. On the way back through the woods at Treasonfield, Matthew had tripped and cut his hand badly on the bottle of lemonade that had smashed as he fell. It was Stephen's quick thinking that had saved Matthew. He'd plugged the gash with his handkerchief and held it to staunch the pumping blood while Claire had run to the house for help. She hadn't thought of Stephen for years. She wondered what he was doing in the war. Matthew would know, although he might not have been back to Treasonfield during the war. Why would he? It had never really been his home. He hadn't wanted to stay there after his mother's death.

Matthew stirred and opened his eyes. His face lit up. 'Claire, oh, Claire, you're a sight for sore eyes. Where on earth did you spring from?'

7

Claire smiled at Matthew. 'We're being moved about — where we might be needed, I suppose. I was down at Roye, but some of us have been posted here in case —'

'No one knows — yet. That was what the raid was about. Trying to nab a German.'

'Did you?'

'I saw one but then I was shot, so I don't know what happened. I seem to remember my lieutenant coming to the dressing station to tell me that all the raiding party were all right. No serious injuries, but I wasn't in any fit state to ask about any prisoners. I don't know if he told me. I can't really remember if Cropper came, or if I dreamt him. I can't remember anything much.'

'Concussion, I'll bet, and fever, Sister told me. She says you still have a temperature.'

'How did you know I was here?'

'I brought you back in my ambulance. They sent an orderly with me.'

'Lord, fancy it being you, and I too gaga to notice.'

'Morphine, I should think. How are you feeling now?'

'Deadly. The pain's bearable, but I don't know what the timeline's going to be — whether I'll be fit enough to get back.'

Claire looked critically at the cheek with its dressing and the strapped-up shoulder and arm. She thought about what Sister had told her. The bullet had been extracted and the wound disinfected, but the shoulder and arm would take time to heal.

'The doctor will come and tell you, I'm sure, but in a few weeks, I should think.'

'Will they send me to Amiens or Abbeville?'

'Depends on the X-rays. In the meantime, is there anything I can do for you? Something from the canteen, cigarettes, chocolate? Do you want me to write to Sir Roland, or your stepfather?'

'Papa Willy? No thanks. We don't correspond these days. As to grandfather, not yet. Not until I know what's what. I wrote before we went up the line, so he knows I'm all right.'

'They might send you to England, you know, to recuperate.'

'What a waste. And I've come so far... To miss this next crucial part, it's rotten. I can't help thinking that raid was no use. All this for nothing.'

'Unless your party did find a prisoner.'

'Could you get to Battalion HQ for me, at Beaumetz?'

'I'd need permission. Our commandant's strict about these things. She likes to know where we are, and I'll have to find a lift. There'll be someone off duty with a lorry or car.'

'Could you...' Matthew faltered. He didn't want to say about Stephen. It was mad. Claire would think... But if a prisoner had been taken and she asked to see him then he'd know, and if it were not Stephen, he could put it down to fever — or something.

Claire could see he was struggling with something. She understood him so well. He felt guilty and ashamed that he'd had to abandon his men. And to be out of action would hurt him. He'd said once that he'd long lost any faith in the idea of honour or right, or the cause of God on their side, but he had to go on. That's what they all thought. Go on for those who'd died. Otherwise, the betrayal would be of the dead with whom they'd fought and suffered. Go on for the living men, too, the ones who stood by your side. Poor darling. She took his scarred hand and gave it a brief kiss. 'I'm sorry.' She turned his hand over and looked at the silver line bisecting his palm and thought of the future. 'You'll be all right, but it will take time. I knew it was you when I saw the scar. My heart turned over.'

'Do you ever think … about Stephen?'

'How funny that you should ask that. I thought about him and Treasonfield when I saw your hand. I remembered that day — we were fishing.'

'I remember. A good day, until I ruined it.'

'Stephen was decent, though, even if he didn't care much for our company.'

Matthew grimaced. 'No, he was older. Didn't want to be around kids. He was a brick to stay and staunch the blood, but he made it clear he thought me an idiot.'

Claire watched his face. His eyes looked haunted. Thinking of his mother, perhaps, and Treasonfield where he had not been happy. The fingers of his scarred hand plucked at the sheets. 'Is something wrong?' she asked.

'It's why I want you — just you — to go to HQ. I saw him.'

'Who? Stephen? Has something happened to him?'

'I don't know. You'll think I'm mad — in the raid, we chucked our grenades to flush them out so we could nab one, and I saw — I thought I saw — Stephen in a German helmet, pointing his revolver at me. I saw his eyes. I think he knew me. It seems impossible, but, Claire, I need to know if I imagined him.'

'But where was he before? I mean, before the war?'

'In Vienna, as far as I know, and then Greta went to Switzerland — for her health, it seems, leaving Papa Willy all on his tod, so grandfather told me. I didn't take much notice. Treasonfield was all over for me by then.'

'But they're Swiss — neutral, so why would he —'

'Swiss-German, studying in Austria. Why would he support England? Claire, I need to know. I can't understand it. Why would I see him? It's not that I miss him or even think about him.'

'It could be simply that the German you saw looked like him, and the mind can play odd tricks. It's strange how people come to mind when you aren't conscious of thinking about them. Something triggers the memory. Remember Doctor Wesel and all that stuff about the subconscious he used to spout? Weasel, you called him —'

Matthew smiled at that memory. 'To annoy Stephen. Anyway, he looked like a weasel.'

'Stoatally,' Claire flashed back, remembering the old joke.

Matthew's face darkened. 'It was on Wesel's advice that Greta went to Switzerland, apparently. An Austrian, one of Papa Willy's buddies. I thought he was a crank, always closeted away with Greta, discussing her nerves, and Stephen following his lead in Vienna. They got on *my* nerves, I can tell you. I wonder, though…'

'What?'

'There was a lot of anti-German feeling before the war. Think of those headlines, "Enemies in England" and all that sort of thing. Uncomfortable for Papa Willy, and for Greta, maybe, a British citizen by marriage, but her loyalties might lie elsewhere. I never trusted her. I think … I think she was Papa Willy's mistress — all that time, when my mother… That's why she and I went back to grandfather's house. Grandfather hinted at it once, but he wouldn't talk about it.'

'Hints and guesses — I knew something was amiss, mother whispering to Greta, shutting up when I came in. Mother was beguiled by her, you know, and the luxury of life at

Treasonfield, and the glamorous people... I understood, though. Life was very dull for her at my aunt's house.'

'They were all thick as thieves: Greta, Papa Willy, Wesel, Stephen — and that school pal of his, Rudolf Schmidt, who stayed at the vicarage with Reverend and Mrs White. That was a queer thing. I don't know who he was. Some connection of the vicar's wife. She was German and very thick with Greta.'

'I remember the vicar's wife. Those plaits wound round her head and the long black skirts. She was so old-fashioned and reserved, but she seemed a harmless sort — rather a rabbit, it seemed to me.'

'True, but — oh, I don't know, I just wonder where their loyalties lie. Last year the French feared that Germany would invade Switzerland and could count on the support among Swiss-Germans. Whose side are they on now?'

Matthew leaned back on his pillows. Claire saw that he was exhausted. 'Don't let's talk too much now. Sister won't be pleased if I leave you tired out. I'd better go.'

'Ask to see Lieutenant Cropper. If he's not there, ask for the adjutant major — damn it, I can't remember his name. Pencil moustache, long in the nose — very highly polished. I'm sure you'll find him. Just tell him I want to know if we took any prisoners and, oh, I don't know, see if you can get any details about Stephen — I mean, if it was —'

'I'll find Mr Cropper or the adjutant, and I'll know what to say when I see one of them. Trust me, Matthew, I'll find a way. Now, just rest, please.'

But Matthew was asleep again, and she had a promise to keep.

8

Claire was worried as she hurried out of the ward. She didn't know what to think. It seemed so unlikely that Matthew had seen Stephen. Impossible, really, and Matthew had gone through so much. Not just the raid, but all that had gone before. Passchendaele in July and Cambrai later, where the 2nd West Lancashires had been overwhelmed as the Germans pushed towards Havrincourt Wood. Thousands of casualties. She'd seen some of them. The gas cases were dreadful. Such things could break a man, and now Matthew had the tension of waiting, of knowing what he might have to face in the coming offensive. Add to that the bitterness he felt about his mother and stepfather, Papa Willy, and Stephen. Suppose all these things had coalesced into a breakdown? He ought to be back with his grandfather for a time — home leave would do him the world of good, and perhaps she might get leave. A few days together in the blessed peace of Hawthorn Park, where they might wander down to the church, think about the future — the wedding…

Claire sighed. It was impossible to think about the future. Matthew's present state was her concern. She'd have to work out how much to say to the adjutant major — that is, if she could find him. Even then, he might not talk to an ambulance driver — a woman ambulance driver, at that. It wouldn't be a good idea to say that Matthew thought he had recognised one of the German soldiers. She could perhaps tell Lieutenant Cropper, but he might have returned to the company's billets by now. She hoped not. He'd be more approachable, and he'd care what was happening to Matthew. She could probably find out where he was to start with.

And what if the prisoner were not Stephen Lang? Then Matthew had imagined him, and that was understandable. She might mock Doctor Wesel, but there was truth in what he said about the subconscious, or was it the unconscious? It didn't matter. There were plenty of stories about soldiers at the front seeing things, stories of ghostly figures in German uniforms appearing in a trench and then vanishing, of a mysterious Comrade in White, supposed to come to the aid of wounded soldiers; there were even stories of whole battalions vanishing. It wasn't surprising, Claire thought, that men thought they saw ghostly figures, given the tension and fear of waiting, the proximity of death, the delirium of the wounded man.

But if it were Stephen — it was impossible to think of, because it meant, perhaps, that Stephen was on the German side and that he had shot Matthew. Stephen. She thought about him. A serious face, sharp-angled, a disapproving mouth and a sarcastic tongue. *Remote*, she thought. She had been a little afraid of him. Could he be on the German side? She supposed he could. He had never seemed to like England much.

Courage, she told herself, making her way to Doctor Simpson's office. *At least get permission to go to Beaumetz. That'd be a start.* She knew Doctor Simpson quite well, a dedicated man who knew very well the stern uprightness of the commandant. Surely, he would give her a note for Captain Riviere's sake.

Doctor Simpson — Major, really — was in his office, where she explained that Captain Riviere, her childhood friend, wished to know if the raid in which he had been wounded had been successful in taking a German prisoner. She thought he ought to know — he was fretting about his men and couldn't remember what he'd been told at the dressing station.

He looked at her kindly. 'I daresay it would be good for him to know. Might aid his recovery, but you should know that it is unlikely that his arm will recover its full mobility for a while. He may have to go home —'

'But he needn't know that yet.'

'No, I suppose not. Find out about that raid first — at least he might have had a success there.' He smiled at her then, a rather sardonic gleam in his eye. 'In the meantime, I suppose you want a note for your commandant, telling her I want you to go to Beaumetz for the sake of my patient.'

'If you would, I'd be tremendously grateful.'

'How will you get there?'

'I saw Sergeant Jouet at the garage. He might take me on his motorbike.'

Doctor Simpson looked at her critically. 'Before you go bowling away with the sergeant, that cut under your eye needs a bit of iodine. You don't want it to get infected.'

She tried and failed not to cough as the doctor cleaned up the cut and dabbed it with iodine.

'I'll give you something for that cough, too. How long have you had it?'

'It comes and goes, mostly at night.'

'Here's some aspirin, and a tot of brandy will help you sleep if you can find some. Now, I'll write that note.'

The commandant read the note, frowned, but gave Claire permission to find a lift. The medical officer's word was law. Claire didn't mention the motorbike — that was a step too far. There was always transport going somewhere, so the commandant would assume that Claire would hitch a ride from a lorry or a car.

Claire went to the garage to see if she could find Sergeant Jouet. She'd seen him tinkering with his motorcycle when she was going to the ward. Paul Jouet was General Byng's man on the move, a Frenchman attached to the British Army. He was an artist, his job being to make maps and drawings of the terrain, and he had a pass to go anywhere he liked on his motorbike, and report on what he had seen and heard. He had been at Gouzeaucourt, examining the land around Gauche Wood. He had stopped off at Ytres on his way back to report to Byng at the Third Army's headquarters in Albert. Claire had met him before, liking his easy smile, yet noting the sadness in his dark eyes which saw the wreckage of his country as he went on his travels. Of course, he was willing to give a lift to Miss Mallory. The road from Beaumetz would take him on to Bapaume and then Albert. She knew she'd have to think again about getting back in time for night duty. She pulled her cap as far down as she could and swathed her face with her muffler.

The motorcycle made short work of the road to the north. Daylight showed the wounded landscape even more harshly, the stunted trees of Havrincourt, the poor, ruined farms and burnt-out dwellings which seemed even more desolate under a weak sun. Not that Claire consciously registered the sights; she was holding onto Sergeant Jouet's waist, feeling the wind, hearing the rumbling throat of the engine and the jolting in and out of potholes. Her head was full of images of the past, black and white pictures, a reel of silent film on a worn-out projector.

Treasonfield, summer, fishing with Matthew, riding ponies across the fields. Her mother and Matthew's mother walking along the lanes. Greta and her son, Stephen, coming on visits. Glamorous Greta with her large hats and creamy lace.

Matthew's mother dying at her father's house where she had gone to live and taken Matthew with her. She had guessed that there was something wrong but, of course, no one talked to her about such things. Those were the days, she thought, when young ladies ought to know nothing. And to think what she had seen and done. Trench feet, venereal disease, lice, rats, young men ruined, raving, naked, gassed, paralysed, limbs amputated, jaws shot away.

There had been something wrong between Matthew's mother and Papa Willy. He married Greta two years after his first wife's death and lived at Treasonfield with Stephen, who became his stepson as had Matthew years before. Swiss-German, but whose side were they on, Matthew had asked bitterly? Not Papa Willy on the wrong side, surely. Willy Lang had been born in England; his ancestors had settled in Manchester way back in the nineteenth century. He was nearly as much an English gentleman as Sir Roland Riviere. Papa Willy, jovial in his tweeds, with his guns and his afternoon teas. But Matthew hadn't got on with them. He felt an exile there, though Treasonfield had been his mother's house, given to her by Sir Roland on her second marriage. Perhaps it was Papa Willy's now.

Matthew had gone to live with his grandfather, owner of Hawthorn Park, the real country gentleman, landowner, and Justice of the Peace. As his heir, Matthew had taken his grandfather's name. He had never known his own father, who had been killed in a riding accident before he was born. He only paid courtesy visits to Treasonfield. The summers when Claire and her mother were invited to stay with Matthew's mother were long gone, but Greta had invited them after she had married Willy, a week in summer and a few days in the autumn. Claire's mother loved going — to live in luxury for a week, away from their stolid house in Oxford where they lived with Aunt Margaret — clever Aunt Margaret. Formidable Aunt Margaret, now in London, organising the welfare of Belgian refugees while Mother dabbed her aching temples with cologne and looked on in horror as her daughter announced her intention of going to France as an ambulance driver. Aunt Margaret had taught her to drive. They hadn't told Mother.

Papa Willy was distantly kind to them when they stayed. Greta was charming, though Claire thought that she took them up in order to have them on her side. She knew what friends Claire and Matthew were — she didn't know they were engaged. No one knew. They'd have said they were too young. Greta knew that Matthew disliked her. Greta wasn't used to that; she was used to admiration — and adoration, Claire thought now. She wouldn't have liked the thought that Matthew loved Claire, that they were out of her sphere. Claire's mother, however, was quite willing to succumb to the charm. Claire was careful not to discuss Matthew with her mother or Greta, despite Greta's wily questions. Stephen was frigidly polite, absorbed in his work, preparing to study in Vienna. Papa Willy, too, was absorbed in his business affairs — a financier with interests in Europe. Claire had only a vague idea of what he did, but they were very well-off in their comfortable home with its odd name.

An odd name in the present circumstances, though the name of the house hadn't anything to do with treason. Claire had thought of distant battles, Cavaliers and Roundheads, households divided, betrayal, and some glorious Cavalier wife defending her manor house against the Ironclads, but Sir Roland had told her that it only referred to an unproductive field in the long-ago past, when Treasonfield had been a humble farm.

A cosmopolitan house, Treasonfield. There were always visitors from America, France, Italy, Switzerland — and Germany. Papa Willy had German relatives, but so did the King of England, though King George V had changed the family's name to Windsor in 1917, and Papa Willy was just William Lang, which might be English or Swiss, or German. A couple of years before the war, Matthew had come to Treasonfield when Claire and her mother were staying. She and Matthew had left the lunch party as soon as they could. Stephen and his friend, Rudolph Schmidt, at nineteen to their sixteen years, had stayed, of course, with the guests. Stephen had nothing to say to Matthew.

Claire thought of Matthew's troubled eyes, his dark brow when he asked his bitter question. He had been serious. Darling Matthew, who had joined in 1915 and arrived in France in late 1916 and had endured. Courage was the thing, and good humour. You kept joking, bantering, chaffing, or you'd go mad. That's what they all said. She thought of the young men who were speechless or raving when she had driven her ambulance back after the disaster of Cambrai. Matthew's bruised fingers plucking at the sheet. Please, not Matthew. Not broken —

Her thoughts were interrupted by the motorbike jolting to a stop. They had reached Battalion HQ in Beaumetz.

9

At the casualty clearing station in Ytres, Matthew had woken up feeling that his mind was clearer. The medical officer had said there was no infection, and the fever had abated. He'd be able to convalesce in a day or two up in Étaples, or he could return to England. He'd be fit to travel with his arm in splints. 'And we'd like to be rid of you,' the MO told him. Matthew knew why. His bed would be needed when... He shouldn't think about that. And seeing Claire had done him good, too, though she'd looked tired. She wouldn't give up, though; she'd get to Beaumetz somehow and find out if they had taken a prisoner and who he was. And what if it was Stephen? How likely was that?

Matthew took himself back to 1906. His mother was dying — of what, he did not exactly know. He had been eleven then, aware for a long time of something amiss at Treasonfield, amiss between his mother and Papa Willy, but he hadn't asked. He hadn't even dared ask his grandfather, and when his mother had died, it was somehow too late. He knew now, of course. Greta had been a very frequent visitor at Treasonfield. His mother had died at Hawthorn Park, where they had gone to live with Grandfather. She seemed to have simply faded away. He hadn't gone back to Treasonfield to live after Papa Willy had married Greta in 1908. He went occasionally with his grandfather, out of politeness, and after all, it was his house, left to him by his mother, though improvements had been paid for by Papa Willy.

Papa Willy seemed to inhabit it wholly. And his guests, too, the German relatives, the Swiss, the businessmen, the bankers, the merchants from Manchester and London, diplomats, politicians sometimes. Important people, whose chief concern was money. He remembered reading a letter in *The Times* before the war, from a Manchester merchant who had argued that on economic and trade grounds war would be a grave error for Great Britain. The writer's name had been familiar, for in late 1913 he had met him, when he and grandfather had paid what was to be Matthew's last visit to Treasonfield. They had been invited to lunch and he had been glad to find that Stephen was not present, but Greta was there, positively glowing. He had been very surprised to find out later that she had departed to Switzerland for health reasons — a weak chest, she said. Greta, always elegant in lace and pearls, her dark hair aglow in candlelight or sunshine, in whose light his mother had always seemed faded.

The other guests at the lunch were the usual mixture of businessmen, whose talk had all been in favour of neutrality and non-intervention in the case of war. Papa Willy had been in earnest conversation with a director of Nobel's Explosives company in Glasgow, in which Papa Willy had interests. A Herr von Bohlen, something to do with shipping, seemed to know Rudolph Schmidt very well — and Greta, for that matter, whose charms he was obviously enjoying. Grandfather talked to the vicar, Reverend White, a surprising addition to the party, though as his wife was German and Greta's friend, and Stephen's school friend Rudolph was related to her, Matthew had supposed that accounted for it. He had talked to her. It was true, what Claire had said about her. She was a rather timid woman who spoke of the ties between England and Germany which she hoped would never be broken, but still, she was part of that circle at Treasonfield, and very close to Greta.

Matthew and Grandfather had left as early as they decently could. Grandfather was silent in the car going back. Only as they reached the gates of Hawthorn Park did he say, 'That woman is all surface, and to think that Lang... Oh, never mind, my boy, I shan't be going again. Let's not think about them.' They didn't talk of them again because Christmas came. In February 1914, Sir Edward Grey talked in Manchester about peace and the interests of commerce. But events overtook his hopeful stance. In June, a nineteen-year-old Bosnian Serb named Gavrilo Princip stepped out in a Sarajevo back street, and shot Archduke Franz Ferdinand, heir to the imperial throne of Austria-Hungary. The fuse was lit, and the flames fanned by the rushing wind that blew through Europe. Austria declared war on Serbia; Germany declared war on Russia, and then by August it was too late for peace. Germany declared war on France. Germany invaded Belgium, and on 4th August 1914, Britain declared war on Germany.

By 1915, Matthew was in training with the West Lancashire Division, whose annual training camps at Kirkby Lonsdale his school cadet corps had visited. It seemed natural to join them. By 1916, he was at the front, surviving — Lord knew how — and then facing the horrors of Ypres and Cambrai in November. And now? Here he was again, but crocked and worried about what that image of Stephen Lang in a German helmet meant. It haunted him. And he was intensely curious about Papa Willy. Where was he? And was Greta still in Switzerland? Whose side were they on?

10

Claire heard the motorcycle roar away. She stood at an open gate to let a wagon go by. A rutted lane led to Battalion Headquarters, which had been a farm. It was now deserted by the farmer and his wife, of course, and their pigs and their cows. Their peaceful fields had been churned into muddy lorry parks, the farmhouse was now offices and the barns were stores. Their yards and orchards were filled with huts, tents, horses and pack mules, waiting for their orders.

Pioneers, signallers, drummers, cooks, stretcher-bearers, drivers and soldiers were busy attaching guns to limbers and packing supplies into lorries. Ammunition, bicycles, water carts, and field kitchens were being packed up. Claire guessed what was happening. Companies were being deployed along the line, where they would set up outposts. They would install communication trenches, signal dugouts, canteens, and field ambulances. Two men in uniform stood watching on the steps of the farmhouse. The red collar tabs and red cap bands told her that they were staff officers. The taller of the two went in and the other came down the steps with his clipboard.

Time to take courage and ask. Drawing closer, Claire saw the three bands round the officer's cuff — a major then. The adjutant major? He turned as she uttered a polite, 'Sir.' She saw his long nose and pencil moustache.

He looked irritated to see a young woman in the uniform of an ambulance driver but was sufficiently polite to ask if he could assist her. As he looked down his long nose at her, she knew instinctively not to tell him that Matthew thought he had known the German in the raid, so she merely told him that she had come from Captain Riviere at CCS 21, and that he wished to know if any German prisoners had been taken.

'Oh, yes, sorry about Riviere. Bad luck, but you can tell him that they took three. Two, not much to say for themselves. Lieutenant Cropper shot the other — saved Riviere's bacon. German blighter's shots didn't kill him thanks to Cropper's quick thinking.'

'The third died?'

'Not dead yet, but no use to us, I'm afraid. Can't speak a word. So, if that's all, Miss…' Claire didn't bother to supply her name; the major was already turning away. 'I'll be getting on. Compliments to Riviere.'

He marched away to speak to someone more important — a quartermaster sergeant major, by the look of the man whom he approached. Claire was left wondering whom she might find who could tell her about the wounded German. She thought it wise to melt away from the precincts of the major. He'd see her as a nuisance. It was then that she spotted a man with a dog collar showing at the neck of his tunic. Surely, the padre would be able to tell her where a wounded prisoner might be.

The chaplain seemed much more approachable than the major and was able to tell her that the German prisoner was being cared for in the barn, which served as the battalion hospital.

'Would it be possible for me to see him?' she asked.

He looked puzzled. 'Might I ask why?'

'For Captain Riviere.'

'Oh, yes, I know him. How is he?'

'He's on the mend, though I think he might be sent home. His arm is pretty bad. You see, we've been friends for a long time, and he asked me … oh, this is difficult. Could I tell you in confidence? It's not something I wanted to share with the adjutant major. He didn't seem very approachable, and it's too personal.'

'Ah, Major Lewis-Guard.'

'Guard?'

'Yes, very apt —' he smiled at her — 'not much given to ordinary conversation. His first name's Nimrod. Rather a burden, I should think. But if you want to tell me, I'll listen. It's my job to receive confidences, Miss —?'

'Mallory, Claire Mallory.'

'Henry Evans, Miss Mallory. I have a quiet room in the barn — just a place where anyone can come to talk or pray if they wish. No one will disturb us, and then we'll see the patient.'

Just inside the open doors of the barn there was a little cobble-floored room, a feed store once, perhaps, with a table and a few sagging easy chairs, probably purloined from the farmhouse. There was a wooden cross affixed to the wall above another battered table on which stood a couple of wooden candlesticks and between them a Bible, and there was a footstool with some worn tapestry to serve as a kneeler. But she guessed that if the visitor were not interested in prayer or the Bible, then he would still be welcome — or she, if a nurse or a VAD just needed to talk. There were cigarettes on the table and a couple of bottles of wine, a paraffin stove, a kettle, cups and saucers. Henry Evans looked to be in his late forties, Claire thought, noting his greying hair and lined face as he removed his cap. He had an air of quiet authority and compassion. She'd bet he was a chaplain who was often seen at the front line. She could trust him.

'Tell me,' he said simply.

Claire told him everything. 'I don't think it is a breakdown and I don't know if he saw Stephen Lang, but I know it's possible to imagine things in the face of death. I thought about all those stories of ghostly figures in the trenches.'

'Oh, yes, the vanishing major and the Comrade in White. It is not an uncommon phenomenon.'

'Or simply one face superimposed onto another. It may simply be that the German prisoner looked like Stephen.'

'That's true, too. But clearly Captain Riviere needs to know. You'd recognise Stephen Lang?'

'I'm sure I would.'

'Well, let's go and have a look.'

They went into the ward, which reminded Claire of CCS 21 with its steel beds packed in rows and the smell of carbolic and Condy's Fluid disinfectant, but there were very few patients — the battalion hospital was quiet at the moment. However, they saw the MO coming out from behind a screen which was used to separate a serious case from the rest of the ward.

'Padre,' he said, coming towards them. 'Too late, I'm afraid. The prisoner has gone — he died a few minutes ago. Shot in the chest, poor devil.'

'The German?' Claire said.

'Yes, did you want to see him?'

Henry Evans explained that Captain Riviere wanted to find out about the German prisoner who'd shot him. 'He thought he'd known him in England before the war, and Miss Mallory here wants to set the captain's mind at rest.'

'Well, it's irregular, but I don't see why you shouldn't have a look.'

Henry lifted the sheet that covered the dead man's face. It was Stephen Lang. How extraordinary that he should be lying here. Claire knew that pale, angular, serious face, and thin lips which rarely smiled. And his height. She remembered how he had looked down at her as if he found her wanting in some

English way. She hadn't liked him much, but she was sorry. He looked young, and why wouldn't he fight for the German side? He had been in Vienna — perhaps he felt loyalty to Austria and to his Swiss-German relatives. His perspective might have been very different from Matthew's. She'd seen young German prisoners — just boys crying for their mothers. Could you blame them for fighting for their country? She thought, too, of Greta losing her only son. Death didn't take sides.

Stephen would be buried with military honours, and the Red Cross International Prisoner of War Agency would be informed so that they could trace his family. Perhaps she could help with that. He must have papers which might tell her where exactly Greta was. Matthew could write to her — he ought to, despite the past, and to Papa Willy, too. Matthew needn't tell them that he was there when Stephen was shot.

Henry made the sign of the cross on Stephen's forehead and Claire bowed her head and said 'Amen' at the end of the padre's prayer, and then they left him.

'You recognised him?'

'I did. He was Stephen Lang. I was wondering if I could help — I mean, I knew his mother, Greta, as did Matthew. She ought to know. She's in Geneva. It would be quicker for one of us to write rather than the Red Cross.'

'Yes, his papers will be with his uniform and belongings in the office in the house. I'll take you. The Red Cross has thousands of prisoners to cope with. It takes ages to trace families. The office will be grateful to save time, given what's to come. Two companies are on the move, as you see. Going further north, to Flanders.'

Inside the farmhouse, Henry showed Claire into a small office where a private was writing in a ledger. Henry told him that the German prisoner had died, and that Miss Mallory had known his family before the war and would be willing to inform his mother, who lived in Geneva, and send on any effects that the private thought could be given up.

'Aye, it's all right, I suppose. Save his ma waitin' for the Red Cross to let her know. Pity for him. He was an officer — he'd have been sent to Switzerland. Could've got home. He would've been better off than them other two. Labour company for them at Boulogne, I'll bet. Still, the Jerries've got our lads buildin' railways over there. Against the Geneva Convention, that is.'

The private brought a parcel from one of the pigeonholes lining the wall and put it on the table. Claire could see the name on the label attached with string: *Leutnant Stephan von Ende*. That puzzled her for a moment, until she remembered that von Ende had been Greta's name before she'd married Papa Willy. The private unwrapped the parcel to reveal a leather pouch with a cord attached. That would be the pouch in which Stephen — or Stephan — kept his *Erkennungsmarke*, or dog tag as the British called it. The tag would give his name, rank, number, and regimental details. She hesitated, seeing the bloodstain on the pouch, remembering Matthew's bleeding hand that summer and Stephen staunching the wound. Now Stephen Lang was dead and so was his German alter ego, Stephan von Ende. Oh, this war.

Henry picked up the pouch and opened the button fastening. He took out the tag, still on its cord. Claire couldn't tell the colour of the cord, only that it was bloodied. Stephen's name was engraved on the oval disc, which was about an inch long. Henry read out the date of birth: 16th May 1891. There was no doubt. He deciphered the numbers and letters for her: "1/b RIR 231/50" which meant 1st Battalion, 231st Reserve Infantry Regiment of the 50th Division; "b" for Bavarian. Not that Claire was any the wiser. She wondered why Stephen had served in a Bavarian regiment.

'Cambrai,' Henry said. 'They were there.'

Had Stephen and Matthew faced each other there? Claire looked at the pouch. Stephen had worn that against his living flesh. 'And this?' she asked, pointing to the oilskin packet that was still in the parcel.

'Two letters,' the private said. 'One gave us an address in a place called Annemasse near Geneva — from his auntie. The other was from him to the lady — it was not finished.'

'Can we can take these?' Claire asked.

'Yes, if the padre'll sign for them. He's a major. Nice an' official, like.'

Henry obliged with his signature in the ledger and taking up the parcel, he led Claire from the office.

'Shall I find you a lift back to Ytres?'

'Yes, please, but I wonder if I can find Lieutenant Cropper first? I'd like to be able to tell Matthew what happened.'

'B Company is one of those on the move. We'll see if we can find him.'

Lieutenant Cropper was standing by a lorry, deep in conversation with another officer. Henry went over to speak to him and pointed to where Claire was standing. He nodded and Henry came back with him, suggesting that they talk in his little room while he went to find her a lift. Claire and Lieutenant Cropper — a young man of about twenty-one with a sensitive face, fair hair and very blue eyes that held the same haunted look she saw so often — went in to sit on the sagging chairs. Matthew had told her that he had studied English Literature; his ambition was to be a poet. She imagined him at Oxford or somewhere before the war, looking eagerly about him with bright, candid eyes. He would have been like one of the young men she saw all the time, speeding along on their bicycles, scarves flying, browsing in Blackwell's bookshop, taking tea, and looking forward to the long vacation and a summer of tennis and cricket, or boating, or writing. Lieutenant Cropper in the shade of a chestnut tree, pen in hand… She realised he was staring at her with an anxious frown.

'I'm sorry,' she said, 'you want to know about Matthew. He's all right — that is, he's on the mend, though he won't be back for a while.'

'I'm sorry. I'll miss him, especially now. The company will miss him. Good of you to come and tell me.'

'He can't remember if you came to the dressing station to tell him about the prisoners.'

'Oh, yes, I didn't think he'd taken it in. I would have come to the CCS, but things are moving. You can tell him that we got three. Pity the officer is dead — the padre just told me.'

'Can you tell me what happened? Matthew's anxious to know. He can't recall much.'

'No, well, the blighter popped up after we'd chucked the smoke bombs in. With the clouds of white smoke it was difficult to see, but the fellow didn't put his hands up. He had his revolver trained on Captain Riviere and then he seemed to hesitate, seeing Matthew pointing his gun at him. The other two blundered out, hands up, and then the officer fired, and I did, almost at the same time, but the captain went down and so did the Jerry. We used our field dressings to patch them up as best we could. Tricky getting back to the dug-out, but we did it. Couple of the privates half-carried, half-dragged the captain and another couple did the same for the Jerry officer. Sent them first so we could cover them. The other two lads were no trouble.'

Claire didn't think it was worth telling Lieutenant Cropper about Stephen — Mr Cropper was on his way north. He didn't need to know that Matthew had known the German prisoner before the war. Better to keep it simple. 'Thank you for telling me. Matthew will be glad to know.'

'Tell him it was a German observation post. They were watching our movements. We found a telescope and notes the officer had made about our positions, so in that sense the raid was useful. He'd have sent his intelligence reports back to their Staff HQ. At least we put the post out of action. Anything to inconvenience the enemy, eh?'

'Yes, it's good to know that what you got was useful.'

Lieutenant Cropper's frown appeared again. 'Still, I'd rather have the captain back. You don't know the timing?'

'I don't. Some weeks, I should think.'

'I'd better get back. Give him my best wishes. Good to have met you, Miss Mallory. Don't know what we'd do without you and your colleagues.'

'Thank you, and good luck.'

They shook hands and Lieutenant Cropper went out. To meet that spring offensive, Claire thought, and she hoped he would get to the end safely — whenever the end might come.

Henry returned to tell her that he had found her a lift. An off-duty driver would take her back to Ytres, but she must have a cup of tea first. While he made the tea, she told him what Lieutenant Cropper had said.

He offered her a couple of digestive biscuits. 'My mother sends me food parcels. I take them up the line for the men. Chocolate's a comfort on a cold night and they like a biscuit, too. Captain Riviere will be pleased that the raid produced something useful. He can concentrate on getting well now.'

'Yes, at least it wasn't a complete failure. And he'll know he wasn't imagining things. It was Stephen, and Matthew didn't kill him. That would have been very hard to hear, and as for Stephen being on the German side, I suppose it was natural. Stephen wasn't English — his mother is Swiss, but his father was German, I think.'

'It's war. There must be many soldiers who are fighting against those they knew before. A chap I was at Oxford with married a German girl. I often think how difficult it must be for him. He loved Germany and they went on holiday to the Rhine every year.'

They talked about Oxford for a while, and all the loveliness of its meadows and rivers and the colleges with their green lawns and quiet quadrangles. When tea was finished, Claire said she had to get back because she was on night duty. She'd see Matthew if she could before she went on duty. Henry accompanied her to the barn door.

'The rider will be here shortly. I asked him to give us twenty minutes. Tell me, how are you, Miss Mallory?'

She knew what he meant. 'Exhausted often. Bewildered frequently, overwhelmed sometimes, and barely understanding what it's all for, yet — oh, I don't know — doing what I can … and wondering if it's futile.' She gestured to the wagons and the hurrying men. 'They're off to more slaughter, I suppose.'

'Most of us feel like that. So many of the men don't believe anymore, even if they did before. Men who face such horrors are more likely to turn to the Devil than pray to a God whom they think is not watching. But, like you, I do what I can. The place where I'm most useful is the front line. At least I can offer chocolates, a cigarette, or just hold a hand, and sometimes we can bring them to safety. I have no answers, Miss Mallory, but I can tell you that you are needed here. The good you do — think of it as a flame in the immense darkness; it gives light to someone who needs it.'

'Thank you, Padre, that is a reassuring idea. I'm sure the men find your light a comfort, too.'

A motorcycle rolled up. *Oh, Lord,* Claire thought, *let's hope the commandant doesn't see me. Still, it'll be quick.*

She shook hands with Henry. A firm grip, she thought, warm and compassionate. He wished her luck, and she climbed onto the motorcycle pillion with Stephen's letters and the pouch safely buttoned into her tunic pocket.

11

Claire just had time to deliver the parcel to the sister at the ward and to leave a note for Matthew, telling him briefly that she'd seen Cropper and that the raid had been successful. She also wrote that Stephen was dead, and she would come as soon as she could to tell him more. Now, duty done, and with no casualties in the night, she made her way to Matthew's bedside, where she saw him reading the letters.

'You're a brick, Claire, my darling,' he said. 'I knew you'd do it. You found Cropper, too.'

'I found the major first, but I could tell he wasn't the right man. I met the padre, Mr Evans, who was very kind. He told me the adjutant's name — Lewis-Guard.'

'Yes, I remember now.'

'First name Nimrod, apparently.'

Matthew laughed and looked more like himself for a moment. 'Never.'

She saluted. 'Honour bright. Lieutenant Cropper sent his best wishes. He's on his way to Flanders.'

'I wish to God, I... Oh well, no use wishing. Good to know that they got something from the raid.' His face looked troubled again. 'So, Stephen's dead.'

'Yes, I saw him. Padre Evans took me to the ward. Stephen had just died, so the padre took me to get his things — he signed for them. I thought you'd want to write to Greta and Papa Willy. The Red Cross will take ages.'

Matthew didn't answer; he just looked down at the letters. Claire hadn't thought he would be so bitter as to be reluctant to write. That was a kind of duty, she reflected, even if they were on the wrong side. Matthew never shirked a duty. Or perhaps he was still thinking that it was he who had killed Stephen. That would be a dreadful burden of guilt.

'Lieutenant Cropper shot him. He said that Stephen was pointing his revolver at you and that he fired just as Stephen fired at you, but you don't need to tell them that. I think they deserve to know that he's dead.'

'I'm relieved it wasn't me, even though he was fighting for the enemy, but I'm certain he knew me. He intended to kill me.'

'Are you sure he recognised you? Maybe he just saw an officer and his instinct was to shoot.'

'He hesitated and in those — I don't know — seconds, he knew me. He looked straight at me, Claire. He knew me.'

Claire saw the conviction in Matthew's eyes and remembered that Lieutenant Cropper had also noted Stephen's hesitation. Matthew was right. Stephen had known him. 'I know you didn't get on, but to shoot you — it doesn't make sense.'

'I think the letters provide an answer. Stephen served with the 50th Division. Greta mentions a Freiherr von Ende who is the lieutenant-general. I should have paid more attention when Greta was boasting about her distinguished family, but I do remember that von Ende was a cousin of her first husband, and a baron. She was very proud of dear Ludwig. It's not surprising that Stephen would want to serve under him, and he certainly wouldn't have wanted to be taken prisoner — not by me. He'd be bound to want to try to save himself. But that's not the reason I'm not ready to write to Greta. It's not bitterness, Claire, and strange things happen in war, anyway. I know that — people who were friends, family even, before the war are now enemies.'

'What is it then?'

'Greta's letter to Stephen is very odd — of course, she sends her love and hopes he is well and so on, but she calls Stephen her nephew. She's looking forward to spring and is certain that it will be a glorious season. She's planting her seeds in the garden, yet she's writing from Annemasse, from a hotel where she says she's carrying on the good work for their beloved Freiherr.'

'Work for von Ende?'

'Not gardening, I'll bet. When did you ever see her with a trowel? Planting seeds — it's nonsense. So what work is she doing for von Ende?'

'I can't think. Not nursing or driving … more like something she can't write about.' Claire looked at Matthew's frowning face. *Beloved Freiherr*. 'Good Lord, Matthew, you don't think she's actually working for the enemy in some capacity, do you? You don't think she's — a spy? It's a big leap from a few remarks about seeds.'

'Why not a spy? There's no doubt about which side she's on, and it's well known that Geneva is a hotbed of spies. I don't know about Annemasse — never heard of it, but she was supposed to be in Geneva for her health. Think about that — never a day's illness. God, when I think of my poor mother… Think about Greta, Claire, think what she was like.'

Claire conjured Greta in her mind's eye. 'Clever, unscrupulous, cunning — she was always trying to wheedle information out of me about you and Sir Roland, trying to get me on her side, asking about the house, and whether you would want to live there again. Of course, she said, they wanted you to live with them.'

'She was worried I might throw them out. Oh, she liked her comforts, did Greta. Lady of the manor.'

'My mother fell for her charm. Greta knew how to use it — do you remember that lunch when she was fascinating that fellow who was visiting from Germany?'

'Von Bohlen, I remember — he'd been inspecting ships at Cammell Laird in Birkenhead, but he'd been at Treasonfield before.'

'Oh, Lord, Matthew, you think she was up to no good then?'

'Grandfather wrote to me about a chap called Peter Dierks who was director of an oil company and who had been a visitor at Treasonfield. He was arrested as a spy in 1914.'

'So many people came to Treasonfield — the arms men, oil men, bankers. There was Mr Ahlers, the German Consul at Sunderland. Lord, Matthew, the name "Treasonfield" takes on a new meaning now. Did Papa Willy know?'

'Must have done. He was thick with all the pro-German, anti-war merchants. I wonder if he was hosting spies. All those arrests of German spies in 1914 and '15. Got a bit hot for Greta, maybe. There was talk that places in the Manchester district were being used as transmitting stations for wireless telegraphy. I wish I could remember the names of others who came from Manchester to see Willy.'

'Is Papa Willy still there?'

'I think so — centre of a spy ring at the Home Front?'

'It seems so, oh, I don't know, fanciful.'

'There are spies everywhere. Unbelievable as it seems, there was an old woman at Bouchavesnes on the Somme who posed as a laundress and gave information to the Germans about the disposition of troops. The washing on her line was her way of signalling to the airmen. Fanciful, eh?'

Claire laughed. 'Not Greta's line, pardon the pun. I mean, can you imagine her disguised as a washerwoman?'

Matthew couldn't help grinning. 'More Mata Hari than the mangle — but seriously, it does make a sort of sense, and Stephen, an observer.'

'What's in his unfinished letter?'

'Well, he knew what was going on. He writes to Greta as "My dear Aunt" and tells her that he is well and that he is carrying on his good work, too. Seeing a lot of the countryside. He mentions Rudolph — that school friend of his — he just says he's heard from him and he's well. I wonder if he's in the German Army? He was some connection of the vicar's wife, Mrs White, I recall. Grandfather never mentions Rudolph, though he wrote that Reverend White had died. Shooting accident, he said, and Papa Willy let Mrs White have a cottage on the estate. And Stephen sends his best wishes to Uncle Max.'

'Doctor Wesel? Where does he fit in?'

'I'm guessing it's Doctor Wesel. Greta went to Geneva with him — under doctor's orders.' Matthew scanned the letter. 'She says here that she'll be returning to the lake very soon and Uncle Max is going to visit Lörrach. That's right on the border — just inside Germany, but a stone's throw from Basel. Handy place for espionage. I wouldn't put it past him, either.'

'So, what do we do about it, if we're sure, that is?'

'We don't have to be sure. Suspicion is enough at the moment. We have to get to Montreuil-sur-Mer.'

'General Headquarters? But you're not —'

'You can drive. They'll give me painkillers. My arm's in splints, but I still have one good arm. I'll survive. They're chucking me out in a day or two anyway. We have to see someone. We can't just sit on this because we don't want to make fools of ourselves.'

'May Lemmon.'

'Who?'

'She's in the WAAC — one of the hush-hush girls at GHQ. We were at school in Oxford together. She was a censor in the War Office — she speaks fluent German. I thought of joining but I thought ambulance work would be more — oh, you know — useful. Anyway, someone in Military Intelligence recruited May. She didn't say who, of course. I met her on the boat to Boulogne when I was coming back from leave. We keep in touch, and I've seen her once or twice when we've scrambled a half day off. There are nice cafés in Montreuil, even tennis courts, would you believe?'

'I bet you won. Crack shot with a tennis ball. You nearly broke my nose once.'

Claire smiled at the memory. 'May's pretty good. It's nice to have a game and a chat. Not that she tells me anything, only that she's a decoder. There's twelve of them, I think, billeted in huts. I could find her. When she knows what it's about, she'll tell us who to speak to. But I'll have to get permission.'

'Ask the MO, Doctor Simpson. He wants me on my way. I'm sure he'll square it with your commandant. I need someone to drive me to — well, I'm supposed to be convalescing in Étaples, but we can make a diversion to Montreuil.'

Doctor Simpson did better than ask permission for her to take his patient to Montreuil; he recommended two days off at the seaside. Miss Mallory, he informed the commandant, had a cough that needed rest and some sea air before it developed into bronchitis or something worse.

The commandant frowned when she read the note. 'Very well,' she said grudgingly, 'two days and no more. One night away. I shall expect you back in time for night duty on that second day.'

12

Major Guy Pelham looked at the overflowing ashtray on his desk. There was hardly room for the cigarette stub he had in his hand. He was smoking too much, but so was everyone else. The fug hovered in a greenish cloud in the coding rooms, the telegraph rooms, the filing offices and the meeting rooms at British Army General Headquarters. Smoking and waiting. Waiting and smoking. Better than biting one's nails, he supposed.

He tossed the contents of the ashtray into the wastepaper basket and resisted lighting another cigarette. It was one of the Virginia cigarettes that his mother sent him from London in packets of a hundred. No use counting how many packets he'd smoked.

Feeling the ache in his leg and the stiffness in his knee, he stood up to pace about the office. It was more comfortable than the dugout he'd inhabited on the front line. He'd been wounded at the Battle of Loos in 1915 and had been transferred to Military Intelligence — being of no further use on the front line, and because he was a linguist. 'You've still got your brains. Use them,' had been his father's robust comment. Guy understood his father's brusqueness. His leg injury had put him out of action, but he was still alive, unlike his cousin John. Guy had been keen to do something useful. And here he was collecting intelligence information from all over France, Belgium, Holland, Switzerland, Scandinavia and Germany. There were reports from German prisoners, information from the pigeons which flew back from behind the lines, and intelligence from the spy networks.

He was crocked but still doing his bit, and not dead like so many of his friends whom he'd seen shot to pieces, torn apart by shrapnel, blown to bits by shell, gassed, poisoned. And they would be so again this spring.

Yet it will come, he thought. Like Hamlet accepting his fate. Early in the year, Military Intelligence had received reports from their agents and from the London Secret Service Bureau that the Germans were preparing for a spring offensive. Just when was the question. "The interim is mine," Hamlet had said. Well, the interim wasn't theirs. Field Marshal Haig and the politicians were at odds over the size of the army. The Prime Minister was deaf to Haig's demands for more fighting men. The Fifth Army was stretched thinly, and the Third. His own chief, Brigadier-General Cox, believed the attack would come at the old Somme battlefield — in effect just down the road, but there was some scepticism about this. It seemed impossible that the enemy would attempt a breakthrough across such a devastated landscape.

Guy paused to look at the big map on his wall and gazed at the web of lines stretching across Europe. *A twitch upon the thread*, as Chesterton had it. A slight pull by some invisible hand and a man lay dead, or an army was decimated. They had to know. There had been news from Switzerland. An agent had picked up a scrap of information about the movement of General von Hutier's army. Von Hutier was famous for having defeated the Russians at the Battle of Riga. The eastern divisions were moving to the Western Front. The attack would come soon enough.

In January, from Denmark where agent D.1 had contacts in munition circles, intelligence had come about the arms factories, notably Krupp gun production; another agent, D.2, had reported on thousands of troops passing through

Hamburg and Hanover from Russia — the information had come from a German soldier on leave and D.2 had heard a rumour about a possible offensive at Verdun. In Norway, N.20 had gleaned information about factories in Flanders being turned into hospitals. From Sweden had come information about high-explosives production. And only last week, S.8 had reported from Sweden that the offensive would begin in four weeks. His informant had been a Swede who had served in the German Army. Lord, that made it three weeks now. March then. The evidence was compelling.

Belgium. La Dame Blanche, that invaluable network of spies which covered most of Belgium and went as far as the railheads at Hirson and Mézières in France. There were bargemen, railway workers, shop assistants, schoolteachers, doctors, laundresses, farm workers, families and their children, nuns and priests, even a midwife whose job allowed her to travel about — all watched troop movements and trains. They could tell an infantry train from a cavalry train with as many as ten wagons for its horses. There were transcribers transmitting reports, couriers risking their lives, travelling at night, escorting British soldiers, delivering their reports about shipping movements and sketch plans of railways and ammunition factories, using shops as letterboxes. Security was good, but inevitably, they had lost some agents. In 1917, a cell had been betrayed to the Germans, but still reports were coming in day and night, as they were from Rotterdam and Antwerp.

Switzerland again. They had agents in Geneva, Zurich, Basel, and Lausanne. London's Secret Service man, Captain Edward Curran, posing as an Assistant Military Attaché at the Consul in Berne, was receiving bits and pieces from behind the German lines, but only bits and pieces, and the other stuff that came through was reports on Germany's domestic and economic problems. Useful to know that the Germans had problems at home, but they wanted meaty stuff about troop movements, whispers from top military types from agents in Austria and Germany. The Swiss Bureau even had a qualified meteorologist go up a mountain twice a day and telegraph to London about the wind conditions for the Air Force. Useful to know which way the wind was blowing, which way the gas would come. But they needed to know where the attack would come. Uncensored German newspapers were available in Switzerland, from which titbits could be found. Titbits — nothing definite.

Guy's eye travelled to Luxembourg, an important railway hub between Germany and the Western Front. The London Secret Service had an operation in Paris where they had recruited a doctor and his sister. The doctor worked for the railways and the intention had been to set up a network of train-watchers in Luxembourg. Unfortunately, the doctor's sister, codename Madame Lamont, had got stuck in Switzerland — last heard of in Geneva where her husband, one of the Secret Service agents, had been killed in a tram accident. You had to wonder about that. Coded messages were coming in, but no news of Madame Lamont. That was a worry. The Germans were active in Switzerland — they had been since before the war, recruiting spies from the local population. Geneva was a centre of espionage, from where spies could cross with comparative safety into France and Germany. Now, the Germans had moved their Antwerp espionage section to KNst Lörrach, near Basel where the Swiss, German and French borders met. KNst — Kriegsnachrichtenstellen — war bureau. Lord, what a language. They'd all be speaking German if things went badly.

Guy looked at the papers piled on his desk. It was going to be a long night. He looked at his watch. Teatime. Now, that was something to look forward to. An hour in the company of his hush-hush girl. May Lemmon. Codename Peel. A silly joke — she wasn't spying in the field, but coding in the Women's Auxiliary Army Corps, the WAACs, but it made them laugh, and the Lord knew how much her bubbling laugh and shining eyes meant to him, and the hour or so they could snatch a piece of happiness. Yes, May and he could forget for an hour. They could know what was to come, but take tea as if it were not.

13

Claire and Matthew were waiting at a table in the English Teashop in Montreuil-sur-Mer, run by an Englishwoman whose French husband was in the army, waiting, no doubt, like everyone else for the big push. Madame Roche, it seemed, worked for the British, but in what capacity, except serving tea, May Lemmon did not explain. Claire, on May's instructions, had explained to Madame Roche that she and her companion were friends of Miss Lemmon's. She had given them a table in a corner and brought tea and cake — a rich fruitcake. They could have had a glass of wine if they'd wanted. Supplies were not short in Montreuil, which had been entirely taken over by the British Army because it was on the road to the coast and halfway between London and Paris. Regular ships came into Boulogne, bringing troops and supplies. The huge training camp at Étaples was only a few miles to the north. Despatches were received and sent between GHQ and divisional headquarters in Arras or Amiens — motorcycles did the journey in less than an hour — and there was a network of telephone lines connecting GHQ to London and Paris as well as the front line.

They had tracked down May at the intelligence branch in the École Militaire, but she was busy, so Claire had only had time for a brief explanation. However, they arranged to meet at the café at four o'clock when she had an hour free. It gave them time to walk around Montreuil, which Claire knew quite well, having met May there on a few occasions. It was a fortified town with huge brick ramparts protecting it. You could only get in through the guarded gateways. Claire led Matthew through the jumble of alleys and cobbled streets, where there were cottages with tiled red roofs and shutters and town houses in which billets were found for the officers and men. There were plenty of cafés and restaurants, too, in the squares. She pointed out the citadel which housed the British Army Communications Centre and they gazed at the tennis court. They passed the theatre used sometimes for concerts and films. There was a hospital for Belgian refugees, as well as other hospitals for casualties. They strolled along the broad walk which crowned the old ramparts, where they stood to look down upon the yellow flowers in the walls, at the trees coming into leaf at the base of the ramparts, and at the peaceful countryside in which crops still grew to be harvested.

'Hard to believe we're only thirty miles or so from the front,' Matthew said. 'The town must have been a lovely, quiet place before the war.'

'I know — if it were not full of army personnel, you could imagine a quiet weekend here, having dinner in one of those restaurants.'

Matthew encircled Claire with his good arm. 'Oh, I can imagine that very well. One day, Claire, one day —' he grinned at her — 'and some nights, too.'

'Oh, I wish…'

'I know, I know.'

They stood gazing at the tranquil scene, listening to an unseen lark pouring out her song to a clear blue sky, innocent as glass. Joy and hope somewhere. At peace for a few precious moments, until Claire said, 'Ah well, we ought to go and meet May.'

The café was charming, with prints of English villages on the walls and white tablecloths and rose-patterned china. They might have been in Oxfordshire, Claire thought, rather than waiting anxiously for their hush-hush girl to look at Stephen's letters. Matthew looked as tense as she felt. Suppose May dismissed their fears or laughed at them? But she wouldn't laugh. She'd listen to Matthew. There was definitely something fishy about those letters.

May Lemmon came, was introduced to Matthew, and drank her tea before she said, 'Don't tell me anything yet. Someone else is coming. He'll know far better than I do if there's something serious about your letters. He's — oh, here he is.'

Claire looked at the tall stranger who came to their table, noticing his pronounced limp — wounded like Matthew, she thought. He wore the uniform of a staff officer with green tabs on his collar to indicate the Intelligence Branch, and the three cuff bands told her that he was a major. However, he had not the long-nosed frigidity of the adjutant major at Beaumetz. He smiled at May who, Claire saw, blushed slightly as she introduced him as Major Guy Pelham and explained that Captain Riviere and Miss Mallory wanted to consult him.

'Good to meet you both. May has mentioned you, Miss Mallory, and the work you do. I wouldn't be here were it were not for the ambulance driver who rescued me.' Pelham turned to Matthew. 'Loos, and yours?'

'A raid. Shot by the German prisoner we are here to see you about.'

Guy Pelham listened intently as Matthew told the story, starting with the shooting and then explaining all that had occurred at Treasonfield. He described his relationship to Papa Willy, Greta, and Stephen, and then they drank more tea as Guy studied the letters.

'A few preliminary questions, if you don't mind. The visitors to Treasonfield. Any names?'

'Ahlers, the German Consul in Sunderland —'

'Arrested in 1914, along with all German residents in Sunderland.'

'Peter Dierks.'

Pelham nodded. 'Swiss, an oil man — arrested, too, accused of espionage.'

'McBain, from Glasgow, a director of Nobel's Explosives. Willy has interests in armaments.'

'Nobel manufacture shell fuses in Geneva, and Switzerland supplies munitions to the Germans as well as the Allies. This is interesting. Anyone else?'

'That man, von Bohlen, Matthew, who'd been inspecting ships in Birkenhead,' Claire put in.

Pelham's eyes widened. 'Ships? Von Bohlen from Krupp's?'

'Krupp's? That name wasn't mentioned.'

'Well, Herr von Bohlen is a chairman of Krupp's, the steel company — direct line to the Kaiser. There was a lot of agitation in the papers about that visit to shipbuilding yards.'

'He'd been to Treasonfield a few times — Greta was very friendly with him, as was Stephen's school friend, Rudolph Schmidt.'

'What was the talk about the war?'

'Well, they weren't in favour, of course. There was a Manchester merchant — a man named Antony Bell. He was a visitor, and I remember a letter he wrote to the papers. He thought there should be no war on economic and trade grounds. The general feeling was that war with Germany was a very bad idea.'

'Hmm, not surprising in commercial circles, but what about when arrests and internment of aliens started, and there was all the talk about traitors in high places?'

'I wasn't there much after the war started, but Claire visited.'

Guy turned to Claire. 'Miss Mallory?'

'Willy was exasperated, I think, rather than angry. He seemed to think it was folly, though nothing ever seemed to really ruffle his good humour. He never gave much away. Greta was contemptuous of the way the British treated foreigners. She had a friend whose husband was pretty high up in the government, yet their Austrian housekeeper was repatriated. She thought it was ridiculous — how was her friend to manage without the housekeeper? Apparently, they lived in a large house in St James's Square.'

'The Langs visited friends in London?'

'Oh yes, Greta preferred London to the country. She particularly liked entertaining their titled friends at the Savoy and being invited to the embassies. At home, there was really only the vicar's wife who was her friend. Local families weren't keen on them.'

'Why the vicar's wife?' asked Pelham.

'She's German. I remember that she was very upset because there had been talk of her as a spy. Willy laughed at that. He said they'd never arrest a vicar's wife. Greta said she'd shoot anyone who tried.'

'Do you know what happened to the vicar's wife?'

Matthew answered. 'The vicar, Reverend White, was killed in a shooting accident and Willy let Mrs White have a cottage on the estate.'

'I met her several times. She seemed harmless enough to me,' Claire said, 'rather timid, and distressed rather than angry about the gossip.'

'She has family in Germany?'

Matthew nodded. 'I assumed so, from what I gleaned from the one conversation I had with her at a lunch — she was very much against any conflict with Germany. I don't know anything about any family, except the school friend of

Stephen's, Rudolph Schmidt, who was some connection of hers. How and why he went to school with Stephen, I don't know. He's mentioned in the letter, but I don't know if he's in the German Army.'

'But he was well-known to the Krupp man, von Bohlen, you say?'

'Yes, Greta and Rudolph were deep in conversation with von Bohlen.'

'Mrs White — was she a Schmidt before she married?'

'I only knew her as Agnes White.'

'Willy Lang — tell me about him and why you didn't want to live with him and Greta.'

Matthew looked surprised at this sudden change of direction. Major Pelham's face didn't give anything away, but he supposed an agile brain was ticking away in his head. *This is an interrogation*, Matthew thought suddenly. Bound to touch on personal matters. He felt uncomfortable, though. Murky waters.

'It's difficult. People liked him. He was always good-humoured, equable, generous, but, you see, I think — I know — from bits my grandfather said, and the fact that my mother and I moved out of Treasonfield, that Greta was his mistress before my mother died.'

'What's his history — I mean, when did he come to England?'

'He was born in Manchester. The Langs were only German way back. They were manufacturers of calico in Manchester in the 1850s, I believe. There was a sizeable German merchant population in Manchester in the 1800s. He's a British subject, as is Greta Lang by marriage. She was resident in Switzerland before she settled in England in about 1906. I knew her as a widow from Switzerland, one of the many visitors Willy always had, except that she seemed to be there a great deal after my mother and I moved out.'

'Did she travel back and forth to Geneva before the war?' Guy asked.

'Yes, to visit family. I went to Geneva years ago when my mother was alive. I don't remember much except the promenade, the steamers, and the coffee. My mother and I saw the sights while Willy attended to his business — whatever it was. We didn't meet any of his friends or business contacts.'

'Presumably Greta Lang's Swiss passport got her to Geneva, despite the restrictions on travel,' Guy observed. 'When did she leave?'

'Late 1915.'

'And Doctor Wesel, who is in Lörrach according to these letters?'

'He was always about, and it was on his advice, supposedly, that Greta returned to Geneva.'

'What kind of doctor is he?'

'He's a psychoanalyst — he'd been in Vienna, where Stephen Lang went to study before the war.'

'Austrian, perhaps?'

'Yes.'

'The von Ende connection — who was Greta's first husband?'

'I don't know — it was a long time ago. I didn't live at Treasonfield after 1906, when my mother died. But I definitely remember her talking about her aristocratic relatives, the von Endes.'

'One last thing — never mind the evidence, do you think it's possible that Greta Lang could be in the pay of the Germans?'

Matthew looked at Guy. The major wanted to know Matthew's deep instinct — nothing to do with whether he liked Greta or felt bitter about her and his mother. Just whether Matthew thought she was capable of treason.

'I do.'

'Willy Lang?'

'I'm less sure about him, despite his betrayal of my mother. It seems more unlikely. After all, he was born in England, and I don't have any evidence except his business interests and the people who were invited to Treasonfield.'

'Miss Mallory, what do you think?'

Claire remembered Greta's contemptuous words about the English. She saw in her mind's eye the hard glitter of her hazel eyes and said, 'I can believe it of Greta, but like Matthew, I can't be sure about Willy.'

'I think that's enough for now,' Guy concluded. 'You've given me a lot to think about, but I don't want to comment yet. What I suggest is that I ask Madame Roche if she can put you up tonight and we'll meet again tomorrow. I'll come here first thing — eight o'clock. Madame will give us breakfast.'

14

'Sorry about our tea, Guy, but I thought you ought to meet them,' May said when they got back to Guy's office, having arranged two rooms for Matthew and Claire. Madame Roche would give them supper and they could have a good night's rest. Guy had seen how exhausted Matthew Riviere looked, and Claire, with her bruised face and cough, looked drawn, too. Not surprising. They'd come from the front line and had brought troubling news. 'What do you think of what they told you?'

'Something in it, I'd say. I just need to pull the threads together and decide what to do. There's the English angle with Willy Lang, and then there's the Geneva connections.'

'You have people in Geneva.'

'We have an agent in Thonon on the French side of the lake, where the French have an information service. They might know about Greta Lang and Doctor Wesel. London Secret Service still has agents in Geneva, but things aren't very satisfactory there. Confidentially, I've heard about an agent who was supposed to be going into Luxembourg, but she's missing. Her husband, one of London's men, was killed in Geneva — tram accident, apparently.'

'Oh, Lord, that's alarming.'

'It is, so you see why I have to think this one out.'

'Late night then.'

'All night, I'm afraid, but it was going to be anyway. You know how things are.'

'I do. I'd better get back, too. I'll have an hour tomorrow afternoon. Four o'clock at the teashop?'

'Yes, if I can.'

As soon as the door closed behind May, Guy studied the letters again. He thought about Lieutenant-General Freiherr Ludwig von Ende; the psychoanalyst Doctor Wesel — possibly Austrian — in Lörrach, where the KNst were based; the vicar's German wife and her connection to Rudolph Schmidt, whereabouts unknown. And Willy Lang, financier with interests in armaments in Switzerland. And Germany? Shares in Krupp's?

Guy thought about the spy William Brown, who had been born in Wales in 1870, whose parents had been German. Brown had been manager of the Krupp's Chemical Works in Shoreham — and Lang was connected to Krupp, whose chairman visited the house called Treasonfield. Appropriate, perhaps. William Brown had also worked as chief draughtsman for Macdonald Gibbs, Engineers to the War Office — and he wasn't the only spy of German descent who'd been found to have infiltrated munitions companies. And there was Greta Lang in Annemasse, where the London Secret Service had set up a spy network. Did she have a contact there? She might be in Geneva, where Madame Lamont had gone missing and where Madame Lamont's husband, an agent for the British, had been killed in a tram accident.

The London Secret Service had not been very successful in Geneva. Some agents had been arrested, whilst others had been duds — taking the money and staying home, fabricating reports. One had been dismissed for drunkenness — a loose-mouthed fool — and one had been compromised over an affair with a so-called Austrian countess, most certainly a spy. And worst of all, there had been one who had betrayed two others, of whom one had been shot for spying in Germany. Add into the mix German spies, Austrians, Turks, Egyptians,

Indians, Bulgarians, Russians, socialists and agitators, and it was a tricky place. Too comfortable and too much money to be had if you wanted to play for both sides, or any side. You didn't know whom you could trust. And the Swiss authorities weren't keen on their country being a nest of spies. They'd had news recently of the arrest of the proprietor of a hotel and three German women, all accused of espionage. They'd be imprisoned, but there were no doubt others ready to take their place. Waiters and chambermaids were often recruited as spies — for both sides. They picked up all sorts of gossip and had access to bedrooms. It was surprising how often papers were left in unlocked suitcases under beds or in wardrobes.

Strictly speaking, Guy knew he should inform the Secret Service man, Edward Curran, about Greta Lang in Geneva, and MI5, the counter-espionage section in London, about Willy Lang at Treasonfield. The first option didn't appeal, given the state of things in Geneva, and GHQ liked to keep their own operations to themselves from time to time. Guy didn't want some drunken idiot compromising an operation. If he sent someone to Geneva, it would be safer if only their own man in Thonon knew about it.

And MI5 could be circumvented for the time being by using Captain Riviere to make the preliminary investigations at Treasonfield. Guy knew exactly what the captain was thinking. Riviere would not want to be sent to England to convalesce. He'd want to be useful. Two birds with one stone. Riviere could be transferred to Military Intelligence, his first mission to investigate Treasonfield, where his presence as an invalid would excite no anxiety in the residents. He could try to find out if Greta Lang was in Annemasse still and if there were any visitors of interest at Treasonfield. And if Willy Lang were not at home, then it would be only natural for Riviere to ask the servants where he had gone. Riviere might enquire of Mrs White in her cottage. Another person of interest — distressed and too timid to be anything but the vicar's grieving widow, dependent on the charity of her rich landlord. Well, maybe not. Agnes White's relative, Rudolph Schmidt, was well-known to the chairman of Krupp's.

And in case of emergency, Guy had recourse to a very handy chum, a man whom Riviere could trust with his life. Uncle Ned could be called on, day or night.

Willy Lang, a money man with diplomatic connections. Guy thought about the news that late in 1917 a secret meeting had been held in Geneva, attended by international financiers, who, it was reported, had met to consider the effects of war on international finance and the possibility of a peace treaty. It was said that British subjects had entered into relations with subjects of enemy powers. His Majesty's Government had said they had no knowledge of such a meeting. Any British subject entering into relations with enemy subjects would be dealt with under the law. Who knew what subsequent 'secret' meetings had been held by those whose financial interests were more important than victory?

Guy thought about Claire Mallory. She knew Greta Lang and Doctor Wesel. Would Claire be willing to go to Geneva for them to see if she could come across Greta Lang — quite by chance? May had told him that Claire spoke German and French, though she hadn't wanted to join the WAACs. She'd set her heart on ambulance driving.

Claire could be in Geneva for her health, of course. That cough would be very useful. She was due back at Ytres tomorrow evening. Suppose her cough had turned into bronchitis or pneumonia? Her friend, May Lemmon, would naturally send a message that Miss Mallory was in hospital. She wouldn't be able to say when Miss Mallory would be well enough to resume her duties.

Very neat, Guy thought. Claire Mallory might look a bit fragile, but she must be tough, doing what she did. She could go to Paris by train. One of the agents from GHQ's Military Intelligence office in Paris would meet and brief her. She'd put Miss Mallory on the train to Geneva with plenty of Swiss Francs and a passport — in her own name, in case Greta Lang saw her first. No cover needed, except the convalescent angle and a bit of geographical chicanery. Miss Mallory at Roye. Never at Ytres. Evacuated weeks ago to Compiegne. That way, she'd know nothing about what was happening on the front line. Letters to a café at Paris-Plage, twelve miles from Montreuil, to Mrs Smith — in reality, Madame Foulon, who sometimes received letters to be sent on to GHQ. No need to mention Montreuil. Just news of Cousin Gertrude, which would mean that Miss Mallory was safe. Handy to stroll to the post office — she might see someone she knew sending letters. Accommodation — a quiet little pension in one of those narrow streets near St Pierre Cathedral or the museum. Run by a friend of the service, naturally. Very genteel for a young Englishwoman with a cough who might take the air on the quayside. And who might be met by an Englishman who had taken a steamer from Thonon. An ordinary Englishwoman. An invisible Englishwoman.

KNst Lörrach — Doctor Wesel slipping in and out of Basel to report to the German war bureau, maybe. A doctor with his black bag — bound to be on the move. And Lörrach was only a few miles from Basel. Guy would send a message to their agent there to keep an eye out for Wesel. Riviere could give him a description, and if Wesel turned up in Geneva to meet Greta Lang, they'd get him there.

Would Claire Mallory go to Geneva? Guy rather thought she would. Was it dangerous? Not more dangerous than driving an ambulance to the front line in the middle of the night with no lights and shells dropping all around you. Spying, however, provided a different kind of danger — you didn't always know who the enemy was. Geneva was full of refugees, revolutionaries, deserters, wounded prisoners, secret agents and spies who could cross into France and Germany. Spies were not protected by the Geneva Convention. It wasn't only German spies that could be arrested. Claire would need back-up. There was Guy's man in Thonon, who would be in constant touch with her.

He thought about Greta Lang. How dangerous was she? A risk-taker, certainly, judging by her history. And contemptuous of the English. Friends in high places — someone who was high up in the British government with an Austrian housekeeper. And that von Ende connection was important, too, he thought. Lieutenant-General von Ende, commander of the 50th Division in which Stephen Lang had served. And what might Greta Lang do for her "beloved Freiherr"?

She'd left England for Switzerland in late 1915, at a time when all kinds of German aristocrats were there — the Prince de Hohenlohe, for example, and his wife, Austrians known to be working for the Germans. A perilous time for aliens in England. Greta Lang would know all about women like Milly Rocker, wife of the socialist-anarchist Rudolf Rocker, held without trial, despite the protests of powerful friends in parliament and the press. There was also Eva de Bournonville, arrested in late 1915, with secret ink and cyanide in her possession; May Higgs, who had offered her services to the Germans; and Gertrude Evelin, the American who was imprisoned for carrying messages for the Germans. And Greta

Lang would certainly know about the rumoured "Black List", said to contain the names of high-ranking traitors.

Anti-German feeling had certainly increased in 1915, with a number of high-profile cases. The German spy, Otto Kruger, had been caught in 1915; Oscar Buchwaldt, alias Baron, and Marshall, had been interned in Reading Gaol in July 1915, his name mentioned on a list of detainees published in the *Daily Chronicle*. Buchwaldt had recruited Heinrich Grosse, who had confessed to spying for the Germans in March 1915. His letters to his paymaster in Rotterdam had been redirected by Otto Kruger. It was a spider's web of contacts, in which the Langs might well be spinning their threads.

Failed spies — the ones who were caught. But as someone had pithily pointed out, the successful spies were the ones you didn't know about.

15

Madame Roche served breakfast when Guy arrived at the café to speak to his potential new recruits. Matthew looked rested, Guy thought, as did Claire, but he felt their tension as they waited for him to finish his coffee.

'I've reflected a good deal on what you told me yesterday,' he began, 'and I think you're right to be suspicious. I've a proposal to make. Captain Riviere, I take it you are afraid that your injury will mean that you are out of action for some time?' Matthew nodded. 'I wonder if you would consider a transfer to Military Intelligence — it's what I did after Loos. My father told me to use my brain. I'm a linguist, so I contacted a chap I knew in the War Office and here I am.'

'What do you want me to do?'

'Go to England to convalesce with your grandfather and pay a visit to Treasonfield. We need to establish the whereabouts of Willy Lang and, if he's there, I want you to find out what he knows about his wife's whereabouts and what she is supposed to be doing in Geneva. And who has been visiting.'

'If Willy is there, am I to tell him about Stephen?'

'No, you shouldn't say anything about knowing he was fighting for the Germans. There must be no foundation for any suspicion about you nor, indeed, should you give any hint that you suspect Lang or his wife. You are in England only to convalesce. Naturally, you will enquire as to how Stephen is — in Vienna.'

Guy saw Matthew's expression darken a little. He could tell that he was uncomfortable with the lie.

'I'm afraid deception is the very essence of our work. Do you have any doubts?'

Matthew looked him in the eye. 'Of course I do. I'd be a fool if I denied that, but if Willy and Greta are working against us, then I must overcome any scruples about lying.'

'If Lang lies about Stephen, then he will have a reason, perhaps a treacherous one, and he will most certainly lie to you if he is involved.'

'How do I contact you?'

'Send a telegram to me at GHQ. I will leave the precise wording to your judgement. No names — just "Father" for Lang and "Mother" for Mrs Lang. Something like "Father unwell" to indicate Lang's involvement. "Mother abroad" is obvious. "Returning as soon as I can" tells me that you're on your way with any information about Greta Lang in Geneva.'

'What happens if I do find out Willy is involved?'

'Then it's a job for MI5. I'll get onto them, and they'll investigate further, following up his connections in England and intercepting his letters. You mustn't do anything. Return here as soon as you can.'

'And if Lang is not at Treasonfield?'

'"Father away." Then I hope you'll be able to find out where he's gone. There'll be servants you can question, but be careful. Servants might not tell you the truth. Are they all English?'

'Yes.'

'Any of them been there a long time?'

'The housekeeper and cook, Mrs Todd, was employed by my grandfather. She's from a local family — her husband is the general handyman and gardener, and there were always local girls in the kitchen, laundry and in the house. A lot of changes, I should think, now the war's on, but Mr and Mrs Todd are still there. They have a cottage in the grounds.'

'Like Mrs White, the vicar's widow. You should talk to her. Find out about Rudolph Schmidt. Stephen said he had heard from him — in the context of the letter I can't help wondering if the reference is significant. I know it's your old home and you know the servants and the widow, but in this line of work, the first rule is not to trust anyone.'

Matthew's brow darkened again. 'My grandfather?'

'Only in so far as you wish to keep him safe. What people don't know they can't tell. We don't know yet how dangerous these people are. The heat's been put on at home — you know that amendments have been made to the Defence of the Realm Act?'

'Yes,' Matthew said. 'Anyone found in possession of information relating to a spy is deemed to be in communication with a spy.'

'Exactly, and you have given me names of people that Lang knew. The contacts in high places. The German contacts and, Miss Mallory, you mentioned Mrs Lang's friend in the government — do you have a name?'

'I'm afraid I can't remember,' Claire answered.

'No matter, I daresay I can find out. There have been questions in the House of Commons about highly placed traitors. There is particular concern about subjects from neutral countries — enquiries into their occupations and antecedents are being carried out. And there's a good deal of unease about spies at docks, passing information about the shipping of supplies and troops. It would not surprise me if Mr Lang has left the country, and if that is so, Captain Riviere, then your job is to look for any letters or papers which incriminate him or Mrs Lang, or anyone else.'

'When do you want me to leave?'

'As soon as you feel fit. I'll get the medical officer to have a look at your arm. When that's done, we'll have another chat.' Guy turned to Claire. 'I wonder if you would consider going to Geneva, Miss Mallory?'

Claire stared at him. 'But what about the commandant? I'm expected back for night duty this evening.'

Guy smiled. 'That won't be a problem. GHQ gives the orders. A message will be sent.'

'Saying what?'

'That you are too ill to return — that is, if you are prepared to go to Geneva.'

'To find Greta?' Matthew asked.

'To find out what she's doing, who she sees, where she goes.'

'Geneva is a big place,' Claire said doubtfully.

'You speak French and German as fluently as Miss Lemmon, Miss Mallory. Where did you and your family stay in Geneva, Captain Riviere? Did Mr Lang have a favourite hotel?'

'The Hotel Belle Vue,' Matthew replied.

'Expensive and known to us as a gathering place for spies with money. The Germans can be very generous. It wouldn't be difficult for you to watch there, Miss Mallory, take coffee or lunch. Is Greta interested in art, the theatre?'

'Anything where she might meet the best people,' Matthew said.

'Galleries then, and the theatre. The best cafés, of course. You are convalescing, Miss Mallory. The Swiss air is very pure. Natural that you would walk about the town and see the sights. There are pleasant walks in the Jardin Anglais and along the Grand Quay. Marvellous views of the lake and the Hotel Belle Vue.'

'What if she sees me first?' asked Claire.

'You will be glad to see her, of course, and you might meet from time to time for lunch or coffee. You know nothing of Captain Riviere, nor of Mr Lang or Stephen, but you will ask about them.' Guy looked at his watch. 'I'll leave you both to discuss the matter. I'll come back at lunchtime for your decision.'

Claire and Matthew watched him go and then looked at each other.

'What on earth have we got ourselves into?' asked Claire.

16

From the snow-covered woods, Matthew looked down on the house in the fading light of the wintry afternoon. There was no one there. Not a light in any of the windows. He had been relieved when Sir Roland had told him that Treasonfield had been shut up for a week already. Mrs Todd had told him that Mr Lang had gone to London on business and that she and her husband had been given a holiday. Mrs White was to look after the house. Mrs Todd had not been pleased — she wondered if Mrs White was trying to usurp her position. Mrs Todd did not care for the German lady.

Matthew looked at the back gardens and beyond to where he caught gleams of the hurrying river. He thought of Stephen in the earlier days, standing there deep in conversation with his friend, Rudolph Schmidt. Two tall figures from whose company he was excluded. Not simply by age, he thought now, but because they hadn't liked him. Treasonfield had been Matthew's mother's house. He had lived there, but he had felt a stranger then. He felt a stranger now. The house looked different somehow, dark and remote, keeping its secrets — secrets which he had bound himself to uncover. Stephen was dead. Nothing could touch him now. What would be the cost to the living of finding out the secrets of Treasonfield? To Claire, to his grandfather, and to Papa Willy and Greta? His eye rested on Larch Cottage, hunched in the trees. No light on there either. He wondered where Mrs White was — not in the big house, he hoped. Not in the dark, surely.

As Major Pelham had instructed, Matthew had asked his grandfather about the accident which had killed Reverend

White and had been told that he had been in the woods shooting rabbits and that the gun had gone off when he had fallen. 'Tragedy,' his grandfather had said, but he had added that White was a fool to go handling a gun. 'Didn't know one end from the other.' It seemed that the Reverend's idea had been that in this time of food shortages, he would establish a kitchen in his church hall to serve food to the poor. Rabbits were free and could make a nourishing stew. 'Good man,' Sir Roland said, 'but he should have left the gun to Todd.'

Matthew fingered the set of keys which he'd taken from the study at Hawthorn Park, having told his grandfather that he felt like a walk after tea. How easily one slipped into deception, but it was better that Sir Roland knew nothing about Willy and Greta yet. He felt no qualms about entering the house secretly, but he hoped that Mrs White wouldn't come to see who was in the house and catch him in Willy's study, which was where he would have to search. His way through the woods had brought him to the back of the house and he passed Larch cottage set among the trees. Fresh snow had fallen and there were no footprints leading from the cottage. Still, he waited to see if any light came on.

He unlocked the back door of the big house which led into the darkened kitchen and switched on his torch. Everything was as it had always been, the big wooden table gleaming pale, the copper shining on the dresser, the old smells of cooking, hams and herbs suspended on hooks, Mrs Todd's armchair on the rag rug by the range, but no fire, of course. He went into the hall where dead ashes lay in the stone fireplace — that fire had always been lit in the winter to welcome the visitors. He was aware of the silence. Even the old clock had stopped ticking. The familiar furniture, the oak chairs and the great chest where he had often left his coat or cricket gear seemed oddly menacing in the shadows. This had been his childhood home, but he felt again that sense that he was a stranger here. An odd thought made him shiver as if he had been touched by an icy finger. No one would live here again.

He stood still, looking up the wide staircase and listening, but the silence held him as if in a spell, and he realised he was nervous. It was the thought of what he might find. He had accepted Major Pelham's commission. Pelham had impressed him — he had been wounded but had found another way of serving. But Pelham had understood some of Matthew's misgivings. The secret world of spying and lying made him uncomfortable, and to deceive his grandfather seemed treacherous.

'Think about what would happen if the Germans win,' Pelham had said. 'High-ranking people in place. We're not only concerned with the Germans and the Swiss you've mentioned. Think of the political and diplomatic circles Lang and his wife mixed in. Traitors like them who'll keep their money — and the rest of us? Under the iron heel. We can't afford to lose this spring offensive, and we can't afford to have traitors spilling our secrets to the German Army.'

Matthew had to agree. 'What am I looking for?'

'Names, of course, papers, letters. Two things in particular concern me. The first is the financial angle — is Lang funding a spy network? Sending money to Switzerland to fund the German activities there? Look out for the name Gustave Mannheim — he's a money man, into the newspaper game, buying up Swiss newspapers to publish propaganda for the Germans. And there's a Florian von Gerlach, a supposed Catholic priest, wanted in Rome for sabotage and thought to be in Geneva now. Secondly there's the shipping business — you may not know, but there are moves afoot to block the

German U-boat routes. Two a day leave Zeebrugge. The idea is to block the harbours of Ostend and Zeebrugge. Top secret. Surprise is the key to success. If something gets out, well, the risk is appalling. Lang and von Bohlen come to mind.'

On the boat from France, Matthew had convinced himself about the rightness of what he was doing. Willy and Greta were probably traitors, and he had felt a cold anger about that. And about the possibility that there were others, maybe British, who were prepared to betray their country. He imagined the marines who were going to land at Zeebrugge being shot to pieces by enemy fire because the Germans knew they were coming. And now, here at Treasonfield, where betrayal had taken place, even the deception of his grandfather seemed a necessary price to pay. After all, Willy and Greta had betrayed Sir Roland — in more ways than one.

Nevertheless, Matthew felt a sense of dread. If Willy had been helping the Germans, he would be arrested and imprisoned. His grandfather would be tainted by the association, as would Matthew's mother, who had been married to Lang. She had suffered enough. To be talked of as a traitor, even though she was dead, was unthinkable. And what of Matthew himself? Willy had been his stepfather. He had lived with him for a time. There might be those who would think that he and his grandfather must have known something. Then he was angry again. God, he hated the pair of them.

Matthew went quickly upstairs to the first floor where Willy had his study. He turned the door handle. To his surprise, the door opened. He pushed gently and he knew immediately by the smell. His torch showed him the fallen chair and the body thrown back on it. And then he saw the outstretched arm and the pistol on the rug, and the black blood on the destroyed face. Lang had shot himself in the mouth.

Matthew was shocked, only because it was the last thing he had expected. He had seen plenty of corpses. He had seen worse than this.. He had grieved for his lost comrades — men he had known and loved as brothers — but he had learned to deal with loss. Mourning was necessarily short in battle. You accepted that nothing could be done and gave the order to move on. He looked at the dead man. Lang, the traitor, who had killed himself. He didn't touch anything and left the room to think what to do next. Pelham hadn't anticipated this, either; there were no instructions about to what to do if he found Lang dead.

Matthew stood on the landing. He was a soldier with his duty to do. So, what would Pelham require? Secrecy, and for Captain Riviere, now of Military Intelligence, to make his search before he did anything else. No one knew he was here. He had time. Lang had been dead for some time. Days, most likely. The dried blood and the smell told him that. It wouldn't matter to him to wait a while longer.

He went back into the study and noted that the curtains were closed. He switched on the light. If Mrs White were in her cottage, she wouldn't see it. The drawers of the desk were open and there were ashes in the grate. Had Lang been burning papers? He thought about what Pelham had told him about enquiries into those who had German ancestry. Had Lang thought that he was suspected and that there was no way out?

Then Matthew saw that the door of the safe was open. There was nothing inside. He had no idea what Lang had kept in his safe. Money? There was none there now. Secret papers? He knelt to stir the ashes and pulled out a few bits of charred paper which crumbled at his touch, but there was a bigger piece on which he could make out a few words in German. It looked like Greta's writing. The words '*Liebe Willi*' told him nothing. He made out the word 'Mann', but whether it referred to the financier Mannheim, it was not possible to say. Had there been news in the letter from Switzerland that had devastated Willy Lang so that he had destroyed his secrets and himself? On another fragment Matthew deciphered the names 'Raulin' and 'Rudi'. Rudolph Schmidt? His name had been in Stephen's letter, and Guy Pelham had been interested in him. Was Schmidt in Geneva, he wondered, part of a spy ring?

He looked at the drawn curtains again. There had been no light on in the room when he had entered, though that might not mean anything. Lang could have shot himself in the mouth in the dark.

Shot himself. Reverend White had shot himself by accident — a man who had no idea how to handle a gun. A man who could have asked the perfectly capable Todd to shoot rabbits in Treasonfield woods. He thought of the dark cottage he had passed. Where was Mrs White, who was supposed to be looking after the house? And why had she been left in charge? Mrs Todd had been housekeeper for years. He felt again that sense that the house had been abandoned, that no one had been here. And Willy Lang had been dead for days. Matthew looked at the mangled face again. Who was Willy Lang? He hadn't liked him for his mother's sake, but other people had. He'd been generous with his employees, had given to the church, made generous donations to local charities, including, ironically, a fund for disabled soldiers. A double life. It was extraordinary how he had sustained it. What had happened to make that equable, easy-going gentleman kill himself in a darkened room?

Matthew left by the back door and walked to the cottage, the torch making circles of light before him. The only sounds were the crunching of his footsteps in the snow, the wind whispering eerily in the tall sycamores, and the low, shushing sound of the river. He stopped from time to time, just to listen, but there was no human sound. The cottage, silent as the big house, gave nothing away. The curtains were closed, and the front door was locked. Round the back, he tried the kitchen door. Locked, too. Mrs White wasn't there, he was certain.

He unlocked the kitchen door and went in. It smelt of disinfectant and was perfectly neat and tidy. The range was cold and the coal bucket empty. The cottage was as silent as Treasonfield. The sitting room was tidy, but he noted the ashes in the grate. Paper, he realised, looking closely. Reaching in, he withdrew what looked like a piece of envelope. The stamp was charred, but it was a foreign one — he made out the number 30 and the letter H — Helvetia. Switzerland. Matthew put it in his pocket and stirred the ashes again, but the papers were well and truly burnt.

There were two bedrooms upstairs. The scent of lavender water suggested that the larger room had been Mrs White's, but the chest of drawers and wardrobe were empty, and the bed stripped of its sheets and coverings. She'd been thorough. The single bed in the other room had been stripped, too, except for a folded eiderdown with a pillow on top. The room smelt of damp and stale smoke, but there were no ashes in its fireplace. Apart from the bed, the rest of the room was stacked with boxes and tea chests. Agnes's household goods from the vicarage, perhaps. They'd have to be searched.

Matthew went downstairs into the small hall and moved the thick curtain that hung across the front door, looking for any letters. Nothing. He went back into the kitchen, where he saw in the corner by the back door a crumpled paper. He smoothed out an envelope and saw that it was addressed to William Lang at Treasonfield. There was a grey stamp with the words "Deutsches Reich". A German stamp this time, but no letter inside. Mrs White — if it were she who had taken the contents of Willy Lang's safe and had burnt papers in both houses — had dropped this on the way out. To where? Had she been alone and made her way to the railway station? He didn't think she had a car. The vicar hadn't had one. That was a thought. Was Willy's car in the barn at Treasonfield? Something to check tomorrow.

The cottage was safe, he thought, walking back down the path. Mrs Todd wouldn't go in, but she had keys to Treasonfield. That was a danger. Matthew's mind worked rapidly as he walked. Lang could be left until he had telegraphed Pelham, but that couldn't be done until tomorrow, and he'd have to go to Kendal for that. He couldn't use the post office in the village — there'd be gossip. Pelham's reply, however, would come there. He'd not give anything away. Matthew doubted that Pelham would want the local police involved. Lang's death would be covered up. He was thought to be in London, and that was where he would die — in an accident, no doubt. In the meantime, Matthew had to be sure that no one entered Treasonfield. He'd have to speak to Mrs Todd, ask for her keys, tell her that he had mislaid the ones kept at Hawthorn. Thin, but it would have to do.

As to his telegram to Pelham, that would have to be worded very carefully. Pelham must know that Lang was dead. The words came to him as he walked back to Treasonfield: *Sad news. Father gone. Staying for funeral. AW not home. Send package to Hawthorn.*

Two deaths by shooting. Accident? Suicide? Or something more sinister? Mrs White had vanished without a trace. To Germany? Switzerland? Geneva? Matthew felt a tremor of apprehension. Geneva, where Claire had gone to find Greta.

105

17

It seemed so ordinary. Claire's contact from Military Intelligence in Paris had bidden her goodbye just before she had boarded the train for Geneva. Two friends hugging before they parted — it was the war, of course. You didn't know when you'd meet again. Charlotte Payne had been very convincing, dabbing her eyes then waving her handkerchief as the train rattled along the platform. Claire watched her walk away, shoulders slumped, handkerchief to her eyes.

Now she was alone and there was time to think. Matthew had made his decision, as Claire had known he would. 'What else is there to do?' he had asked. He couldn't simply sit around while his men were going up the line. He couldn't idle about at Hawthorn Park, waiting for his arm to heal when he was able to walk, and he felt perfectly well. And he needed to find out about Papa Willy and Greta. She could tell by his troubled eyes that the uncertainty gnawed at him. The idea of treachery in his childhood home was deeply shocking. He wouldn't rest until he knew the truth.

The bustle of their flight to Montreuil, the haste and anguish of Matthew's departure, and for her, Major Pelham's instructions about names, invisible inks and coded letters, the study of maps, the rigorous and speedy directions about what she should do in Geneva, how to protect herself, whom to contact if she needed help, and her journey to Paris had meant that a sort of excited tension possessed her, as if she were wound up taut as a wire spring. But now the shock of it all chilled her. It was possibly — probably — true that the Langs were spying for the enemy.

Major Pelham had turned to her after Matthew had agreed. She'd said yes because of Matthew. They had talked it over, lying on Matthew's bed in Madame Roche's back bedroom. Of course there were unknown dangers, but Matthew had faced worse things and so had she. They couldn't say no to Major Pelham, but it was for Matthew that she was on the train, wearing her uniform, lace-up shoes, a shapeless hat and spectacles with plain lenses. Her suitcase, suitably travel worn, was on the rack with her simple grey coat. She had a couple of nightdresses, underwear, two grey cardigans, white blouses, two skirts, a black dress in case she needed one for an evening, a pair of black shoes with heels and marcasite buckles, stockings, a washbag, and under the false bottom three hundred pounds in Swiss francs. Charlotte Payne had been very efficient. Everything was second-hand, but everything fitted, even the shoes. There were even laundry labels on the nightdresses, underwear and blouses. Claire had left Montreuil with nothing of her own, though her things would be collected from Ytres. The uniform was deemed essential for the journey and needed to be seen when she arrived at her digs — the brave ambulance driver recovering from pneumonia who had been sent from Roye to the hospital in Compiegne to recuperate. And should anyone ask, an aunt was funding her stay in the little pension in a quiet street between the cathedral and the Madeleine church. Not that Aunt Margaret or Mother knew that she was on a train to Geneva.

But nothing about the situation was ordinary at all. Claire was alone and going into unknown territory in which the first rule was to trust no one. Before, Claire had known whom she could trust. She'd trusted the other women in her ambulance unit. The commandant might be frozen-faced and humourless, but she was straight as a die. Doctor Simpson; Sergeant Jouet on his motorbike; the padre, Henry Evans, whom she hardly knew, but had trusted on sight. Matthew, of course. Aunt Margaret, too. Capable, strong-minded, and loyal to Mother. Mother — weak and foolish at times but trusting and to be trusted. May Lemmon, who had not hesitated to help them. Major Pelham — he might be doing secret work, but his eyes were clear and honest, and he had been straight with her.

Pelham had told her that spying was always dangerous. He didn't know what dangerous contacts Greta Lang mixed with in Geneva, so Miss Mallory must be careful. Act her part. Be ordinary. Invisible. Observe. Memorise. Try not to write anything down. The letters to Paris-Plage from Geneva were part of her cover. Only banalities needed to be written in those, but they would tell him she was all right. A young woman convalescing must write to someone. The man from Thonon would pass on any important information she had discovered to GHQ. She'd send a telegram to the man in Thonon if she needed to get out.

That last part chilled her, as did the thought of the little pistol sharing the space at the bottom of the suitcase with the money. Pelham had asked her if she had experience of guns. She had. He showed her how it worked and gave her the bullets. 'Keep it loaded in your pocket,' Pelham had said, 'just in case you find yourself in difficulties. Remember, trust no one.' Except the man from Thonon, she presumed, who would be on the steamer which travelled the lake. She'd see him from the pier. For the first meeting, he would wear a red scarf and would stand in the same place on the top deck by the flagpole on the side which overlooked the pier. She was to raise her newspaper to tell him that she had arrived. He would take off his hat and smooth his hair, but he wouldn't disembark, and she must watch until the steamer sailed away. After that first contact, he would be in his place two days later, then three days after that. When she had information, she should board the steamer, go onto the upper deck and stand at the rail, looking out onto the lake. He would approach her.

It was all so unreal, as if she were playing a part in one of the spy films which had been so popular before she came to France. Thrilling, full of action; she remembered the one featuring a deadly female German spy with black-ringed eyes, wearing a headdress of peacock feathers, a slip of a black dress and impossible shoes. Aunt Margaret had laughed cynically, observing that any fool would have known what the minx was up to. The French officer who had fallen for her obvious charms must have been an idiot.

Well, Claire thought, no one would take her for a minx in her outfit. That was the point, of course. Dowdy, bespectacled, invisible Miss Mallory would hardly be taken for a spy. She looked at her fellow passengers. How quickly Major Pelham's lesson was being learnt. The passengers looked ordinary, too, but what were they hiding? The well-dressed woman with the little boy on her knee had a sweet face. Dress her up in peacock feathers and she might be taken for a spy. That red-cheeked lady knitting in the corner seat looked like a farmer's wife — Pelham had told her of a case in which messages had been knitted into a scarf by a very respectable lady. The man in the frock coat, a lawyer, perhaps, but what secret papers written in invisible ink might be in his briefcase?

Claire's view of the world had changed. If Greta and Willy Lang could be traitors, so could anyone. She thought of the bespectacled, dowdy vicar's wife, Mrs White, in whom Major Pelham was so interested. *You never know*, she thought, looking out of the window at the quiet landscape unfolding under the winter sun. This was unoccupied France, away from the front line. It seemed unreal, too. Untouched farmhouses with smoke curling from chimneys, cows in the fields, a man looking up at the sky, children waving, a woman hanging out her washing. She thought of the laundress who signalled to the German airmen with her washing on the line. Nothing was what it seemed anymore.

Claire alighted from the train at Cornavin railway station and walked down the Rue de Montblanc. From the bridge she could see the lake glittering in the sunshine, the steamers plying to and fro, the mountains gleaming white in the distance, all as pristine as a picture postcard. Across the bridge were the shining white buildings with their ornate balconies and shutters, red roofs, and the spire of the cathedral soaring up. Somewhere, tucked into the narrow streets, was her pension. The luxury hotels, the apartments, shops, cafés and restaurants all looked prosperous. You'd never know that there was a war on — except for the spies, of course. Major Pelham had told her all about the spy networks in Geneva, including the ladies who drank cocktails at the Hotel Belle Vue.

Claire crossed the bridge and sat down on a bench on the promenade, watching the well-dressed ladies and gentlemen, some of whom were in military uniform. She recognised the green uniform of a cavalry man. So smart in his gleaming boots. He looked like a toy soldier from the ballet. She thought of Matthew on a stretcher in his blood-spattered khaki. There was plenty of fur — full-length coats, fur muffs, collars, and hats. An elegant woman walked by in dark blue velvet trimmed with white fur; neat two-tone boots buttoned at the side in the latest fashion showed under her ankle-length skirt, rather narrow at the hem. Her companion wore a long fur coat, too, and highly polished boots. A silver-topped cane completed his look of wealth and ease. Furs and velvet for the children, too, but a sensible tweed cape for the young woman who accompanied them. A nursemaid, perhaps. Claire was struck by the pink-cheeked healthiness of the passers-by.

And suddenly she longed to be back at CCS 21, huddling round the paraffin stove, drinking Bovril and gossiping with her friends, waiting for the alarm. It was dangerous and heartbreaking at times, but she was used to the cold, the hunger, the perilous driving, the injuries, even the deaths.

She looked again at the passers-by. What did they know or care about what she had seen? She hated their smug, well-fed faces, the gleaming boots and gold braid. And she thought of Greta Lang, no doubt swathed in furs, drinking hot chocolate in one of those luxurious cafés. Anger propelled her to her feet. She had a job to do.

Pelham's map showed her the way down the Rue de la Fontaine, past the Madeleine church towards the Cathedral de Saint Pierre where she found the discreet pension in a small house on the narrow Rue de St Marie. A good many saints, she thought, and hoped they were in a protective mood.

Madame Grenier looked at Claire's passport but asked no questions, just showed her up to a clean and tidy room on the first floor, pointed out the bathroom, and said that she could have a light supper at eight o'clock. The woman had a rather severe face that gave nothing away, shrewd black eyes and black hair, shiny as paint, drawn into a bun at the nape of her neck. She wore a simple black dress — no ankles showing — topped by a starched white apron. Was she, Claire wondered as she unpacked her case, another Madame Foulon to whom she was to address her letters to Paris-Plage as Mrs Smith? Lord, she was at it again. *Trust no one.*

She put some of the Swiss francs into her purse, hesitating over the pistol. She could hardly imagine any of those fur-clad ladies taking a pot shot at her — or even the gentlemen. She left it in the suitcase. She would hardly need it at the Pension Saint Marie. She was just an English woman recovering her health.

Now, a bath in which hot water was to be had. Soft white towels and a cake of sweet-smelling soap. Luxury. She might as well enjoy it. No use feeling guilty. She enjoyed the omelette and fried potatoes, too, prepared by Madame Grenier. There was no one else in the small dining room, where there were only three tables with two chairs at each. The absence of tablecloths and cruets suggested that no one was expected.

Claire slept dreamlessly in her soft bed and woke to the sound of chiming bells, surprised to find that she was not in her bunk at Ytres under a thin blanket, her frozen feet sticking out at the end. Of course, the cathedral. Geneva. A bathroom and hot water again. She hadn't felt this clean since 1916. Fresh rolls, jam, and hot chocolate for breakfast, and a few enigmatic words in English from Madame Grenier.

'The air is very good on the promenade. There is a kiosk which serves coffee. From there you can watch the people coming and going from the fine hotels and see the steamboats come into the pier. It will be very interesting.'

Claire half-expected her to wink to indicate that she was speaking in code, but Madame Grenier's face was inscrutable as Claire left. She hoped the man from Thonon might be a little more readable, or anyone else for that matter.

18

Sorry about sad news. Meet home. Last train. All best, Ned.

Matthew had deciphered the telegram received in response to his, though he had no idea who Ned might be. Sent by Guy Pelham, he supposed. He knew that the last train stopped at the little station nearby at nine o'clock, so he had arrived at Treasonfield in plenty of time and was surprised to see three men climbing out of a lorry which halted before the front steps of the house. The men were dressed in rough coats, caps and workmen's boots. Two of them carried sacks. The oldest of the three, and the senior, Matthew guessed, introduced himself as Ned. Matthew saw a man approaching forty years, with a broad, genial face and generous lips revealing strong white teeth, but grey eyes that were shrewd and calculating. This was no ordinary workman.

Matthew told him about the empty safe and the fragments of letter with the names 'Raulin' and 'Rudi', explaining the possible link with Agnes White, the vicar's wife who had vanished.

'Yes, we're trying to find out about her. We'll let you know.'

'I found an envelope with a German stamp, so she's in touch with her relatives, maybe.'

'Very likely. Now, we need to get the chappie upstairs away tonight. We'll clean up as best we can. Anyone else have a key to the room?'

'No, it'll stay locked. The housekeeper might come to the house, though.'

'Best let her if she does — keep it ordinary. Lang's in London as far as anyone knows. She won't ask about his room?'

'She has no need to, and I've got the keys to Mrs White's cottage as well,' Matthew said. He didn't ask any questions. He knew they wouldn't be answered. Mrs Todd wouldn't expect to go into the study. He wondered about the blood on the rug. Well, it was only a rug — it could be thrown away.

Matthew stayed downstairs, but he could hear the low murmur of voices upstairs in Willy's study and the sound of furniture being moved about. They would bring the body down and take it away in the lorry.

He heard them on the stairs, and one of the men went up carrying a canvas stretcher, the kind Matthew had seen so often on the front line. Together the three men manoeuvred the stretcher down the stairs. Matthew looked at the shape on the stretcher as they carried it out. He was impressed by the efficiency of the operation, but he was chilled by its ruthlessness. He didn't feel much pity for Willy, but it was unnerving to know that he would make his last journey on that lorry to some unknown destination, and that his body might turn up on the banks of the Thames. And then he thought of the men he had seen bundled onto stretchers, the bearers staggering away in the mud to the dressing station. He thought of the men who had drowned in shell holes, and the men who lay out there, their bodies lost to human sight. Lang deserved it.

The senior man came to speak to him. 'We've cleaned up as best we can, but we need to get a move on. Did Lang keep or use a pistol?'

'I don't know. There's a gun cupboard with all the usual shotguns for pheasant, rabbit and so on. He might have kept a pistol.'

'Ah, well, we'll test it. Make sure it's the one that shot him. We've searched for papers in the usual places — desk, shelves, up the chimney, but we might have missed something. I'll leave it to you, and that cottage. I've locked up. Here are your keys.'

'And if I find anything, is it for you or Pelham?'

Ned showed Matthew a slip of paper. 'My number. Memorise it.' He grinned at Matthew. 'If there's anything, ask for Uncle Ned.'

'Anything urgent, you mean?'

'We can't take for granted that it is suicide. It looks that way, but the study door was unlocked, so you never know. Someone might be waiting for news of the discovery of the body and when no news comes, they might be back, so keep a watch on the place and your wits about you.' Ned paused, looking up the stairs. 'If it is something else, he'll have left a trace. They always do.'

Matthew watched until the taillights of the lorry disappeared into the night. *If not suicide, then murder*, he thought. This was a different world in which he had no idea who his enemy was. Even a sniper was a known enemy, despite being hidden from sight. One shot awry and you knew what he was and where. He lit a cigarette and watched the smoke in the cold air. A cloudy night presaging more snow. Time to go. He locked the door and turned to go down the steps when he saw the answering red glow of a cigarette in the woods opposite. *Sniper*, he thought, suddenly back in the trenches and about to duck. His laughed at himself, and his heart steadied. Not a sniper in these woods. Poacher, maybe?

But he was aware of a prickling at his neck, and of the stillness and the dark. Matthew didn't take his eyes off the place where that tell-tale red had shown, but it was gone. He knew, though. His sense of danger had been honed during the long nights at the front. Someone had been watching this house where a man had died. Possibly murdered. He thought about the smell of smoke in that second bedroom, and the folded eiderdown and pillow on it. Mrs White's bed had been stripped completely. Had someone left a trace? *They always do.*

19

There was some comfort, Claire thought, in seeing the red scarf and the man who had taken off his hat and smoothed his hair. At least he knew she was in Geneva, and she had made contact. She didn't feel quite as alone, though it would have been better if she had been able to make out his face. As it was, the contact had been so fleeting that his face had been a blur as he turned away. She had only raised her newspaper in a very brief gesture.

Well, he was gone now. Time to follow instructions. She was to spend her first day exploring her surroundings and working out the routes back from the lake to the pension. She should use different routes, making sure she could find her way through the narrow, medieval streets of the old city which wound about the cathedral. She should have her map, take note of the buildings and the street names, try out the shortcuts, and make sure she knew the blind alleys.

She strolled along the quay to have a look the Hotel Belle Vue, which faced the Jardin Anglais and looked very expensive. Claire had no difficulty in imagining Greta in there and she would certainly see her if she came out of that grand entrance. There were plenty of well-dressed people coming from the hotel into the garden, but she didn't linger. It was time to work out her way back to the Rue de St Marie, taking a different route from the Rue de la Fontaine.

Claire made her way back to the cathedral where she climbed up some steep steps under a covered way into the cathedral precincts, and from there she found her way out into the Rue St Pierre. Another winding passage took her back to the

Madeleine church. She retraced her steps several times. It was easy to get lost, so she was careful to note the names of cafés, the different types of shops, the tall houses with their heavy wooden doors. She memorised shields and nameplates as she passed them, a curious lamp on the corner of the Rue Perron, the bookshop at the entrance to the Passage de Monetier, the wrought-iron sign over a little café, the marble plaque over the entrance to the large house on the corner of the Rue de St Marie. Finally, she looked up at the lamp over the door of her own pension, by the side of which she entered another narrow street which took her back to the cathedral and into a square. Now she saw that Geneva wasn't entirely composed of smart cafés and elegant hotels; here the houses were shabbier, the cafés poorer and the people looked as if they worked for their livings.

Claire took out her map — better to look like a tourist who had lost her way. She took the Rue Belle Filles. That was a mistake, as she realised from the curious glances given by a few men gathered at the entrance to a bar, and she looked up to see a couple of young women in dressing gowns gazing down at her. *Belle Filles*, she thought. No one could possibly think she was touting for business. A swift right turn took her into another narrow passage, and she saw a sign which told her that she was passing the Café Martin, a name she knew. Pelham had told her that it was a meeting place for agents who were to be sent into France by their German handlers. Not a place where Greta Lang would be found and better to keep her distance. A place for low-life types. Claire hurried on, and after a few twists and turns she was back near the cathedral. She walked onto the Rue St Pierre where she found a café, a sandwich and a coffee. She was satisfied that she knew her way round — in daylight, at any rate, but she supposed she'd have to walk at night, too, though not in the Rue Belle Filles. She settled down to watch the passers-by.

Idle curiosity made her watch the couple standing across the street in front of an open door by the entrance to what looked like a narrow passage. A man wearing a long dark coat and a fedora hat was talking to a woman, also in black, who was putting what looked like an envelope into her bag. When the woman looked up, Claire saw a face she knew. Claire picked up her map to shield her own face and managed to peep over the top of it to get another look. The man had vanished — into the house? Or down the alley? The woman crossing the street towards the café was Agnes White.

Claire froze in her seat, but the woman passed by, and then Claire was up and out of the café and following the woman into the precincts of the cathedral and out into the Rue de la Fontaine, where she kept her in sight until she watched her go into the Hotel Belle Vue. After a minute or so, she followed. Claire stepped out of the revolving door and caught sight of the woman at the reception desk, where she was handed a key. Claire stepped smartly back into an empty section of the revolving door and was then out again on the promenade. So, the vicar's poor widow was staying at the plush Belle Vue. With her great friend, Greta Lang, perhaps.

Claire was astonished to see the man in the red scarf taking off his hat and smoothing his hair as he watched her approaching the steamer pier. She had intended to board the steamer to tell him that she had seen Agnes White. It was definitely Mrs White. Claire had seen very clearly that thin face, the narrow lips, the spectacles, and the grey hair under the fur-trimmed hat. Agnes White had looked every inch an ordinary woman with her shopping bag and stout boots. But what was the vicar's widow doing meeting a man in a quiet Geneva street?

She strolled to the kiosk, not looking back. He must have news, she thought, since he had disembarked to wait for her. Claire heard his footsteps come closer and as he passed her, he murmured, 'Tram to Cornavin. Sit behind me.'

The tram rattled across the bridge, and Claire looked out to the lake where the steamers plied, pennants and Swiss flags fluttering, passengers on the decks pointing at the water and the mountains beyond. The war seemed a long way away. And yet here she was, carrying a pistol in her handbag on a tram to somewhere, waiting for a stranger sitting a few seats away to signal what to do. All as if it were the most natural thing in the world. But then Claire had once picked up a patient's severed hand, handed it to the orderly, and walked back to her ambulance to help unload the next patient whose jaw had been smashed to bits.

Once across the bridge, the man from Thonon stood up. Not the railway station then. Claire followed him off the tram and onto the quayside. He entered a café and she joined him at a table in the furthest corner. They chatted in French about Geneva and train times until the waitress brought two coffees. Now, sipping her coffee, she had a good look at him — just an ordinary man with brown hair and serious eyes of no particular colour in a thin face. He wore a pencil moustache and revealed crooked yellow teeth when he smiled. The gap between his two front teeth gave a fleeting impression of vulnerability. Yet he must live on the edge of danger, and he certainly knew his job, for he looked round casually before he said quietly, 'English now. I've important news which mustn't get lost in translation.'

Claire noticed his northern accent. 'All right.'

He kept his voice low and took her hand. 'We are lovers,' he said with a wry smile. 'Keep your hand in mine. News from

Pelham. Papa is dead — shot, maybe suicide, maybe not. Your cousin is investigating. The vicar's wife seems to have gone away without a word.'

Claire leant forward so that their heads were almost touching. 'She's here. I saw her with a man in the Rue St Pierre. She took what looked like a letter from him. I could only get an impression of his dark hat and long coat. I saw her face, though, and followed her to the Hotel Belle Vue. She went in and took a key from the reception desk. I'm thinking that Mama —' Claire was careful not to use names — 'might well be staying there.'

'Uncle G. wants you to make contact, so if they are both in the hotel, then find them. You've nothing to hide — you're just convalescing. Uncle G. wants to know if they know about Papa's death. Seems likely, considering you've seen the vicar's wife, who was supposed to be looking after Papa's house. If they lie, then you know. It's urgent now. There must be a reason for the sudden death and a reason for her leaving Papa behind. Take a room at the Belle Vue. You've enough money?'

'Yes, but Mama wouldn't expect to see me there —' she gestured to her coat — 'not my sort of place.'

'You have the right accent. Anyway, tell her you're only there for a few days.'

'I'll say it's the only place I knew.'

'Good idea. Make sure you know where their rooms are and how to get in and out of the hotel on the quiet — you never know —'

Claire thought about the gun in her handbag and Major Pelham's serious eyes when he had told her there might be danger. She nodded. 'I will.'

'It might just be a matter of simply finding out what she knows about Papa and who she sees. She's no reason to be suspicious, and she might spill some names. Two names have cropped up in the fragments of a burnt letter at Papa's house.' He let go of her hand to show her a piece of paper on which she read the names 'Raulin' and 'Rudi'.

'The second name could be the name of a connection of the vicar's wife. He went to school in England with Mama's son,' said Claire.

'Would you know him?'

'I think so, but he might not recognise me — I was a young girl when he stayed at Papa's house, but if he's at the Belle Vue, Mama's bound to introduce me.'

'You'll be delighted to see him, I'm sure.' The man from Thonon took her hand again and lowered his voice to barely a whisper. 'Raulin, we know about — Swiss Army man, supposed to be, but suspected German sympathiser. Could be passing on military information from his British connections. Known to Mama. See what you can pick up.'

Claire nodded and took a sip of her coffee.

'Also a Mr Mannheim. Money man. His name is worth listening out for. I'll give you a couple of days and I'll be on the steamer on, let's say, Wednesday. Take your hat off if you're coming on board. Look out for a green scarf and a fur hat. I'll signal as usual. If you need help in the meantime, telegraph from the post office to —' Claire looked at the words on another piece of paper: *Sutton, Post Office, Quai de Ripaille and Mochat Import/Export, Avenue de L'Église.*

'They know me at the post office. They'll find me. "Auntie sick" will do for a telegram. Don't use your own name. The other is my address — in case you have to get out. Memorise both. Take this.' The man from Thonon — whom Claire now knew as Mr Sutton — pressed a key into her hand and put the paper back in his pocket.

'What about the pension? Uncle arranged all that.'

'I'll see the landlady before you do. She'll understand. Can you find your way back?'

'Oh, yes, I've been doing a lot of walking.'

He kissed her on both cheeks when they stood up to leave. Claire walked to the tram stop. Mr Sutton, she thought, or not, perhaps. From the north, though. Manchester, maybe. He hadn't hidden that. Perhaps he had known Willy Lang.

She didn't look back. On the tram she thought about Willy's death. Maybe suicide. If not, then murder. Murder at Treasonfield. That was a frightening thought.

20

Agnes White was in the breakfast room of the Hotel Belle Vue. Even though Claire couldn't see her face, she recognised the coiled grey plaits looped over the head, the thin, hunched shoulders and the long black skirt. *No skulking,* Claire told herself, putting the spectacles in her pocket. *Take the initiative.*

'Mrs White,' she said cheerfully, touching the woman's shoulder.

Startled, Agnes White twisted round and looked up. 'I'm not — oh, Miss Mallory —'

'How lovely to see you. What a surprise.'

'Indeed. What are you doing here?'

'I'm on leave. I was in France doing ambulance work and then I got pneumonia, so I'm convalescing for a few days.'

'In this hotel?'

'Yes, it's the only place I know. I shan't be staying long. Is Mr White here?'

'Oh, you haven't heard. My husband is dead — an accident.'

'I am so sorry, Mrs White. I expect you wanted to get away, and it is rather lovely here.'

'I am here with Mrs Lang.'

'Oh, golly, how marvellous.'

'Not exactly. Her health is not very good.'

'Oh, I see. Is Mr Lang here, too?'

'No, he is far too busy. He is in London just now.'

Probably a lie. Claire determined to press on, though she could tell by the terse answers that Agnes White was keen to get rid of her. 'Have you been here long?'

'A week or so. I came to keep Mrs Lang company.'

'How is she now?'

'Better, of course, but not well enough to return to the wind and rain in Westmorland. We are thinking of leaving Geneva for the mountains, where the air will be good for her.'

'I'd love to see her if she's well enough. You will tell her I'm here, won't you?'

'Of course. Now, if you'll excuse me.'

'Oh, yes, I didn't mean to disturb your breakfast, but I was so cheered to see a familiar face.'

'Yes, well, I'm sure we will meet again before Mrs Lang and I leave for the mountains,' Agnes White said, picking up her newspaper. *Der Tag*, Claire noticed, a German newspaper, full of the news of German glory.

Her coffee unfinished, her fresh rolls untouched, Agnes White left the dining room and Claire took a seat at another table. Well, she had disturbed Mrs White's breakfast. That was telling, as was the probable lie about Willy Lang being in London. Agnes White must know that Willy was dead — why else would she be here? As she buttered her own hot roll, Claire pondered. Agnes White looked the same, but something had changed. There was something hard about those pale eyes behind the spectacles, the expression of which had not changed when she'd spoken of her husband's death, and it was perfectly clear that Claire's unexpected appearance had rattled her. And she had said "I'm not"— I'm not Mrs White, perhaps.

Claire thought she had acquitted herself rather well, but those cold eyes warned her to be on her guard. Agnes White had vanished from Treasonfield and might well vanish from Geneva with Greta. Greta was clever. She had been here in Geneva for the last three years. If she were a spy, then she had

had plenty of practice and Claire Mallory was new to the game. She must not be complacent.

The summons came to take tea in Greta's suite, to which Claire presented herself at four o'clock. She already knew the way. She had spent a satisfactory hour exploring the hotel, its dining rooms, bars, the terraces and gardens, and the back stairs down which the chambermaids went. This led to a corridor, the kitchens, and to an outside door into a large yard where lorries and carts parked and from where you could take a path into the garden. At the odd moment when she met a maid, she only had to flutter about being lost to be directed back to her room.

Very luxurious, Claire thought now, taking in the long windows of the suite which gave onto a balcony with a view of the shining lake. The room was furnished with gilded and brocaded sofas with plush velvet cushions, a desk inlaid with gilt with a silver inkstand and hothouse flowers in a crystal vase, and a tea table with a silver teapot, dainty cups and saucers, tiny sandwiches, and even tinier cakes. Through an open door she glimpsed a four-poster bed, draped in blue silk. Another closed door must lead to Agnes White's room, and there would be a private bathroom for each of them. Claire hardly dared speculate what such opulence might cost, and she remembered Major Pelham's cynical observation that the Germans paid well.

Greta looked exactly the same. Her afternoon dress was stylish, showing neat ankles encased in pale blue suede shoes with fashionable wine-glass heels. The dress fell in folds of matching pale blue crepe from the frothy lace collar that showed off her dark hair, piled in waves on top of her head. She looked beautiful and not at all unwell, but no doubt she could act the part of an invalid when necessary. Agnes, in her funereal black, looked as if she had come from the undertaker's. Claire wore a grey skirt, a white blouse, and a cardigan. Her hair was tied in a demure bun at her neck. She had aimed for a rather English governess look. No fashion sense, of course. Invisible woman. She was pale enough to pass for an invalid, however, and the bruise on her cheek added to her look of fragility. She could cough to order, too.

Greta put on a convincing display of delight at Claire's unexpected appearance at the Hotel Belle Vue. She kissed her gently on both cheeks and Claire watched the soft hand with its clean, buffed nails wave her to the sofa, aware of her own roughened red hands — the hands of a woman who had driven through nights of freezing cold and rain. The blue crepe folded itself perfectly as Greta sat and looked at her, smiling fondly. Of course, she was too polite to hint at any curiosity as to how Claire could afford the Belle Vue. She expressed sympathy for Claire's illness, explaining that she, too, had problems with her lungs — the damp in England. Of course, darling Willy didn't mind it — he had lived there so long, but she was used to the pure Swiss air. Yes, she would go back after … the war must end soon. Then again, they might live in Switzerland. It was hard to say what one might do at present. Things were so uncertain. Claire would go home, yes? Oxford, wasn't it? Lovely city. Or would she go back to France? Where was it she had been? How long had she been ill?

The questions were skilfully slipped into the general conversation, but Claire was ready. *Tell as much of the truth as you can about your ambulance work*, Guy Pelham had said. *It's all right to mention Roye — far enough from the front line, but you've been ill since January. You were evacuated to a convent in Compiegne. That way, you'll know nothing about the front line now.*

She explained to Greta and Agnes, who was knitting and certainly listening, that she had been ill for more than a month. She had been evacuated from Roye, where she had been stationed as an ambulance driver.

'Brave girl,' Greta purred. 'That must have been very taxing.'

Claire coughed a genuine cough and sipped her tea. 'It was. We were often so cold and tired that I suppose I got run down and it turned into pneumonia. I was taken to a convent hospital in Compiegne. The nuns were very good, and the food was better.'

'Oh, my dear, such a long time to be ill. From the beginning of January, you say? It was very cold then, of course. But you will get better here, I've no doubt. You should perhaps go somewhere quieter than the city. Nyon is very charming. I have friends there in a lovely chateau. I will take you there for a visit. And there are the mountains, of course — very good air for the lungs.'

Claire let her rattle on, not minding that her jaw ached from smiling. Agnes White was not a smiler, but Claire was aware of the flash of her spectacles when Agnes looked up from her knitting, and she sensed those cold eyes on her.

'And dear Matthew?' Greta asked. 'What news of him?'

'I don't know, Greta. I haven't heard anything, and I was so ill, I couldn't write. I've written to my mother, of course.'

Claire felt she had made a mistake to mention letters when Greta said, 'And you haven't heard from dear Sir Roland?'

'No, as I say, I haven't been in touch with anyone except Mother.'

'Sir Roland will know where his grandson is. I must write to him. Matthew will be in France with his regiment, I expect.'

'Yes, I should think so.'

'You don't go back to France, Miss Mallory?' Agnes asked.

'I doubt it, Mrs White. I was terribly ill, and I think my mother would like me to go home.'

'Quite right. A child's duty is always to the mother.'

That gave Claire the cue she had been waiting for. She felt a little guilty about the question she was going to ask, knowing what she knew, but these two were consummate liars. It was her turn. 'Oh, and Stephen, Greta, how is he?'

'Studying hard in Vienna with Doctor Wesel. You remember him, Claire?'

'Of course, such a clever man, and Stephen, too. I expect he is doing awfully well.'

Claire didn't ask about Rudolph Schmidt. She had hardly known him. It would be inappropriate. She coughed again several times and said it was time for her to rest. As she was leaving, Greta suggested she join them for cocktails and dinner. There were interesting people to meet — if Claire didn't mind a cosmopolitan group and after all, the Swiss were neutral, even if some of their friends and relations were German or Austrian.

'Here in Geneva, one must take people as they are, my dear. One must not be judgemental about one's old friends.'

'No, I'm sure not. I've seen some of the young German soldiers very badly wounded. I couldn't help thinking it wasn't their fault. It is all very difficult. Sometimes I don't know what to think.'

Greta was all sympathy. 'I know, life is so complicated in these times. I feel a little guilty being here, but it is my home, and I must look after my health for Willy's sake. Now, poor dear Agnes has come, so I must look after her, too. Do say you'll come to dine. We should both like it.'

Claire doubted that Agnes White would like it, but she said as innocently as she could, 'You are both very kind. Thank you, I shall be glad to come.'

'Excellent, it will do you good to meet some new people. Now, run away and have a nice lie down.'

Claire went up the stairs to her own room. Greta Lang was very convincing if you didn't know she was lying. What, though, was her game in introducing Claire to her friends? She and Agnes seemed very interested in the length of Claire's illness and her evacuation from Roye.

Claire was introduced to the other guests in the gilded private anteroom. She wore simple black crepe and buckled shoes. No lipstick or powder, of course, but she left the spectacles in her room, and the pistol in her suitcase.

Greta was gracious in silver and white fur. Agnes White was still in black like the spectre at the feast. A couple of other women, shining hard as crystal, wore silk and diamonds, one blonde and the other dark, both with smiling, carmined lips and very good teeth. Madame Brahms and — Claire's ears pricked at the next name — Madame Mannheim cast an appraising look over the black dress, saw nothing of interest and murmured polite greetings. Two men in tails bowed. There was one man in uniform. Swiss, Claire recognised. Major Pelham had instructed her. She knew a Swiss uniform from a German one, a cavalry uniform from an infantry one, a dress uniform from a field uniform, and the gold and dark blue of the aristocratic-looking man bowing to her was certainly the attire of a high-ranking officer.

'Colonel Raulin, this is Miss Claire Mallory, an English friend of mine.' Greta spoke in English.

The colonel's English was faultless. He expressed his pleasure in meeting her. Claire murmured politely that the pleasure was mutual. Cocktails were served by a waitress in black and white, but Claire declined — a clear head was needed. Mr Sutton had said Raulin was a suspected German sympathiser. And in any case, the rather gauche Englishwoman wouldn't be much of a drinker, perhaps.

'You would prefer something else?' Colonel Raulin asked.

'Just soda water, if I may.'

A soda water was summoned and appeared in an instant. The colonel asked what she had been doing in France. Nursing, perhaps? For the Red Cross?

'I drove an ambulance for the Red Cross.'

Raulin extolled the virtues of the Red Cross in Geneva, its work with prisoners of war, and congratulated her on the fine work she had done for the wounded. Claire sipped her soda and smiled politely until a bejewelled blonde woman claimed his attention.

'Regine Diane,' a voice murmured in her ear. A gentleman introduced himself as Monsieur Thomet, director of the Belle Vue hotel. 'Very chic, is she not, Mademoiselle Diane — a French singer.' Claire agreed that the lady was very chic, and wondered what her relationship with Colonel Raulin might be. Monsieur Thomet hoped she was enjoying her convalescence at the hotel and if she wanted anything, she must, of course, ask. Claire smiled at his bland, rosy-cheeked face, and wondered. Convalescence, indeed. *Trust no one.*

Dinner was announced, and Monsieur Thomet escorted Claire to her seat in the next room, where she found herself between Greta and a man whose name was Doctor Brahms. It seemed that Greta had informed the whole company of her recent illness. Doctor Brahms agreed that her treatment in the convent hospital at Compiegne would have been very good — the nuns made fine nurses.

'And where did you serve before you fell ill?' he asked.

'At Roye.'

'Ah, yes, a scene of much bloodshed, but the French had their victory, thank God, last year. But we will not talk of the war tonight. Poor Greta thinks much of Willy's stepson serving at the front — er — Matthew, I think?'

'Yes, I think of him, too, but I don't know where he is now.'

'It is all so difficult, I know. Enough, tell me about Oxford where Greta says you live.'

Greta, hearing her name, moved smoothly into the conversation and it was to her that Doctor Brahms now gave his attention while Claire was able to eat her veal in peace and to study the guests who were reflected in the mirrors on the walls. Colonel Raulin was talking to the blonde woman, Madame Mannheim, who clearly found him charming. Agnes White was deep in conversation with the gentleman whose name she had not caught — Monsieur Mannheim, maybe, as his wife was there? Claire wondered if he were the man in the fedora whom she had seen in the Rue St Pierre with Agnes. Agnes's spectacles caught the candlelight and Claire sensed she was being watched, but she bent her head to her glass and caught the name "Wesel". She dropped her napkin and fumbled for it, hearing then that Doctor Wesel was expected very soon. 'From Vienna, of course,' she heard Greta reply. When she raised her head, the talk had turned to the theatre, a concert of music by Gustave Doret at the Victoria Hall, and an exhibition of paintings at the Galerie du Moos — Claire noted the names. They might be useful.

A pudding came with a sweet wine. There might be rationing elsewhere in Switzerland, but clearly not at the Hotel Belle

Vue. Claire had had enough suddenly. She asked for more water, at which Greta looked at her and said, 'Oh, my dear, you look exhausted. Forgive me. Would you like to retire?'

Claire coughed and nodded and was escorted to the staircase outside the dining room by the solicitous colonel, who said he would be enchanted to meet her again and show her around the city. She could only nod and hold her handkerchief to her mouth.

In her bed at last, Claire wondered what she had learned. Doctor Wesel was expected. Not from Vienna. Major Pelham had told them that Wesel was in Lörrach, not far from Basel. Doctor Brahms had been very interested in where she had served. So, she had names: Doctor Brahms and the blonde lady, Madame Mannheim. She didn't know if the man to whom Agnes White had spoken at such length was Mr Mannheim. And then there was Colonel Raulin, whose name had been on the paper that Matthew had found in Willy Lang's fireplace, and who wanted to meet her again. *Colonel*, she thought, recalling Major Pelham's account of the affair of 'the two colonels', a scandal involving two officers of the Swiss Intelligence Service who had passed information to the Germans. She had assumed that the colonel was an army man, but that uniform could well hide a spy.

She was woken by the sound of laughter outside her door and then voices murmuring in German. She was out of bed in an instant and tiptoeing across the soft rugs to the door. Colonel Raulin was asking about a room, and she made out Greta whispering back, '*Still sein*,' telling him to hush. She heard her own name and the colonel laughing softly about the '*kleines Mädchen*' — the little girl. Greta laughed, too, and Claire heard the name 'Agnes' and Greta saying, 'She sees everything. Upstairs.'

Claire heard footsteps and then they were gone. She listened for a minute or so more. All was quiet. She went back to bed and lay thinking. Greta and Colonel Raulin. Going to his room, perhaps. So much for Greta returning home to her husband.

21

The man from Thonon was in his usual place. Claire noted the green scarf and raised her hand to take off her hat. At that moment, she felt someone touch her elbow and Colonel Raulin's voice saying in English, 'Mademoiselle Mallory, you are going on board?'

'Gosh, you startled me, sir. No, I was just enjoying watching the boats and wondering where they are going.'

'You can take a steamer round the lake. You would enjoy that, I am certain. You will see all the towns. The cabin is very sheltered if you feel the cold, and you can take hot chocolate on board. I am going to my house at Nyon, which is not more than an hour's sail. Perhaps you would care to accompany me? You will like Nyon very much.'

Claire thought fast. Her instinct was to decline, but she wasn't in Geneva to stand on the jetty doing nothing. Raulin's name was connected to Willy Lang, who was dead. She looked back at the boat. Mr Sutton was still there, and she felt Colonel Raulin's persuasive hand on her elbow. She hadn't much choice. 'I would be delighted to come,' she said, 'if it is not inconvenient to you.'

They were the last to board, Colonel Raulin keeping hold of her. He told her that the upper deck gave a fine view of the lake and if she felt cold, he would be delighted to buy her hot chocolate or coffee if she preferred.

He steered her to the staircase before she could reply. It was all done gallantly, but she could hardly break away. Mr Sutton was still at his post, but he didn't look at her. The colonel pointed out the towns of Versoix, Coppet, and Céligny, all of which, it seemed, had fine castles and chateaux, and parks and gardens where one could walk and picnic. The castle at Coppet was of great interest, as it had been the home of Madame de Stael, about whom the colonel spoke at some length before exclaiming that he was '*désolé*' that Claire looked too cold, and that he had not remembered how ill she had been. She wasn't particularly cold, but he had her by the elbow again and turned her away from the rail.

Mr Sutton was looking their way, but he turned swiftly back to his contemplation of the lake. It was probably a good thing that he had seen Colonel Raulin — the colonel in his uniform was not someone you would forget, but Mr Sutton must have seen him come up behind Claire at the pier, and he might have seen that hand on her elbow and guessed that she was being coerced — gently, she thought, but she hadn't been able to refuse him. She wondered if Mr Sutton would get off at Nyon.

There was time for a hot chocolate in the smart first-class salon with its panelled walls, thick floral carpet, chandeliers and crisp, white napery. Colonel Raulin was still perfectly charming. Like her, he was on leave, but fortunately in good health. He would like to spend more time at his house, but he had duties in Geneva every day. However, it was very pleasant to meet old friends in Geneva like Madame Lang, whom he had known for a long time. Miss Mallory was a childhood friend of Captain Riviere, was she not? And the captain was the son — no, stepson — of Monsieur Lang? Claire nodded, wondering where this was leading. Captain Riviere was at the front in France, yes? The West Lancashire Division, he believed. The Third Army was in the line, he had heard. He hoped that the captain was well after the terrible events of 1917. He was, no doubt, preparing for the rumoured spring offensive by the Germans. She had heard about that? Not much; she had been at the convent since January. It was upsetting, but she had no idea where Captain Riviere was.

Colonel Raulin was as skilful as Greta with his questions. Claire answered as she had answered Greta, being careful to look directly at him. Mrs White, he thought, was rather a sad woman. So recently bereaved. What a terrible thing that her husband had died in a shooting accident. Claire agreed, though as an infrequent visitor to Treasonfield, she had not known Mrs White or her husband very well. And the poor lady, the colonel continued, how difficult life must have been as a German in England at this time. It was a cause for great sorrow that this war created so much division. He was glad to be in a neutral country and hoped that the end would soon arrive.

'I hope so, too,' Claire said, wondering if she dared ask whether the colonel thought that Britain and her allies would gain victory. She dared. 'I know Switzerland is neutral, Colonel Raulin, but I can't help asking, as you are a soldier, if you hope the Allies will win?'

Raulin sighed, blowing out smoke from his cheroot. 'I hope it will end, Miss Mallory, in peace for us all. Who does not? I do not think there will be such a thing as victory in a war like this.'

Claire felt he had patronised her with his high-minded answer. He had looked at her as if he meant what he said, but he was having an affair with Greta Lang, and he had followed her from the hotel to the pier. *Trust no one.* Certainly not the gallant colonel in his fancy uniform.

He asked no more questions when they reached Nyon, where he turned into a tour guide again, pointing out the twelfth-century church, the gate of Saint Marie, the avenue of chestnuts. He told her about the porcelain factory and the

Roman amphitheatre, which she must try to visit on another occasion. They had lunch at a café in the Place de Chateau, where Raulin ordered in French. The waiter obviously knew him very well and was most attentive, inviting the *cher* Colonel to come to the counter and choose one of their best wines. After they had eaten, Raulin looked at the watch on his wrist and exclaimed that he must escort Claire to the boat. He had hoped to show her his house, but alas, there was not time. He hoped she would come back to Nyon with Madame Lang, perhaps. He would be enchanted to give them luncheon.

Claire stood by the wooden rail on the boat. Colonel Raulin was standing watching as the steamer pulled away. She waved, but he offered no response. He wasn't looking at her, but at something or someone on the top deck. She hoped it wasn't the man from Thonon. She waited until she saw the colonel stroll away. He didn't seem to be in any particular hurry now, though he had seemed keen to get rid of her earlier. Had he no more questions for her? Those questions, especially those about Matthew and the spring offensive, sympathetically as they had been asked, were probing. He had spoken to her in English, and he had spoken to Greta in German outside her hotel room. And in French to the waiter in the café. Who exactly was Colonel Raulin?

Claire waited at the kiosk, just out of sight, after the boat docked in Geneva. She watched the passengers come down the gangway. There was a man in uniform with a beautiful young woman on his arm, a lady with two children, and a clergyman in his black woollen cassock and round hat. She remembered the name of the priest, von Gerlach, who was wanted in Rome, but how would she know? Another priest in the same garb met him and they strolled away together. Her heart fluttered a little when she saw a man with a green scarf come down onto the quay, but he walked off in the other direction. She couldn't tell if it was Mr Sutton. Another man followed him. A man wearing a fedora hat. She shivered in a sudden gust of wind coming off the lake. *Trust no one.* Colonel Raulin, Greta, and Agnes White must live by the same code. And Colonel Raulin's attentions perhaps meant that they didn't trust her. Greta had said that Agnes saw everything. Those flashing spectacles watching her. Raulin seemed to know a good deal about Matthew's army service. What else did he know? Suppose they all knew that Matthew was at Treasonfield and had discovered that Willy Lang was dead, and that Agnes White had disappeared. The man from Thonon knew. Guy Pelham knew. The icy wind gusted again. Maybe a murderer knew. What if he were still at Treasonfield?

22

There was no discarded cigarette butt, but Matthew saw the trampled ferns where someone had stood watching and had crept away. Whoever it was had walked towards Larch Cottage. He followed the trail to where the woods opened out and revealed the back door of the cottage. There were no footprints, but then he had woken to snow first thing. Matthew unlocked the back door and went into the kitchen.

There were faintly damp marks on the flagstones. Someone had been in since Matthew had left the previous day. But there was no sign in the parlour. Matthew went upstairs and looked at the single bed in the second bedroom. The folded eiderdown and pillow were still at the end of the bed, but someone had smoked in here recently. He could smell it. He looked under the bed and pulled out the chamber pot. It had been used. *He'll have left a trace. They always do.* So the man called Ned had said.

Who? Matthew asked himself. The man who had murdered Willy Lang and who had concealed himself in this cottage for some days. Why had they waited? For instructions, perhaps. Or to see what happened. A sudden thought sent Matthew out of the front door and along the path to Treasonfield. He went round the back and saw that the barn door was open. Willy Lang's car was gone. No tyre marks in the snow. Gone before light and snow. He closed the door and locked it. Better that no one knew the car was gone.

He drove back to Hawthorn Park in his grandfather's car to use the telephone, which was tucked into a space under the stairs. A female voice told him to wait just a moment and then another, deeper voice said, 'Uncle Ned.'

'Father left something for us. Just a few bits and pieces. Traces in the cottage. Oh, and the lad's taken the Alvis. The number's DA 4852 if you want to catch him before he leaves.'

'Handy to know.'

'Anything definite on the consignment you moved?'

'Ah, still not sure. I'll let you know if there's anything.'

There was a click and the line went dead. Nothing more he could do. It was time to speak to Mr and Mrs Todd. Matthew went into the panelled hall to find his grandfather looking at his letters.

'You were out early, my boy. Come in and get your breakfast.'

Over breakfast, they chatted about the sheep, the dairy, the broken fence down by the river, and the loss of Bill Clemmet's son at Cambrai in 1917. Bill Clemmet farmed at Black Beck with his older son, Jack. 'Nearly broke Clemmet,' Sir Roland said. 'Thank the Lord for Jack — he's carrying on.'

Then there was silence except for the sound of tea being poured and the clink of Sir Roland's spoon in his saucer. Matthew sensed that it was a silence full of meaning, of unspoken questions. He felt the weight of secrecy between them. Sir Roland wouldn't ask, but Matthew knew he'd have to tell him something. He'd notice all this sneaking off to Treasonfield and Kendal, and the brief telephone calls about which Matthew made no comment.

'I went to Treasonfield this morning. Agnes White has gone.'

Sir Roland put down his cup. 'Gone? Where?'

'Don't know. Germany, I wonder.'

'Doesn't Mrs Todd know?'

'I haven't asked her yet. The thing is — I'm not supposed to say, but I've been transferred to Military Intelligence.'

'Spying?'

'That's it — I couldn't just hang about waiting for my arm to heal, and something happened…'

Sir Roland's eyes narrowed. 'Germany, eh? Lang not here — supposed to be in London. They — the intelligence men — think Lang's involved in something and have sent you? They think Lang's in cahoots with Mrs White?'

'I don't know. I daren't tell you too much — it's all a bit murky, maybe dangerous, but I wanted to put you on your guard.'

'You mean if he comes back here?'

'I don't think he will come back, but he's suspected, as is Greta — in Geneva.' Not entirely a lie, but not the truth, either. Safer, he thought. What Sir Roland didn't know he couldn't tell.

'Hotbed of spies, Geneva. Two were arrested for spying for the Germans earlier this month. It was in *The Times* today. Military Intelligence really think —'

'They do. Lang had connections. Remember that chap who'd been inspecting ships — name of von Bohlen?' Sir Roland nodded. 'Well, he was a chairman of Krupp, and there was talk of a spying operation in Manchester, so Lang is in the frame, and with Greta being in Geneva, you can see why Military Intelligence are interested.'

'They must have something on Greta in Geneva.'

'I can only say that they do, and they have people there watching her.' Matthew didn't dare mention Claire. 'It's just — I'm not keen on all this cloak and dagger stuff, but I'm in it now, and I want you to be watchful. If there are any strangers about, maybe don't take your shotgun to them.'

'Sounds a rum business to me, but I'll be careful. No shouting "Get off my land" to some blighter in a spiked helmet, I suppose.'

Matthew had to laugh, but he warned Sir Roland to let his gamekeeper and the servants know. 'Just tell them not to approach anyone. Get a description and report to you.'

'Defence of the Realm Act, I suppose. All hush-hush. Well, you know what you're doing, I expect. However, same to you — be careful.'

'I'll have to go back to Treasonfield,' said Matthew. 'I need to search his papers, see if there's anything —' Sir Roland looked pained — 'I know, it's a grubby business, but if he was — is — in league with the enemy —'

'I understand. If Lang's a traitor, then he's to be stopped. I just wish it didn't have to be you.'

'The fellow who recruited me was wounded at Loos; he said he couldn't stand doing nothing. He's damned clever and he's convinced me that we need intelligence. Not what I wanted, but he was damned persuasive. I'm in it now — but not for long, I hope.'

'Well, I won't ask anything more.'

'I'll have to ask the Todds about Mrs White, and about any strangers. I don't want them going into that cottage.'

'Just tell 'em nothing needs doing and you've locked it up on my say-so.'

Mrs Todd, red-faced and floury, frowned at the name of Agnes White and her rolling pin banged down hard on the unfortunate pastry as she heard Matthew say that there was no sign of Mrs White at Larch Cottage.

'Just let me put this lid on the pie, and then we'll have a cup of tea. Kettle's boiled.'

When tea had been poured out and a slice of plum cake had been served with a flourish of a sharp knife, Mrs Todd, still red-faced, was ready to talk about Agnes White.

'Fancy Mr Lang leaving her in charge, and now she's upped and gone. Not that I ever liked her —' she glared at Matthew — 'and not because she's German, though there was them as said she could be a spy. Silly nonsense. Frightened of her own shadow, that one. Mr Lang were all right — paid us fair, and very good-humoured, but that Mrs White were always whisperin' with Mrs Lang. What Mrs Lang saw in her, I'll never know. Streak o' misery, that Agnes White, and as for the Reverend, not a patch on Mr Williams — you know, at the Holy Ghost.'

Matthew did know. Reverend Enoch Williams had been vicar of the Church of the Holy Ghost, the small parish church, for forty years before Reverend White came. By which time, Matthew and his mother had moved to Hawthorn Park and worshipped at St Andrew's. A thought struck him. 'Where did the Whites come from?'

'Manchester, I believe. Mr Lang knew 'em from there, I think. She weren't the type to talk, and he, well, he were in a world of his own, I always thought.'

'Pity, though — I mean the accident.'

'Me and Todd, we could never understand that. Whatever were he thinkin', takin' a gun from the house —'

'The cottage?'

'Nay, the gun cupboard at Treasonfield. Mrs White said he'd borrowed it. Rum do. Mr Lang said he couldn't remember. He might have given him permission. Anyway, it didn't matter who said what, the man shot himself. Accident, the coroner said. Suppose that's why she's gone — mebbe back to her family in Germany. Best place for her. She wouldn't have told me, and I'd no reason to go to the cottage.'

'I've made sure it's all locked up. Sir Roland said to leave it for now.'

'Oh, aye, but you'll want me to do the house while Mr Lang's away?'

'Oh, yes, just keep an eye on things. Sir Roland says he doesn't know when they'll be back. Mrs Lang is still in Switzerland, and I suppose Mr Lang might go there. Sir Roland has asked me to have a look round while I'm here. Check the locks and so forth.'

Sir Roland's words were law to the Todds, so Mrs Todd just nodded and said, 'Mebbe they won't come back until after the war — whenever that's to be. What about you, Mr Matthew? Will you be going back?'

'Soon, I hope, when my arm's ready to use.'

'I can't help hopin' the war'll be over before you have to go. Too many good lads have been lost. You've heard about Farmer Clemmet's lad? And there's Tom Nelson from Barbon way — married with a lad of his own — Mary Nelson heard only the other week. Dear Lord, Mr Matthew, it's a bad business.'

'So it is, Mrs Todd. When I go back, I'll be doing it for them, all the ones who've gone.'

'You're a good boy, Mr Matthew. I'd like it if you was to come back to live here someday. Mebbe settle down, eh? Miss Claire's a nice young lady.'

Matthew laughed. 'She is, and a brave one, driving her ambulance in France.'

Mrs Todd heaved a sigh. 'What girls do today. Why, even Skin Taylor's lass has left home to work in munitions up in Carlisle.'

Skin Taylor, the poacher, Matthew thought. 'Skin still about then? I thought I saw someone in the trees near Larch Cottage the other evening.'

'Nay, he bust his leg a fortnight since. Up to no good, I reckon, but he says he were just takin' a walk and tripped up. Drunk, more likely. Tell Sir Roland, Skin's out of action.'

'I will, and you tell me or Sir Roland if you see anyone hanging about. I heard a tale about fellows driving from Kendal or even further to poach on estates round here.'

'Todd'll have his gun at the ready.'

'Tell him not to kill anyone, or the police will have him up before the magistrate. He's just to frighten them off, and if he catches one, then fetch me or Sir Roland.'

'Aye, I'll tell him, but I haven't seen anyone.'

'No one's asked about Mr Lang?'

'Nay, everyone knows he went off to London. There wasn't so many visitors after Mrs Lang went to Switzerland. Just a few fellows for lunch — businessmen, I suppose. Oh, and that lad came.'

'Stephen?'

'Nay, the other one as was related to Mrs White — Rudolph summat — you remember him.'

'I do. Recently?'

'Before Mr Lang went away. A week back, I reckon. He never came to the Reverend's funeral, but then I saw him with Mrs White coming up the drive and they went in to see Mr Lang. He were only here a day or two.'

'Do you know where he came from?'

'He came on the train, but I don't know where from.'

Burly Mr Todd came in to greet Matthew as an old friend. Harry Todd had taught Matthew to shoot and to fish. Matthew couldn't remember a time when Mr and Mrs Todd had not been there, always kindly, reassuring, stalwart presences in his life. What he had been fighting for really, these good, honest folk who looked you in the eye and spoke plain truths. *Trust no one.* But he would trust these two — with his life.

Once Mr Todd had taken his tea and cake, Mrs Todd told him that Matthew had seen a stranger in the woods. Mr Todd had seen no one, but he'd heard about them townies as came poachin' and he'd keep a look out. He was surprised to learn that Mrs White had gone, and he did remember the lad, Rudolph, coming.

'All grown up now. Went across and spoke a word to him, but he didn't say owt about what he was doin'. Summat off about him. Cagey, you know. Ted Punch's lass — the one with the limp — well, she did some charring for Mrs White and says that he had a coat like them as she'd seen soldiers wear — heavy like, with leather buttons and epaulettes, so I wondered if he were in the army?'

'A British Warm?'

'Sounded like, but I can't reckon he'd be fightin' for us. A German?'

'It's possible — he was at school in Lancashire. He could have stayed in England — not wanting to join the German Army.'

'Mebbe he went to Switzerland — they're neutral. He came back just to see Mrs White.'

'I don't suppose we'll ever know. Anyhow, I'm going over to the house now.'

'Want me to come?' asked Mr Todd.

Trust him with your life. 'Good idea.'

On the way to the big house, Matthew made a decision. He stopped Mr Todd when they were well away from his cottage.

'I want to tell you something, Todd, but I want you to keep it to yourself.'

'Oh, aye, you mean not tell the missus.'

Matthew looked him in the eye. 'No one.'

Todd held his gaze and nodded. 'Aye. I'll keep me word.'

'I know you will. I can't go back to the front until my arm's functioning, so I've been temporarily transferred to Military Intelligence — investigating possible treachery here at Treasonfield.'

Todd looked shocked. 'Blimey, and you think Mrs White is involved?'

'I can't give you any details, but it's odd that she should have left without a word, and that Rudolph Schmidt should have been here. That British Army coat — good cover. A young man on a train in mufti might draw attention, but a British soldier on leave, that's not unusual.'

'You saw someone in the woods.'

'Someone watching the house — there were signs in the ferns, and I think someone's been staying in Larch Cottage. Whoever it was has gone now — in Mr Lang's car — but don't say anything about that, either. Keep the barn locked.'

'I will. Anythin' else you want me to do?'

'Be vigilant. I've told Sir Roland what I'm doing, so if you see anything unusual, go to him.'

'Right. What about Mr Lang? Is he likely to be back? I mean, what do I tell him?'

Matthew didn't want to tell Todd that Willy was dead — it would be too hard to keep to himself. 'Sir Roland said he's not likely to be back before the end of the year. Business, I suppose. You needn't worry about him.'

Mr Todd looked over to Larch Cottage. Then he said, 'That were a queer do — the vicar shootin' himself.'

'Mrs Todd said the gun was borrowed from Treasonfield — Mr Lang thought he might have given permission.'

'Who'd have been daft enough to let a shamblin' fellow like him take a gun? That's what I thought, but Mr Lang were satisfied that it were an accident.'

'You weren't?'

'As I say, a queer do, and now there's what you say about his missus. It was she as found him.'

'I'll bear that in mind, Todd. Just keep it all to yourself for now.'

Todd left him and Matthew went into the house. He stood in the hall, contemplating the empty fireplace. *A queer do.* So it was. Could Agnes have killed her husband because he had found out something? And Rudolph Schmidt had been here for a couple of days before Willy Lang was supposed to have gone away; Rudolph Schmidt possibly wearing a British Army overcoat; Rudolph Schmidt, whose name was mentioned in Stephen's letter to his so-called aunt. It was significant, no doubt, in a coded letter. Did "well" mean that Rudolph had pulled something off? And Rudolph had been mentioned in Greta's letter to Willy Lang with the name Raulin.

Matthew went upstairs to unlock Willy's study, where there was a telephone. He dialled Ned's number and heard the familiar voice asking, 'How's tricks?'

'So-so, just a call about Smith — you remember him?'

'Old red nose? Haven't seen him in a while.'

'He was up for a couple of days to see his aunt, Agnes Grey.'

Matthew heard the chuckle in Ned's voice as he responded quick as a flash, 'Jane's sister.'

'The very one. Smith's been up again for a day or two. Borrowed the car. Going back to his regiment, I think. Didn't say where, but he'd his warm coat on.'

'Never expected him to serve.'

'Neither did I. Odd how things turn out.'

'Certainly is. By the way, the consignment you mentioned, it's hard to say. Could be one thing, could be the other. Cousin Guy'll be in touch soon. Cheerio, old thing.'

Matthew put the receiver back on its candlestick holder and stared at it. Ned was a clever chap. He'd understand what all that implied, and anyone listening at the exchange wouldn't have a clue. Murder or suicide, though? If Willy Lang had been murdered, then by whom and why? Matthew sat and thought. Could Willy be innocent? Could he have found something on Agnes White? Perhaps she then whistled up Rudolph, who killed Willy before he could go to the authorities. Or was Willy a traitor, under investigation as Matthew had first thought? He could have told Agnes White of the danger, prompting her or Rudolph to kill him before he could be questioned by the British. Perhaps Agnes then took flight, while Rudolph, in the pay of Germans, stayed to see what happened.

Matthew looked at the bloodstain on the rug. Evidence of something violent. *Get rid of it*, he thought, *just in case*. He knelt down to roll it up and felt the give of a floorboard under his knee.

23

It was not at all surprising to see so many men wearing a fedora hat, but it did make it difficult to identify the man to whom Agnes White had spoken in the Rue St Pierre. Claire was watching passers-by from a restaurant near the concert hall, where she intended to spend her evening. The idea of dinner in the hotel and the possibility of having to make conversation with Greta or, worse, Agnes White, had not appealed. She had no wish to be under Colonel Raulin's scrutiny either. She couldn't do anything until she had given her information to Mr Sutton tomorrow. He had certainly seen her on the steamer, and he might have noticed that before the colonel had interrupted, she had raised her hand to take off her hat, showing her intention to board, which meant that she had information for him.

She'd thought about the man in the green scarf who had disembarked the steamer after her and walked off in the opposite direction. Surely it couldn't have been Mr Sutton, and in any case, it seemed there were as many green scarves as fedoras this evening. Leaving the restaurant, Claire entered the concert hall and purchased a ticket for the back of the stalls, from where she could slip out before the end.

The Victoria Hall, named after Queen Victoria and gifted to the city of Geneva by a British ambassador, was immensely grand. She wondered what the Germans thought of it. The music advertised was by Gustave Doret, whom she remembered had been mentioned by someone at the dinner. Claire had seen a poster in a shop window. It would be interesting to see if anyone she knew came, so she stationed herself in the foyer well before the start time, carefully concealed behind a handy palm tree, and watched. Sure enough, Greta arrived with the colonel, the singer Regine Diane, and Doctor Brahms and his wife. Where, she wondered, was Agnes White? Perhaps she didn't care for Swiss music, or, more likely, Queen Victoria. Regine Diane was greeted by another man. She watched them all mount the steps. They'd have a box, no doubt.

The lights were dimmed on the magnificence of the hall, all red, gilt and stucco. Claire tried to concentrate on the music played by a wind orchestra, but she couldn't stop the anxiety gnawing at her. She couldn't help fretting about the man in the green scarf who had come off the steamer and walked away. He had been wearing a fur hat, but like the fedoras, fur hats were ten a penny in Geneva. If it had been Mr Sutton, then why had he not made contact? And if it had not been Mr Sutton, where was he? He had seen her on the boat. She thought he must have stayed on board. Surely, he would have waited, or even got off and followed her and Colonel Raulin. He was a spy — he must be practised in the art of not being seen. He could have taken off his hat and scarf, and put on spectacles. Even she knew that the latter was a spy's trick. She had returned that morning to the jetty at the usual time, but the man from Thonon had not come. She had taken the tram to the other side of the river and looked into the café, but he wasn't there.

A burst of applause interrupted her thoughts. Lord, people were getting to their feet. It must be the interval, and she hadn't heard a thing. Poor Mr Doret — she wasn't much of an audience. The second half was to be an organ concert with sacred songs. Claire couldn't imagine sitting through another hour, trying to concentrate. She might as well fret in her room with hot chocolate. She left her seat and mingled with the crowd streaming out into the foyer, where she saw Greta and Colonel Raulin walk out of the great doors. She stood on the steps in front of the doors and watched them stroll away in the direction of the Hotel de Ville. Perhaps they were more in the mood for champagne rather than sacred music.

Claire watched them go into the hotel, then she crossed the road and took the narrow street that she knew would take her back to the cathedral and the Rue St Pierre. There was a lamp at the corner of the street. *Ah, the Rue de Perron*, she thought, but she didn't recognise the alley in which she found herself. She hesitated, aware that she was alone in the dark. Go on or turn back? She went on, painfully aware of the sound of her footsteps on the cobbles. In her hurry, she slipped and had to hang onto a wall to get her breath, feeling the prickle of sweat at her back. The alley ended in a flight of steps. An archway with a lamp hanging above did nothing to reassure her, only creating moving shadows at the entrance and ink-black dark within.

Then she heard the footsteps behind her, coming along the alley. A man's tread, she thought, heavy and rather menacing in the circumstances. Claire risked a glance back but could see nothing. She went swiftly up the steps and shot through the archway, then went down another set of steps, treacherous in the dark, slowing her down. She heard the scrape of a boot or shoe behind. At the bottom of the steps she took the first turning she came to and ran along a passage, at the end of which was the cathedral precincts. Claire stopped to look which way to go, then whirled round at the sound of footsteps behind her. A man in a black cassock and dog collar smiled at her and asked in French if she was lost. She thought of the priest on the ferry. Von Gerlach following her?

She replied in French that she was wondering if she could go into the cathedral at this late hour.

'You are English, I can tell. How nice to meet a compatriot,' he said. Claire was relieved. He was English. 'Of course, do go in. Just follow those two gentlemen. Good evening, my dear.'

Claire saw a couple of men in dark robes going towards the cathedral door. She followed and was in the candlelit space in a moment. She slipped into a pew where there were a couple of women praying and bowed her head. There was no service going on, and she heard the footsteps of the two priests walking away and then a door closed somewhere. She didn't dare look up. She had no idea if someone had followed her, but if someone had, he might have seen her come in and be waiting outside. *Sanctuary*, she thought, half-laughing. Perhaps she could cry out the word and someone would come to her aid, and what a fool she'd look, saying that she thought she'd been followed.

She waited, hearing footsteps come in and the rustle of clothes indicating that someone was sitting down in the pew behind. The whiff of scent suggested it was a woman, but she didn't look. She heard footsteps leaving and the door opening and closing several times with a creak and a cold draught round her ankles. Claire sneaked a look at her wristwatch — ten o'clock. Not that anyone would be missing her at the hotel, but she couldn't sit here all night. *Follow someone out*, she thought, and at that moment the woman further along the pew picked up her walking stick and fumbled past Claire, who stood to slip out after her. She glanced at the pew behind but saw only three bowed heads in seemingly identical black hats. Impossible to know if any of them had followed her. The lady with the stick was making her way to the door. *Follow her*, she thought. *She's elderly — not dangerous, surely*. She had an impression of a fur coat and a large hat. Respectable — maybe walking back to a respectable lighted street. She followed the woman, hesitating slightly as the lady approached the covered way which Claire remembered from her first visit to the cathedral. It looked horribly like a tunnel in the dark, but the lady went in, and she heard the tapping of the stick as the older woman went haltingly down the steps. Claire looked down the steep steps and remembered that they led into the square from where she had wandered into the Rue Belle Filles.

At the bottom of the steps, she risked a look back. There was a dark shape at the top of the steps — somebody there, standing quite still. Man or woman, it was hard to tell at a glance. Move on. Her elderly lady was gone — into the square? It was well lit and there were more people. Which way, though? An entrance to a passage. She saw lights, a café, an open door. Customers coming out. Claire darted in and slipped through the crowded tables, hoping for a back exit. No one paid attention, but she was aware of uniforms and voices and laughter. She found the ladies' lavatory and waited. If he — if it were a man — had seen her come into the café, then he'd wait. Another way out?

A young woman came into the lavatory. She took off her black hat to reveal almost white hair that looked silver in the gaslight. She took off her long black coat, under which she wore a neat black velvet jacket trimmed with fur and a gold-coloured skirt in what looked like taffeta, black stockings and button boots. She smiled at Claire as she went to look at herself in the mirror. She powdered her nose and touched up her lipstick, standing back a little to admire the improvement. 'Ah,' she said, '*c'est bon.*'

Claire spoke to her in French, asking if there was another way out other than the front door.

'You wish to avoid someone?'

'I was followed from the cathedral — a man.'

'You know him?'

'No, I just heard his footsteps behind me.'

The young woman looked at Claire critically, seeing the dull grey coat, the spectacles, and the unmade-up face. 'Well, there are some dangerous men about here, it is true. You are English? Where do you stay?'

'The Belle Vue.'

The young woman's mouth turned down. 'Very nice — for rich people. But this is not the place for you, mademoiselle — it is for working girls.'

'Oh, I see, but can I get out another way, please?'

'I will show you — I work here behind the bar.' She laughed. 'Many girls want to escape through the back way if they do not like a particular man. They like the English, of course, and the French are very *charmant*, but, others, well… Come, it's easy to slip out. You know how to get back to your fine hotel?'

'I have no idea.'

'I'll show you.'

Claire followed her down a narrow corridor. Now she was close to, she could see that the velvet jacket was worn, and the golden skirt torn in places. A working girl, but a good-natured one in her ragged finery. She thought of Greta in her furs and silk — cold as ice. At the end of the corridor, a door was propped open. A young man in a shabby raincoat and a battered fedora appeared and stood waiting. Claire heard a sharp hiss of breath from the woman, who said sharply, 'Not now, Emil, I'm busy.'

'Who is this?' Emil spoke in French, but his accent was German. There was a hard edge to his voice.

'A friend — who's in a hurry. Why don't you wait in the bar? I'll be back in a minute.'

As Emil passed, Claire could smell his unwashed staleness, the musty damp of his shabby coat, and cheap tobacco. This wasn't the person in the cathedral. Two black eyes stared hard at her, and she had a glimpse of a yellowish, unshaven face.

Her guide didn't speak until they heard the sound of a door closing. Claire saw the spark of anger in her eyes when she said, 'Someone I'd like to get away from, too.' She led Claire across the yard and told her to turn left at the end of the alley and she would come to the Rue de la Fontaine, which would take her back to the Grand Quay.

Claire looked out into the night and then back at her rescuer, thinking about how useful it would be to have a friend. 'Thank you, may I know your name?'

'Giselle.' She must have seen something in Claire's face, for she scrutinised her again. 'If you are in some danger, mademoiselle, send a note to me here at Café Martin, but do not come back.'

Claire hurried along the Rue de la Fontaine, past the cathedral and the Madeleine. The Café Martin — a meeting place for German agents, Pelham had told her, for low-life agents which she'd passed on her walk that first morning. Pity she hadn't recognised it again. Emil was one of the agents, perhaps. *German*, she thought. He'd certainly given her a hard look. And Giselle, she must know what went on at the Café Martin. That remark about danger. Maybe Giselle thought she had come to the Café Martin for a purpose and warned her off.

Claire risked a look back along the promenade as she joined the people entering the garden of the Belle Vue. She approached the front steps and was startled when someone touched her arm.

'A thousand pardons, Mademoiselle Mallory.'

It was Doctor Brahms, whom she had last seen going up the stairs at the Victoria Hall. He was looking down at her sympathetically. 'I did not mean to frighten you.'

'No, of course, I was just surprised.'

'You have been seeing the sights? So late, mademoiselle, to be out alone.'

'I just wanted some air — I thought a walk on the promenade might help me sleep.'

'You do not sleep? I can give you a powder to help. Not strong, but enough to relax you. You seem very tense, my dear.'

Claire forced a smile. 'I'm still a bit feeble, I think, after my illness. I must go up to my room. And no, I don't need a powder, but thank you for the thought.'

Doctor Brahms followed her into the revolving door — he was so close that she could smell the brilliantine on his dark, shiny hair, a scent of musk and rose, the scent she had caught from someone sitting behind her in the cathedral. Women used brilliantine for their hair, too, but still… She felt his gaze on her and looking up, caught a fleeting expression of amusement, but the next moment she was stepping out of the door, thanking him again, and going up the staircase. Turning the corner on the first landing, she glanced down to see the doctor looking up. The man next to him was wearing a fedora hat.

In her room, Claire thought of the dark shape at the top of the steps by the cathedral. It was impossible to say if it could have been Doctor Brahms, but how odd that he had materialised just as she was approaching the front door of the Belle Vue — almost as if he had been waiting for her. She amused him, did she? Well, let them think she was a fool.

Claire opened her suitcase and contemplated the pistol — she had not thought to take it to the concert. She would not make that mistake again.

24

Matthew lifted the rug and saw the loosened floorboard. He prised it up and found the little space below. It was empty. Whoever had emptied Willy's safe and burnt his papers had known what they were doing. If there were any evidence, it would be at Larch Cottage, though he doubted they would have left anything incriminating. *They* — it made sense to presume that Agnes White and Rudolph Schmidt were working together, and that it was Rudolph who was the man in the woods, the man who had slept in the cottage. What he needed, he thought, was information about Agnes White — who was she? And what was the connection between her and Rudolph Schmidt?

It was not particularly extraordinary that he and Claire, Sir Roland even, should know nothing about Agnes and Rudolph. That was the way of things. It wasn't polite to ask questions — the vicar's wife was the vicar's wife, and Agnes White had been very good at camouflage. She had seemed timid, rather distressed about the enmity between Germany and England, and had been taken under Greta's wing — what was there to suspect? No doubt plenty of spies operated in the same way. Major Pelham had mentioned a headmaster's wife in a naval port who had been sending coded letters to her sister in Germany — outwardly a pillar of society.

Matthew smelt damp as he climbed the stairs to the spare bedroom in Larch Cottage. The place seemed colder, the air of abandonment more pronounced. He looked at the boxes and tea chests which he had assumed had been brought from the vicarage. He had no compunction about forcing the tea chests open with a knife. He was sure Mrs White wouldn't need these things again. He made short work of the chests, looking at a dinner service, tea sets, glassware, decanters, candlesticks, cutlery, linen, napkins, tablecloths, all the accoutrements of domestic life, none of it particularly valuable or attractive. An unworldly man, the Reverend White, Matthew reflected looking at a box of books — *Crockford's Clerical Directory*, Bible commentaries and sermons, mostly, by forgotten clerics. Struck by the awful irony of the words, he picked up *The Christian Watching Against the Suddenness of Death* and saw inside a dedication to Mr White by the author, one Reverend Doctor Makepeace, and the address of Lincoln College, Oxford. The year was 1888. Matthew imagined two pious young men toasting muffins and counting angels on a pinhead. How on earth had White come to be married to a German wife — who had possibly killed him?

Shakespeare, Wordsworth, Tennyson, Cowper, Scott, Dickens — all the authors he might have expected were boxed up, but Matthew made sure that there were no letters or papers accidentally concealed. It was a dispiriting job — partly because these were the remnants of what seemed to him a half-life. Mrs Todd had said the Reverend White was not a patch on the former vicar. Matthew remembered very little about White, which was telling — it was dispiriting, too, because the job was possibly a waste of time.

There were more sermons and a dog-eared bundle of *The Philosophical Transactions of the Royal Society*. *Not much help in the spying business*, Matthew thought to himself, but he was quite wrong, for slipping out of the tattered papers was a slim volume of Goethe's poems, and inside that an inscription in German: *To My Dearest Agnes, my love this Christmas, 1892, your Ernst*. Matthew felt his heart quicken, for inside the cover was written the name Agnes von Ende. So, Greta and Agnes were somehow related, and most importantly to Greta's "beloved *Freiherr*", Lieutenant-General von Ende of the 50th Division.

He opened the book and out fell a folded paper. A letter, in German, of course. There was an address in Frankfurt, the salutation was to Agnes, and the signatory, 'your affectionate cousin, Berta.' Matthew scanned the letter to see if there were any mention of the von Ende name, but there was not. However, he did see the name 'Rudolph' and the name 'Schmidt'. Matthew's German was nowhere near as good as Claire's, but he made out the word 'baby' — he looked back at the address. The letter was dated 1893. He managed a somewhat halting translation, but he got the drift. Berta Schmidt, Agnes's cousin, had adopted the baby boy, Rudolph, who would henceforth be called Schmidt. Ernst would never know — he had deserted Agnes, and he had no right to know about a child he had not wanted. Agnes must refuse to see him. She must make her life in Manchester now — the Adolphus family would be kind to her.

Manchester, as Mrs Todd had said. Mrs White must have known Willy Lang there. Who'd have thought Agnes to be the object of passion and betrayal? Agnes would have been in her twenties, perhaps, in 1893. Matthew realised he had no notion of how old Agnes White might be. She had made herself invisible in a way, and yet here was proof that she had not been. Ernst — whoever he was — had loved her, but when he found out about the child, he had left. The child had been adopted and Agnes had gone to Manchester to live with the Adolphus family. Then there was the von Ende connection. Agnes's son Rudolph had been at school with Stephen von Ende. Whatever the convolutions of these relationships, one thing was clear: Rudolph Schmidt had to be on the German side, as Stephen had been. Rudolph had visited Agnes White; he knew his way around Treasonfield and Larch Cottage. He knew about Lang's car, and now, Matthew thought, he must know that Lang's body had been found, who had found it, and that the matter had been hushed up.

What had the Reverend White been doing in Manchester? He had not come to the parish of Middlethorp straight from Oxford — that was too long ago. Perhaps he had met Agnes von Ende in Manchester? Ah, *Crockford's Directory* which he had tossed aside. Granted it was dated 1912, but White must be in there. He was:

White, Cuthbert, the vicarage, Middlethorp, Westmorland. Lincoln Coll, Ox, B.A. 1892; c. St Mark's Hulme, Dio. of M/C 1894–1904; ch. to Lancaster County Gaol 1904–1912.

So, White had been curate in a Manchester church. The question was if Agnes White's friends, the Adolphus family, had anything to do with St Mark's church and might White have met his bride there? He looked under 'A' and there was Adolphus, Otto — of German extraction? Educated at Oxford, too, earlier than White, and author of the *Compendium Theologicum* — whatever that was. And vicar of St. Mark's where White had been his curate, and where White had met Agnes. Adolphus was Canon of Manchester Cathedral, too. Eminent, then. Mixed in good society like Lang? Did a favour for both White and Lang by recommending White after he'd done his stint as chaplain at Lancaster Gaol. He looked at the entry again. Otto Adolphus had achieved his B.A. in 1865, so that made him surely in his sixties. He might still be in Manchester and able to shed light on Agnes White's von Ende connections and possibly Rudolph Schmidt.

An image came to Matthew which sent him dashing back to Treasonfield and the room which used to be Stephen's before he went to Vienna.

Two framed photographs stood on a table, one featuring some of the boys from Stephen's school — older boys, sixth formers, perhaps — and next to it, a photograph with four people in it: a seated man wearing a dog collar and what looked like a tweed suit, behind him a moustachioed man in a white sweater, and two young men, about eighteen, not unalike in looks. They had serious faces, their muscular arms were folded, and they wore collarless, short-sleeved shirts, cricket trousers and white shoes. The caption read: *The School Gym Pair, 1911.*

Matthew took off the back of the frame and slid out the photograph. The names on the back in Stephen's crabbed writing confirmed that the young man on the left was Stephen himself. The one on the right was Rudolph Smith — well, that made sense. Nothing easier than to have a Swiss mother and, probably, a dead English father. Sponsored by the wealthy William Lang, who would care?

The man in the white sweater was A. H. Smythe — the gym coach, perhaps, and the seated master, C. von Rahn Nicholl. Part German — not that that signified anything. There'd been a Herr Strange at Matthew's school. No one thought anything of that in those old days before 1914.

He peered at the faces. The gym pair looked like any of the boys in the sixth form at his old school: upright, young, earnest, taking their success seriously. Stephen — Matthew thought of the blue eyes staring at him as the smoke cleared. He felt sad. He hadn't liked him. He was the enemy — yet here he was. Just a boy, not knowing what was to come. He studied the other face more closely. There was a resemblance, but Rudolph looked older, more confident, and had an arrogant tilt to his head. There was something cold about the narrowed eyes, too. Not innocent, Matthew thought.

Curious about Mr C. von Rahn Nicholl, Matthew turned to the bookcase. Stephen had left his school textbooks — Latin, French, German, Physics, Chemistry and so on — but Matthew was looking for the school register. All the public schools published a register of headmasters, assistant masters, and pupils every few years. He saw the Fernhall register, found the lists of assistant masters, and turned to the 1900s. Conrad von Rahn Nicholl had been educated at Lincoln College, achieved an MA and was ordained in 1892. Well, well, a friend of the Reverend Cuthbert White, perhaps. Mr White might not have known that Rudolph Schmidt was his wife's illegitimate son, but an orphaned relative, say, whom Willy Lang was willing to educate because Greta von Ende asked him to. What better place than Fernhall, where his old friend with the half-German name was now a master? All very neat. Conrad von Rahn Nicholl had left Fernall in 1913 for — good Lord — the University of Lausanne on Lake Geneva. A veritable spider's web of connections.

And while he was there, Matthew looked in the lists of assistant masters for A. H. Smythe, the man in the white sweater. He was there: *Ashton Hamilton Smythe, B.A. Prep. Sch. Left 1912. Kamuning Rubber Estate, Sungai Siput, Perak.*

Malaya. Rubber more lucrative than gym coaching, perhaps. Smythe — not German at any rate.

Matthew stood up. He looked at the other photograph. All those solemn, innocent faces, he thought, schoolboys in 1911. How many of them were dead in Flanders now? He thought of his own school friend, Charlie Macpherson, school captain and fearless cricketer. Royal Flying Corps and dead. Tom Proud, killed at Cambrai. And the others. Proud. They had all been proud. Play up and play the game. What folly. What waste.

He put the register of names back on the shelf. No use brooding. A phone call to Ned next.

25

Claire was still in her nightclothes when the knock came at her door. She felt a tightening in her chest. She was still anxious about Mr Sutton. Her intention was to meet the ferry again and if he were not on board, she would go to the post office at Thonon. The knock came again, more loudly this time. She hoped it wasn't Doctor Brahms come to offer her a powder.

She opened the door to find a smiling Greta swathed in furs. Claire could only manage a surprised, 'Oh.' Remembering her manners, she let Greta in. 'I'm sorry I'm not dressed. I've only just got up.'

'You are not sleeping, my dear?'

Had Brahms spoken to her? 'The cough keeps me awake.'

'Too much walking about late at night, perhaps. A trip on the lake will do you the world of good. We are all going to Colonel Raulin's house at Nyon — Agnes, Doctor and Mrs Brahms, and me, so you must come — the colonel so enjoyed showing you around the other day. He was quite charmed by you. It will be a lovely day out. We are taking the steamer at ten o'clock to be in time for lunch.'

Claire sat down on the bed with what she hoped was a convincing show of feebleness. 'Oh, no, I feel so tired this morning, Greta. I just want to stay in bed today and sleep.'

The smile stayed in place, but Claire had already noticed a strain about Greta's eyes which had not been there before. Had something happened, she wondered, that meant they wanted her out of Geneva — and maybe for longer than a day?

'Ah, that is very disappointing, but another time will present itself, I'm sure. Shall I send Doctor Brahms to you before we leave?'

'No, thank you — I'm just tired.'

'Very well, as you wish, but I will speak to Monsieur Thomet and he will make sure that the maid brings you some coffee and rolls this morning, and lunch later. Then you won't need to leave your bed.'

Claire found it difficult to suppress her impatience as Greta insisted on plumping up Claire's pillows, helping her into bed, smoothing the counterpane, pouring some water, and advising her to sleep away the day. Eventually, feigning weariness, she lay back and closed her eyes.

The fidgeting hands were stilled. 'That's it, my dear, you must rest, of course.'

'Thank you, you are very kind, Greta.'

Claire heard the door close and lay still. There was something restless and nervous about Greta, who was usually so serene. Something to do with last night, perhaps. Nevertheless, it was a relief to think that they were all away for the day and Claire could go to the jetty without fear of eyes watching her every move. And then she thought of something else. If Greta's suite was empty, it might be possible to get in and search. There might be letters or papers which she could pass on to Mr Sutton. Claire didn't think she could do much more. They didn't trust her, and she might have been seen at the Café Martin. She might even have been seen with Mr Sutton. Mr Sutton would advise her about getting back to Montreuil.

Claire dressed and slipped the pistol into her pocket before making her way along the corridor to Greta's suite. The door was open, and she peeped inside. The sitting room was empty, but the other doors were open to the bedrooms, and she could hear the sound of running water from within the bedroom she had thought to be Greta's. The maid, perhaps, cleaning the bathroom? The heavy brocade curtains at the balcony window were open, so she slid behind one and waited. The chambermaid came out. Claire heard the clank of a bucket then the click of the door closing. She waited, motionless and holding her breath in case the maid came back.

Somehow, she thought it more likely that Agnes White would have information. It was she whom Claire had seen in the Rue St Pierre next to that narrow alley. The geography of the old town was hard to fathom, and Claire wondered now about the man in the fedora who had given Agnes a letter, and the Café Martin. Had Agnes come from there with the hard-eyed Emile?

Claire crept gingerly out from behind the curtain and into the room she guessed was Agnes White's. The wardrobe revealed a couple of black dresses, shawls and blouses, and at the bottom a suitcase, locked, and what looked like a portable writing desk with its key in the lock. Inside were little ebony-lidded compartments for stamps and pen nibs, and little silver-topped ink bottles in two neat compartments. Not ink, Claire thought, unscrewing the top of the first bottle. Just water. She remembered Major Pelham's talk about invisible inks. She lifted the writing slope and in the space beneath found sheets of blank paper with the hotel's name and address and spare blotting paper, and pens with nibs.

Aunt Margaret had had one of these desks with a secret drawer. You just had to find the button which released it. Claire fiddled about and found the little button, and a drawer opened to reveal a paper packet with what looked like salt crystals inside — sugar of lead, perhaps, which, dissolved in water, made invisible ink. Heat the writing and it would turn black. There was a sheet of paper with faint markings — a letter received, waiting to be deciphered? Proof of something, but what? Claire put it in her pocket, put back the paper packet, turned the key of the writing desk and put it back in the wardrobe. She went back through the sitting room into the other bedroom and looked in Greta's wardrobe — the silks and furs all carried Greta's perfume. She looked at the gold-topped scent bottles, jars, and powder boxes, and opened drawers in the dressing table. Boxes of jewels — pearls, diamonds, rubies — rings and bracelets. Greta wouldn't leave all this behind. The war was making her a very rich woman by the looks of it.

In the sitting room, Claire examined the desk. The blotter contained used blotting paper on which she could see words in reverse. She made to take the paper out of the case and stopped. She picked up a glass paperweight and froze because all of a sudden she knew that she was being watched. Claire turned to see Agnes White gazing at her. Horrified, she saw the gun: a little, deadly-looking pistol, not unlike the one in her own pocket. And then she knew they hadn't trusted her. Agnes White had intended to come back and check on her.

'I knew you were up to something,' Agnes said, her spectacles fixed on Claire. 'You were sent here, weren't you?'

There didn't seem to be any point in answering, so Claire just stared back at the flashing lenses. There was something horrible about being unable to see Agnes's eyes. It was like looking at someone unreal, rather nightmarish. She kept one hand behind her back.

'No matter, I know. I have heard from England that your friend, Matthew, is spying at Treasonfield and here you are, doing the same. No one will miss you for a while, though. It is such a pity you would not come with us to Nyon. You'd have been comfortable there, until our work is done.'

'What work is that?' Claire was surprised at the coolness of her own voice.

'Our war work. Germany will win this war, Miss Mallory. We will make sure of that. The spring offensive will sweep all before it. What will happen will rock Great Britain to her foundations and the government will submit to a peace treaty. You are not important to the British. Spies who are unmasked are regarded as expendable. No one will come looking for you — not even your friend from Thonon.'

Agnes began to raise the gun. Simultaneously, Claire threw the paperweight. It hit Agnes in the middle of her forehead and felled her with a sickening thud. The gun skittered across the parquet and the spectacles flew into the air. Agnes didn't move, and neither did Claire, who stood frozen in shock, staring at the sprawled figure. For how long she didn't know, but when she came to, her first thought was, *Oh God, I've killed her.* She knelt to feel for a pulse. Nothing. She looked into the blank eyes. Death had erased Agnes's malice, her bitterness, her twisted loyalty to her country. Then Claire saw the blood seeping from her ear. The fall must have killed her, though the paperweight had caused the fall. It didn't matter. She couldn't leave the body here. She had to act.

After the initial shock, Claire suddenly felt completely calm. She had always thought that some part of her — and most other people in conflict — switched off in moments of peril or dreadful trauma. You had to deal with the events happening in front of you — a man screaming in agony, a severed limb, a destroyed face, a shell bursting on the road. And now a dead woman. Claire bolted the door to the suite from the inside.

Agnes White was very light. It was easy to drag her into her own bedroom. Claire took Agnes's room key from her coat pocket. *Don't think. Lock up the room. Buy time. Agnes will be found, but not for a while if the others really are at Nyon for the day. Time to clear out.*

She locked Agnes's door. If the maid came back, she might assume that Agnes was in her bedroom. She wetted her handkerchief in Greta's bathroom and wiped away the blood from the parquet. There was only a faint stain, which wouldn't be noticed immediately. She put Agnes's gun in her pocket, took the blotting paper from the desk in the salon, remembered the paperweight — she'd chuck it away with Agnes's room key and her gun. She listened for any noise in the corridor outside and slipped out.

Back in her own room, Claire dared not think about what had happened, except to reflect that she'd have been dead had she not thrown that paperweight, and the paper with the secret writing would have been lost. She'd have to clear out altogether —

A knock on the door turned her blood to ice. 'Yes,' she called, her voice suddenly hoarse.

A light female voice. A French voice. 'Room service. Your coffee, mademoiselle.'

'*Un moment, s'il vous plait,*' Claire replied, leaping into her bed, pulling the covers up to her chin and then calling for the maid to come in, hoping that she wasn't being fooled. She recognised the young woman who entered with a tray, but that meant nothing. She could be in on it. Major Pelham had told her about the maids in Geneva hotels.

She smiled at the maid. 'Oh, that is kind, thank you.'

The maid put the tray on the bed. 'May I bring you anything else?'

'No, no, I won't need anything else. I shall go back to sleep after this.'

Claire was out of bed as soon as the door closed. She poured out a cup of black coffee and spooned in several sugar lumps. She couldn't face the rolls and jam. She needed time to think. Agnes had come back to spy on her. She'd probably knocked on Claire's door to check that she was still in bed. The others must know that Agnes was at the hotel. They'd know it was Claire who had caused Agnes's death. They wouldn't call the authorities to have Claire Mallory locked in a cell, where she could spill the beans. Oh, no, they'd look for her, and they'd be ruthless. Agnes had told her she was expendable. She would have to go to Thonon and find Mr Sutton. But no, Agnes had said "your friend from Thonon" — they knew. Claire felt a chill run down her spine. Oh, God, where was Mr Sutton?

Had Agnes come back alone? Was someone waiting for her down in the foyer or at the jetty to take the steamer to Nyon? And would that someone come looking? So where should she go — to Madame Grenier at the pension? Military Intelligence had organised all that, but Mr Sutton had been there. They probably knew she'd stayed there. Giselle, maybe? She thought of the man in the fedora, of Emil at the Café Martin. She thought of Giselle's offer if she was ever in danger and her obvious dislike of Emil. Send a message, she had said. Claire could hardly send an errand boy in his smart uniform from the Hotel Belle Vue, but she had to leave now and find sanctuary.

She'd have to risk it. No suitcase, obviously. Just her handbag, money, passport, and her gun and the papers, of course. The paperweight and Agnes's gun were in her coat pockets. She must get rid of those as soon as possible.

Claire left everything as it was — as if she had just gone out for a walk. She felt a pang about her uniform. She'd have to stump up for a new one. She closed the door. No one about. The maid's staircase would take her out the back way.

26

Matthew stepped off the Oxenholme train at Lancaster, where Ned was waiting for him. Matthew had told him on the telephone in the vaguest of terms that Agnes was connected to Greta's family and that she had a son. He mentioned casually that he thought of making a trip to Manchester where 'Agnes Grey' had lived. Ned had news and asked him to meet at Lancaster station. Ned had taken the sleeper train for Scotland and had changed trains at Preston. They took refuge from the bitter wind in the station buffet, where there was a fire and hot, if tasteless, coffee. Matthew told his news — it was a relief to speak freely.

Ned looked at the photograph. 'They look like your typical public schoolboys — something a bit sly about the eyes of our Rudolph, though. God's gift to Germany, eh? And crikey, another clergyman in the case, this von Rahn Nicholl in Lausanne — a boat ride from Geneva. Let's hope God's not on their side. Anyhow, it'll be Pelham's job to find him — they've a man in Thonon on Lake Geneva. Praise be to the school register for the address.'

'I thought of going to Manchester in search of Otto Adolphus, the vicar of St Mark's, to see if I can dig up anything on Agnes White and the von Ende family.'

'Hear what I've to tell you first — it might change things.'

According to Ned, Willy Lang's Alvis had been left at Lancaster railway station. Ned had worked out that Schmidt wouldn't keep the car for long — too easily traceable. The railway police at Preston, Lancaster, and Manchester had been alerted. The Lancaster police had a piece of luck. A lad who was mad about cars, a sharp-eyed little perisher, who noticed everything about them and their drivers, had asked the driver of the Alvis if he wanted it minding while he was away — the lad often spent the day at the station, picking up a bob or two as a minder. The driver said he was not coming back for a bit; he was going to London. The lad described the British Warm coat — his dad wore one — and the cap. An officer's cap, he noticed, but there was no badge, and the lad knew his stuff, according to the sergeant who had interviewed him. There was more — the London train came in just as the lad was inside, buying chocolate from the cart. He saw the Alvis driver get on the train. Now, according to the lad, only a couple of other chaps got on, and he saw the Alvis man get into a first-class carriage. Naturally, the sergeant went to ask about the single first-class passenger who had travelled to London.

'And?' Matthew asked as Ned drank some of his coffee.

Ned put his cup down, grimacing at the taste. 'He asked about a connection to Folkestone.'

'Bloody hell — on his way to France?'

'I reckon so, and I reckon he's got to be Schmidt. We now know the connection to the von Ende lot, and therefore it's probable that he's Agnes White's son. And there's this —' Ned held up a key — 'found in the car, slipped down the side of the driver's seat. Blighter didn't notice. Not as clever as he thinks he is. I recognised it. Same as the one you lent me to lock up after we removed the body.'

'The key to Willy's study. So, he *was* there. Clever enough to leave the door unlocked but slipped the key into his pocket without thinking.'

'The question is, where is he? Masquerading as a British soldier — no one would pay much attention to a missing cap badge except for that lad, but it tells me he's wearing borrowed finery.'

'And he'll have papers to get him to France and on to Switzerland, maybe.'

'Papers and plenty of money from Lang's safe —'

Matthew interrupted. 'You know, I've thought about that. Why murder Willy if he was in with them? Did you have anything on him before Pelham contacted you?'

'Not a thing. You're right, it's damned peculiar. I can imagine a bloke like Lang topping himself if things were getting hot, but as far as I know, there wasn't a whiff — not even about the wife. And yet, if Schmidt did for him, why?'

'I wondered if Willy found out something that he didn't like — said no to something and became a liability to them.'

'Hard to say — the postmortem was inconclusive. No prints on the gun other than Lang's. The gun was on the rug as if he'd dropped it. Could have shot himself in the mouth. Could have been shot.'

'Like the poor old vicar, Cuthbert White. Mrs White found him. Suppose he found out what his wife was up to?'

'Cold-blooded, ain't she? She might have shot Lang for all we know.'

'Any sign of Schmidt at Folkestone? Booked a passage or anything? But then we'd need to know a name, an English name, maybe.'

'Plenty of army men with foreign names — look at Philip Sassoon, Haig's secretary. And that poet fellow, Siegfried Sassoon. Siegfried, eh? Fellow called Meinhardt in my section. His father's Swiss, and his first names are Clifton Ulrich. Known as Cliff to his friends. No one thinks much about these things if a chap has the right accent and has been to public school.'

'Rudolph went by the name of Smith at school. He speaks perfect English — I'll bet he could pass for a native.'

'The young lad at the station thought he was English.'

'What next?'

'Fancy a trip down south?'

27

Claire, with her spectacles on and her hat pulled low over her brow, huddled in a doorway some yards down from the entrance to the Café Martin. She felt frozen, sick with dread and with waiting. The shutters of the café were still closed and there was no sign of life. Of course, the place might be open only at night and Giselle might not come for hours. And then what? She'd have to try Madame Grenier at the pension. But not until dark. She thought of those twisting alleys round the cathedral. *Please, Giselle.*

Claire didn't dare move. The doorway was deep in shadow on this side of the alley and the house behind her was silent. She hoped it was empty. Maybe the café opened late in the morning for coffee. Her watch showed that it was almost eleven o'clock. Less than an hour since she had left Agnes White at the hotel. Those blank eyes came back to her, but she shook them away and concentrated on the café door and her plan. She would go round the back when Giselle came, enter the bar from the lavatory corridor and hope that Giselle might see her. It was all she could think of.

Eventually, Giselle arrived, more soberly dressed than the previous night in a blue coat with a fur collar and a matching hat. Claire watched her open the front door. Thank God she was alone. Claire went back into the Rue St Pierre and into the alley behind the café. The yard door wasn't locked, so she slipped easily into the corridor. And heard the hiss of a breath. Too late. Someone grabbed her, yanked her arm up her back in an excruciating moment of pain and before she could cry out, she was shoved against the wall. She knew who it was by the smell. Emil.

He kept his grip on her arm. She felt his thick, stale breath on her neck as he leaned into her, his other hand fumbling at her breast, his knee between her legs. 'English bitch, I know about you. You should be in Nyon, out of the way. Too bad for you.'

Emil dragged her towards the door of the lavatory. Where she was going to die, Claire thought, if she didn't do something. She found her pocket with her free arm, but she didn't resist as he pushed her. He relaxed his grip on her arm as he made to kick open the door. Claire stumbled and as he pulled her back, she lashed out backwards with her foot, hoping to get him between the legs. She missed but caught his knee. He was so surprised at the blow that he staggered backwards and let go. Claire whipped round, gun in hand, saw two vicious black eyes, and struck him in the face with the gun, but he was back at her, snarling in fury, knocking the gun out of her hand, grabbing her collar and swinging her round so that her head hit the stone wall. He had her by the collar, lugging her backwards. She could see the open door at the end of the corridor and in her own surge of fury, made a desperate lunge to get away, but Emil was so enraged that his strength was greater than hers. He pulled so hard that her feet slid from under her, and then she was down, trying to wriggle away from him. She heard a door and a cry. Then Emil was down too, almost on top of her, and Giselle was beating him about his head with the gun until he collapsed unconscious.

'*Merde*! Help me drag him into the lavatory — we must hide him there.'

Claire helped Giselle stuff Emil into one of the cubicles. She watched with a kind of frozen horror as Giselle took a knife from her pocket and plunged it into his eye. His head fell forward, and blood spurted out.

Giselle dropped the knife and found Emile's gun in his pocket. She looked at Claire again. Claire noticed for the first time how pale her blue eyes were and how unmoved her cool stare. She felt a tingle of apprehension. Had she made a mistake?

'We might need this,' Giselle said, putting the gun in her pocket. She shut the lavatory door, snatched a piece of greasy card from the washstand and hung it on a nail in the door. It read in clumsy block capitals: HORS D'USAGE.

Claire gave a half-smile as Giselle said contemptuously, 'Out of use — he is now.' She continued in her rapid French, '*Mon Dieu*, you look terrible, but you must stay here in the next cubicle. I will get my things. We have to go.'

Claire sat on the lavatory seat. She was dazed and exhausted. She'd just seen a murder and had committed one herself. Her arm felt as if it had been wrenched from its socket and her head was bruised from where it had hit the wall. She must look a wreck. *Go where?* she asked herself, though she hadn't the strength to care much.

Giselle was back in her hat and coat. 'We leave the back door open. Someone got in. That's the story. I've locked the front door. I'm late opening up, that is all. No one will come yet, but we must be quick. Now we go to my lodging. You can walk?'

Claire nodded and Giselle took her arm. A few twists and turns through the alleys and she recognised the Rue Belle Filles. Then down another passage, up some stairs onto a landing, up another flight and into a room with a day bed, a table, two chairs, and a fireplace with a grating on which there was a saucepan. Giselle sat Claire down on the bed. 'Brandy,' she said.

Claire almost choked at first and then she felt the warmth sliding down her throat. She looked at Giselle, who was regarding her with that look of cool appraisal and — what was it? Amusement? Whatever it was, Giselle in her blue hat and coat did not look scared.

'*Merde*,' she said again, 'what have you got me into?'

'I'm sorry. I didn't mean for you to —'

'He deserved it. It's war. He'd have got you the next time. I have to go back to work and open up. We'll talk later. Just rest. There's coffee in the pan. Bread in the crock. Don't answer the door. I'll tap and say my name when I come back.' Giselle took Claire's gun from her pocket and put it on the table. 'You'd better have this back — you'll need to clean off the blood. I'll keep his.'

Claire looked at her gun and felt the bile rise in her throat. Emil's blood.

Giselle didn't give it a second glance. 'I'll light the fire before I go. You need to get warm.'

'What about Emil? What will you do?' Claire asked as Giselle put a taper to the wood.

'I'll be the one to find him. I'll scream the house down and someone will fetch the police. No one will care about him.' And with that Giselle was gone. Claire heard her heels clacking on the stairs. A woman who knew where she was going and was intent on getting there, Claire thought, overcome with weariness. She closed her eyes on the blood-stained gun.

28

Ten hours from Lancaster, stiff with cold, fuddled with too many cigarettes, hungry and exhausted but glad of the sea breeze, Ned and Matthew walked to a narrow, terraced house just off the High Street in Folkestone.

'The landlady puts up our Belgian friends, but she keeps a room for special guests, shall we say. Military Intelligence pays the bill, so she doesn't mind what time — and she'll feed us.'

Despite the discomforts, it had been an instructive journey for Matthew. He now knew who Ned was. Or at least who he said he was — Ned had a dry sense of humour. Superintendent Edward Turner, Special Branch, he told Matthew, a sort of roving commission. Here and there when he was wanted. He knew Guy Pelham, of course — good lad — and if GHQ wanted a job done on the quiet on home territory, then Pelham was likely to contact him. Chums from way back. Ned worked from a flat in Westminster — three lady assistants from the Secret Service bureau on eight-hour shifts. Clever. Methodical. Knew all the secrets and kept them. Matthew told him about Claire and her ambulance driving and that she was in Geneva. He hadn't heard anything about her, which was beginning to worry him.

'Pelham must have seen something in her, my lad. He wouldn't have sent her if he hadn't thought she was up to it. You have to have nerves of steel in the ambulance racket. Amazing what these girls can do these days. I'm all for it. My sister was a suffragette. Force-fed in Holloway. Bloody awful business.'

'I'm all for it, too. Claire's —'

Ned looked at him shrewdly. 'Like that, is it? Still, you'd not want her languishing on the sofa with her crocheting.'

Matthew laughed. 'She was never that type.'

'Plenty of women in the spying game — on both sides. It's a dangerous business. There are the networks in Belgium. La Dame Blanche, for one — nuns, teachers, housewives — and all of them just as brave as men. Risking everything. It's war and the women are in it. I'd raise a glass to them — if I had one on this creeping thing that calls itself a train.'

Ned had gone on to talk about the Belgian refugees. He explained that many who had flooded into Folkestone were used by the Secret Service, including women. A chap called Cameron was in charge of the Folkestone Bureau on Marine Parade and had an extensive intelligence network in Belgium, sending coded reports on troop movements, artillery — Matthew would know the sort of stuff, beans for soldiers, coffee for canons — train-watching, aviation, aerodromes, and shipping movements from Zeebrugge and Ostend. They also kept an eye out for enemy agents trying to get to Britain. Useful chaps to know at the Folkestone Bureau, where they could make enquiries about Schmidt or Smith. A long shot, Ned said, but they might have had a sniff of him. Nothing to say Schmidt hadn't passed himself off as Belgian or Dutch. The bureau had a roster of women who worked with the lady volunteers at the Harbour Buffet. The women's job was to look out for likely wrong 'uns — news came in about types under suspicion coming in or going out on the boats, or trying to get out with false papers. They could show the photograph to the ladies — someone might have seen him, though that was a long shot, too, as thousands of troops went in and out of Folkestone.

Mrs Lamb, landlady at Buckingham House — royalist and loyalist — proved to be meek as her name and rather fond of Uncle Ned. Her supper of fried fish was excellent, her beds clean and comfortable, her water more than tepid, and her breakfast kippers succulent. Fortified, Ned and Matthew went to Marine Parade to see a man Ned knew. Well, he would, thought Matthew. A man of many parts, Uncle Ned. The man Ned knew was a major in Intelligence, but a bit of a duffer. Some queer story about his wife, too. 'Mustn't gossip, though,' Ned said with a wink.

They were taken to the musty, smoke-filled office of Cameron's deputy, Captain Strange. Matthew was struck by the coincidence of names — Herr Strange, he wondered. Lord, how quickly he had learnt to trust no one. Ned hailed the captain briskly and introduced Captain Riviere on GHQ business. Strange listened intently as Ned unfolded the story of Rudolph Schmidt and his connection to Treasonfield, the home of the now dead German financier, Willy Lang, whom Captain Riviere knew. He told of the removal of papers and money, the German stamps and envelopes, the theft of the car, and the suspect's flight, possibly to Folkestone.

'Wondered if you'd had a sniff of him — masquerading as a British officer in his British Warm. He has an officer's cap but no badge. This is the blighter.' Ned handed over the photograph, pointing out Rudolph Schmidt.

Captain Strange didn't speak for a while, his eyes fixed on the photograph. When he looked up, his eyes were wide. 'Where did you get this?'

Matthew answered. 'At Treasonfield. The other lad is Stephen von Ende, Lang's stepson. He and Rudolph Schmidt were at school together — Fernhall, up on the Lancashire coast.'

Strange turned a ghastly yellow colour. 'Von Ende? You mean —'

'Lieutenant-General Freiherr Ludwig von Ende, 50th Division, German army. Baron, too,' Ned cut in.

'A relation of William Lang's wife, Greta, who is in Switzerland. Rudolph Schmidt is a von Ende, too,' Matthew explained.

'Wrong side of the blanket.' Ned had a trenchant way with words.

Strange turned even yellower. 'But he can't be —'

'Who can't be what?' Ned asked, eying the major as if he were an escaped lunatic.

'This man can't be Rudolph Schmidt — he can't be a von Ende. It's impossible.'

'Nothing's impossible in this game, old son. It's obvious you know something about him. Spill the beans.'

Strange looked like a drowning man and as such clutched at a straw. 'This photograph — you're sure it's genuine? From Fernhall School?'

Matthew nodded. 'I took it from its frame. Look on the back. It tells you it is from Fernhall School, and that writing is Stephen's.'

'And the bloke in the middle is one Conrad von Rahn Nicholl, sometime master at Fernhall, now residing in Lausanne on Lake Geneva where Mrs Greta Lang has gone for her health — or maybe for the health of the German state. Now, be a good egg, Captain, and tell us what you know.'

Strange looked nervously at Ned, pointed to Rudolph Schmidt in the photograph, and said, 'I know that man as Ashton Hamilton Smythe. He can't be — I mean, he's one of ours. A walk-in — you know, asked if he could do something for us. Public school, of course. Yes, Fernhall. Sportsman, cadet corps, Swiss mother, father dead. Couldn't join a regiment — dicky lung. Sound chap, we thought. Straight bat. And bright — right sort of man for intelligence work —'

Matthew interrupted. 'Look at the photograph again, at the man in the white sweater, and look at the back.'

Strange turned the photograph over. When he looked up, they saw the face of a terrified man. 'Good God, Ashton Hamilton Smythe —'

'Rubber man in Malaya now.'

'No, no, I can't believe — Malaya —'

'And not available for comment, I shouldn't think. Maybe dead, but he's the real deal, old boy, and your man Smythe is Schmidt. Very convenient name change. So where is he?' asked Ned.

'Posted to the British Military Intelligence Mission at —'

'French GHQ. When did he go?'

'A week ago.'

'No, he didn't. He was up in Westmorland embracing his ma — she's in Geneva now, by the way — and probably murdering William Lang when he could tear himself from the maternal bosom. He's a bloody double agent.'

29

Claire woke up, every joint aching and as stiff as a wooden doll. She looked round, momentarily disoriented by the unfamiliar room; then she remembered. Two dead bodies, Agnes and Emil, and she was responsible for both.

She suddenly felt shaky, but she forced herself to stand by, levering herself up on the arms of the chair. The fire had died down and Claire saw from the skylight that it was dusk outside — a blue-grey light whispering at the glass, tender and dreamlike. A night for a stroll on the quay with a lover. Oh, Matthew… But the ice in her veins was real, as was the memory of Emil. Giselle, icily calm with the knife in her hand. An eye spurting with blood. Scarlet blood on the tiles. The stink of the lavatory, of his clothes, of his breath on her neck. Agnes White's blank eyes, a pair of broken spectacles, blood on the parquet floor. And a gun with blood on it.

Claire moved to the table, but she couldn't bring herself to touch the gun. She covered it with a towel. She put some wood on the dying fire, holding her cold hands to it when the blaze blew up. The warmth made her feel better and when the pan of coffee was heated up, she gulped down two cups, black and sweet.

Another tot of Giselle's brandy stopped the shaking; Claire drew the chair to the fire and sat until the ice in her veins melted and she felt calmer. Not the time to give in. Time to think. How to get to Thonon? Agnes White had mentioned Thonon, but Claire would have to risk it. She must see Mr Sutton. He had to know about Agnes, and he must help her get away. That thought reminded her — the blotting paper and the letter from the writing box. Now was the time to hold the letter to the fire and see what it contained before Giselle came back. She ought not to involve Giselle in that. She'd already put her in danger … though when she thought about it, Giselle had tackled Emil and stabbed him without a qualm. Who was the woman with the silver-blonde hair who had sensed that Claire might be in danger and who had shown the utmost contempt for the German?

Well, she couldn't think about that now. She could only trust Giselle to help her get away. In the meantime, she had the letter and Greta's blotting paper with its squiggles and blots. She took them from the inside pocket of her coat, held the letter to the fire and watched the black writing appear, as if by magic. German — well, she had expected that.

The recipient was addressed as 'Aunt Agnes' and at the end of the letter there was simply the initial, 'R'. Rudolph Schmidt? She saw the word 'Treasonfield' and the word 'Kapitan' followed by the initials 'M. R.' Matthew? She went back to the beginning — there was no address, just the name of a house. Where was Ivy House? Claire began to read very slowly and carefully. R had seen Captain M. R. at Treasonfield. The body of the fool, L, had been found. It was his own fault — he was a coward in the end. The body had been taken away in the night by a group of men — intelligence people, no doubt. The captain must be in intelligence, too, but it was too risky to attack him. He would be armed, and the Todd man was always snooping about.

Claire stared at the black letters. It was true, then — Willy Lang had been murdered. Why was he a coward? Perhaps he had fallen out with Greta and the others — wouldn't do what they wanted. She felt the ice in her blood again. Rudolph Schmidt had contemplated murdering Matthew. Her fears about what Agnes and the others had known were confirmed. They had known she was a liar. She read on.

R was preparing for *Einsatz Admiral König Vulkan* in February — what did that mean? *Einsatz* meant operation. So, a military operation of some kind. Who was Admiral König? *König* meant king and *Vulkan* meant volcano. Agnes White had said that Great Britain would be rocked to her foundations and would sue for peace. Something to do with the spring offensive that they were all preparing for? Or something in England — some mighty explosion that Rudolph was planning? Was Rudolph still in England? In London, maybe?

Whatever it was, it was to happen soon. In February — but when? She must get to Mr Sutton. Get away from Geneva and if Mr Sutton wasn't in Thonon, then she could make her own way to Montreuil if she had to. She had money and her passport. And she could telegraph Major Pelham from Lyons. The plan comforted her for a few minutes, until she found herself consumed by anxiety. *Oh, Giselle, come soon.*

Claire examined the blotting paper, holding it up to the fire. It was almost impossible to tell what the blots and marks were. But there were letters. Upside down and back to front, of course, so the 'M' was a 'W'. She made out the word 'Willi'. She looked again and deciphered 'von' and 'End'. Von Ende? Was Greta writing to her relative, the lieutenant-general?

Pacing the small room, Claire watched the skylight darken, but the hours were painfully slow. It was still only eight o'clock. She eventually sat in the firelight, drinking coffee and eating bread and butter, trying not to think about Agnes or Emil. She tried to take comfort in the thought that Matthew was not dead, that he was at Hawthorn with his grandfather. Or was he somewhere with Major Pelham? On some other mission, searching for Rudolph Schmidt?

She started as she heard the gentle tap on the door and the low voice telling her it was Giselle. She heard the key in the lock and Giselle came in with some ham and cheese. 'Supper for you,' she said, 'from the café. It's fresh.'

Claire was surprised to find she was still hungry, and she ate while Giselle drank coffee and brandy. Giselle's eyes were triumphant as she told Claire what had happened. She had quite a story to relate. Claire was so entranced by the vividness of the tale and the teller, she almost forgot it was real.

'I screamed the place down — the neighbours came and called the police. Well, of course, I was almost fainting — the dead body — what a shock, but I managed to answer some questions. So brave! Oh, yes, I knew Monsieur Emil, a regular customer, but not a nice one — mixed with low-life types. He took drugs. The women didn't like him — but then he was a German, a criminal. One of the neighbours, an old lady with nothing to do, said she saw a man hiding in a doorway, watching the café in the morning. She didn't know him, but he looked like a criminal, with a long coat and a dark hat pulled down low over his eyes. Of course, another old dear saw him go into the Rue St Pierre —'

'But it was me,' Claire protested.

'Oh, I know them, they make it up. They enjoyed themselves, being the centre of attention for once, and telling the police what they wanted to hear.'

'I'm glad they did. The police believed them?'

'Of course, case closed. A criminal off the streets. They won't care who killed him — a German low-life. Serves him right.'

'What shall you do now? I need to get to Thonon — there's a man I must see.'

Giselle gave her a long look. 'I'll help you, of course, but I think it's time you told me what you are doing here. After all, how do I know I can trust you? Not everybody is who they seem in Geneva. I don't think you are.'

Claire felt she had no choice. Giselle had saved her from Emil. She explained in as much detail as she thought best, telling Giselle about Greta and Colonel Raulin, who were spying for the Germans, and that they had found out that Claire had been sent to spy on them.

'A British spy? I knew there was something that night. An Englishwoman alone at night at the Café Martin. When you asked my name, I knew that you had some secret. The man in Thonon is your contact, I suppose. English?'

'Yes.'

'He will be waiting for you?'

'He will wonder why I've not contacted him.'

'You can send a message — I have trusted friends.'

Claire knew she mustn't involve anyone else, however trustworthy they might seem. She'd taken enough risks already. 'Better not,' she said. 'I must see him in person.'

Giselle shrugged. 'No matter, but tell me, why did you come to the café this morning?'

'Because Agnes White was going to shoot me. I was in her room... I threw a glass paperweight to stop her. It hit her right in the face, and she fell onto the hard floor —'

'Good shot,' Giselle interrupted.

'Well, it was, but I think the fall killed her...' Claire remembered the sickening thud as Agnes had fallen. 'I can't help hoping so.'

'It doesn't matter — she would have killed you. And Emil would have killed you. He's in the pay of the Germans. He's the type they use for murder — there was a woman from

Luxembourg found in an alley near the railway station. The killer was never found, but there was talk at the café that she was working for the Allies.'

'Thank goodness you came in time.'

'They're ruthless. Emil would work for anybody for money. He was a pimp and dealing in drugs for the Germans who send agents into France. If they're caught, they say that they're only dealing in drugs. Emil gave women and drugs to the Russians and the Turks, anybody who'd talk. The Germans paid him well. I'm glad he's dead.'

'So am I, but how can I get out?'

'You can't yet. Those others, Greta Lang and Colonel Raulin, they will send someone to look for you. They must know you were at the café.'

'I was followed the other night, but not by Emil — someone else from the hotel.'

'I'll go to the Belle Vue tomorrow morning. See if the police are there. No one can stop me walking in to take coffee.' You must describe the Lang woman and the colonel to me, but later. I must go back to work now, and for the next day or two — in case the police come back, or anyone else. It would look odd if I disappeared. I don't want any police or any German thug coming here.'

'And then?'

'I'll ask for a day off — shock, I'll say. My boss will understand. And then we'll go to Thonon. Two of us will be less noticeable, but you can't go as you are. I have some ideas about that — I'll get us some clothes. Our own mothers wouldn't know us. Now, that day bed unfolds for me to sleep in. We'll have to share.' She looked kindly at Claire. 'Try to have a sleep while I'm gone.'

Claire lay on the bed, looking at the letter again, her mind racing. Admiral König — Admiral King. A ship, perhaps. Major Pelham had told her that the British were planning an important naval operation and that she should listen out for the names of places like Zeebrugge and Ostend. Not that she'd heard anything. It was all so complicated — all these tentacles of war stretching out across the seas and lands of the wide world. And here she was, trapped in an attic room, harbouring what might be a key piece of intelligence. Giselle was right, of course. It would be folly for Claire to move now. If she were caught, then her information would be lost. Should she get Giselle to post the letter folded inside another to the Paris-Plage café under cover of Madame Foulon? But she hardly knew Giselle. What if Giselle were caught or the letter intercepted?

Claire tossed and turned in the lumpy bed, got up, drank some more brandy, and fell asleep for a while, a sleep disturbed by images of faces peering in at the skylight. Greta, Colonel Raulin, two moons turning into Agnes's spectacles, into a bloody eye, all watching and waiting, and then Mr Sutton in his green scarf, walking away from her into the dark. And, even more horribly, she dreamt of Giselle. Two cold blue eyes. Giselle in her blue coat and hat at the Belle Vue. Giselle being embraced by Colonel Raulin. Claire sat up then, sweating, her heart pounding, and possessed by a terrible misgiving.

Trust no one. But she had. A woman about whom she knew nothing; a woman who had stabbed a man in cold blood. And joked about it.

30

Captain Strange seemed to shrink under the cold eye of his chief, Major Cameron, and the glare of Ned's contemptuous gaze. Matthew had never seen a man so cowed. He looked like a dog under a whipping.

Captain Strange told them — in halting words — all about the man whom he had believed to be Ashton Hamilton Smythe — the walk-in. Matthew had learned that the term meant someone with the right papers, someone with excellent language skills who offered his services to an intelligence agency. Smythe spoke fluent German —

'Oh, God —' Strange faltered, realising the terrible irony of his words — 'I thought —'

'I know what you thought. Get on with it.' Cameron's voice was steel.

Smythe had been in Belgium and France, and behind the lines, train-watching, picking up information about German troop movements. He'd even filched German military compilations. He'd been into Belgium and brought back very useful stuff on shipping movements out of Zeebrugge and Ostend.

'Did he know about the plans for the raid? About Deal?' Cameron barked.

Strange looked like a man condemned as he whispered, 'I don't know — I mean, he could go where he liked. I didn't —'

'When was he last in Belgium?'

'I don't — I can't —' His desperate eyes looked at the implacable faces staring back. 'Earlier in the month — February the seventh.'

'The day after — Schmidt knew?'

Ned interrupted. 'What happened on the sixth?'

Cameron answered. 'Orders went out to raise a Royal Marine Battalion in Deal for one specific operation.'

'The raid on Zeebrugge?'

'Yes, the plan was approved back in January — to land a thousand troops on the mole, the navy to bombard the lock gates and fortifications, blockships to enter the harbour. There's an appeal going out for volunteers. HMS *Vindictive* is in Chatham for a refit. Ferries are being converted in Plymouth.'

'A loose mouth or two at the docks, maybe. Schmidt will have had plenty of money from his paymasters,' observed Ned.

'No doubt, but Schmidt wouldn't have known about Zeebrugge if there hadn't been a loose mouth here.' He glared at the trembling Strange. 'You gave him stuff he shouldn't have seen.' Cameron's voice was tight with anger, but he didn't let it spill over. 'Tell us.'

'I didn't tell him — he had a key to my office. I didn't know if he... He knew about my wife — he had drugs — morphine, cocaine — he gave me them and I gave him the key — she can't do without it. I can't afford... I don't know where to get it. I wanted to stop, but he said he'd tell everyone. I didn't want it all bringing up again — I couldn't stand it.'

'Blackmail!' Cameron snapped, and that finished Captain Strange. He gave a strangled sob, his head down and shoulders heaving.

'When is the raid supposed to be?' asked Ned.

'Between March the fourteenth and nineteenth. The fleet is due to sail from Swin Deep, off Clacton.'

'That gives us time.'

'If you can find him.'

'Where was Schmidt billeted?' Ned asked. 'I need to see his rooms.'

Strange couldn't answer. Cameron signalled them to leave and walked out without looking back. They left him, a broken man. Cameron shut the door on the sobbing.

Cameron sent a clerk to find the address. Then he told them that Captain Strange's wife was a morphine addict who had been arrested several times for shoplifting and had served a prison sentence. She'd been in various clinics. She was a liability to Strange, but he had stood by her. Of course, private clinics cost money. She'd almost bankrupted him and Strange wasn't from a moneyed background. Pity, though — he had done good work in Givet on the Franco-Belgian frontier. He had handled various agents to glean intelligence from inside Germany and was at GHQ for a while when GHQ was in St Omer. He was an able man — Cameron had had faith in him. He had come back because his mother-in-law had died, and his wife needed him.

'Bloody fool,' he said. 'This'll finish him.'

Ned didn't comment on that. Strange was Cameron's problem. He wanted to get to Schmidt's lodgings. When the clerk came back with the address, he asked for a car.

Ned drove them out of Folkestone, past the hotels, the hospitals and rest camps, past the observation posts, the station, and the harbour where the ships bound for France blew off smoke as they waited to depart. Out at sea, Matthew could see the funnel of a minesweeper. He thought of Zeebrugge. They needed to find Schmidt, or the raid would have to be called off. But would it? There was no actual proof except that Schmidt had been to Belgium on February the seventh — it was thin now he thought about it.

Ivy House at Alkham where Schmidt had lived was about five miles from Folkestone and proved to be a half weatherboard and flint cottage down a quiet lane which didn't lead anywhere, though they could see an oast house across some fields and orchards. They had had to ask the way twice.

'Nicely tucked away in the heart of England,' Ned observed as he parked the car on the grassy verge, from where they could see the house. Not very big. Four windows, a dormer in the roof, and a door half open. A brick path cutting a line through lawns and empty flowerbeds led up to the front door, where a bicycle was leaning against the porch. 'I wonder who's at home.'

They'd worked out a plan which depended on whether the house was empty, and if occupied, depended on the person they might encounter. Empty — well, they'd just break in. Official army business, if anyone asked. If a landlady were at home, they'd ask about Smythe and tell her that he was missing. They were worried about him. A soft heart, Ned hoped. Fond of the blighter, with any luck, so she'd let them search his room.

'We'll use our charm,' Ned said. Matthew didn't doubt the efficacy of Ned's charm. They'd be taking tea in the parlour within minutes.

They walked up the brick path and listened at the door. There was the sound of light steps coming down the stairs. The landlady, Matthew hoped.

A freckle-faced young woman in an outdoor coat and hat opened the door fully. 'Oh, I saw you from the window, but I'm going out, I'm afraid. I've only a few minutes.'

Ned introduced himself and Matthew and they showed their identification. She looked trustingly at Matthew in his uniform.

He said, 'We're here to ask about Lieutenant Ashton Hamilton Smythe.'

'Ash is in France, I'm afraid. You'd better ask at Headquarters in Folkestone. Captain Strange will tell you.'

Ash, Matthew thought. *Intimate*. He saw the same thought flash across Ned's face. More than just his landlady? This might be tricky, but Ned was already asking if they might step in for a few minutes.

'Oh, dash it — I'm on a shift at the Harbour Buffet on the mole. Folkestone, you see. I've to cycle there.'

'We'll be quick. It's just that — well, I think we should come in, please.'

'Oh, all right —' she grinned at them — 'I suppose I'll get there if I pedal hard.' She was an appealing young woman in her bright green hat with its jaunty feather and her red curls springing beneath it. Matthew hoped she was just the landlady.

The young woman led them into a narrow hall, where Matthew noted the fishing rods and umbrellas in a brass stand. There were waterproofs hanging from hooks, an old tweed hat and a couple of sou'westers. They went into a neat parlour and she motioned for them to sit.

'We've just come from Captain Strange,' Ned continued. 'It's a bit awkward — er — Miss —?'

'Cresswell — Anna Cresswell. Is there something wrong with Ash?'

'He's missing, I'm afraid — in France.'

The colour drained from her face, and her hand flew to her mouth. Her green eyes opened very wide. 'Oh, God,' she said. 'What do you think's happened? I know he's on something very secret — he's not told me, honest, but I know, I sort of guessed —'

Ned spoke mildly. 'You don't know where he is exactly?'

'Oh, no — he would never say — the darling. You don't think he — I mean, I know it's all dangerous —'

They knew then that Anna Cresswell wasn't the enemy. She was a useful tool to Schmidt, perhaps.

Matthew spoke. 'We don't know anything, Miss Cresswell. We thought you ought to know, but I'm afraid you mustn't tell anyone. Does anyone know that you and Lieutenant Smythe are...' He trailed off.

Anna blushed, but she sat up straight and there was flash in her eye. 'Lovers,' she said defiantly. 'I shall have had that ... if anything happens to... I don't care what you think.'

'We don't think anything, Miss Cresswell,' Matthew said gently. 'We're just concerned about Lieutenant Smythe.'

'I love him. I'm not a fool. Of course, it was secret. No one knows, not even the girls at the café. My gran was his landlady — she's dead, and this is my house now, but Ash said we oughtn't to tell. He might be compromised. Major Strange wouldn't like it — he'd be afraid that Ash might tell me things. He still keeps his own room — at the top of the house. No one knows when we are up there.'

'I'm sure he wouldn't betray any secrets,' Ned said, 'but I wonder if there is anything in his room that might give us a clue to his whereabouts.'

Anna certainly wasn't a fool. 'Captain Strange must know all about that.'

'Not always,' Ned told her. 'Sometimes it is necessary for someone on top-secret business to keep his cards very close to his chest until he brings back results. I'm thinking about contacts — names that might give us a clue as to where he might have gone. He hasn't been in touch with Captain Strange, you see.'

'There was a man in Deal.'

Ned didn't blink. 'Someone you met?'

'I didn't meet him, but we went there at the beginning of the month. Ash had to meet this chap at a pub near the docks. I went for a walk. Ash said it had been a successful trip.'

'Do you know his name?'

'Just Bill.'

'Ah, well. Did he have meetings elsewhere?'

'We went down to Plymouth for the weekend. I think he met people there, but he didn't tell me, I swear. He's absolutely committed to his work.'

'Would you mind if we looked at his room? You don't need to stay if you want to get off to the café.'

She looked doubtful but made up her mind. 'If it helps you to find him, and I don't want to be late. The key's in the door. Lock up and put it under the mat, will you?' Her face changed again, misery in her eyes. 'And you will let me know any news — please?'

'Of course — as soon as we hear anything.'

They watched her wheel the bicycle down the path, and when they were sure she had gone, Ned turned to Matthew. 'I wonder if she's one of the Bureau's ladies at that café — best not to enquire into that. We don't want her getting into hot water. She's been used. Let Strange take the blame. Good job Schmidt wanted secrecy. She'll never know what happened to him.'

'Perhaps it's better that she thinks he's a casualty. She'll never need to know how he deceived her.'

'She thought we suspected him of spilling secrets — Lord, what an irony. She's the casualty. He's a bastard. Come on, let's see if he's left us a handy guide to his whereabouts.'

'He must have told her he was coming back. He won't have taken everything.'

'Good thought, my lad.'

They went upstairs to the attic room in which there was a double bed, a chest of drawers with a mirror on top, a wardrobe, and a chair by the bed.

Matthew took the wardrobe and Ned the chest of drawers. They worked in silence for a while, except for the sound of opening drawers. A tweed suit in the wardrobe, a Norfolk jacket and breeches, a pair of flannel trousers, jodhpurs, two waistcoats. Matthew tried all the pockets. Not even a stray handkerchief, which was suspicious in itself. He thought of the clothes in his wardrobe at home; he was always finding things in the pockets — notes, matches, bits of chewed pencil, string, a conker once. He contemplated the clothes. Not new, but good quality — just what you'd expect an English public-school man to wear. He looked in the hat boxes on the top shelf — a bowler hat, a trilby, a straw boater. He looked in the drawers — a few shirts with the name A. H. Smythe, underwear, socks. Nothing remarkable. Schmidt was good, even down to the fishing gear in the hall. Miss Cresswell wouldn't suspect a thing.

Ned was fishing under the bed now. A suitcase — locked. Ned took out a set of skeleton keys. The locks clicked. It was empty. 'He's damned good, ain't he?' Ned said.

There was a bathroom downstairs. On a shelf they found a shaving brush and bowl and a razor. No pills or drugs. They went across the corridor to what they assumed was Anna Cresswell's room. A single bed, furniture in the same Victorian style as that in the attic. The top drawer of the chest revealed jewellery boxes. A diamond ring — a pledge of some future life falsely promised? She hadn't dared wear it. An old-fashioned heavy gold bracelet, some earrings, and a gold cross. Handkerchiefs and a very fine Indian cashmere shawl, inside the folds of which was a photograph of Rudolph Schmidt outside a French café. He was not looking at the camera. There was a waiter with his sleeves rolled up, bending to speak to Schmidt. It looked like a seaside resort: a sandy beach, a tower, the café on a promenade, umbrellas at the tables, straw hats, and parasols. Summer, anyway. Had he taken Anna Cresswell to France? Maybe she'd sneaked the photograph, which was why it was hidden.

They went down to the parlour and contemplated the bookshelves, both thinking of the time it would take to look through them all. These were Anna's family's books. Was it likely that Schmidt would have hidden something in any of those? Not very, they concluded. He'd cleared out, leaving only so much as to allay any suspicion on Anna's part.

'Aye, aye,' Ned said, 'what's that?'

At the end of one of the shelves something was sticking out. Ned handed Matthew a couple of slim linen-backed volumes, *Pleasant Kent Walks* and *A Guide to Rambling in Sussex*. A third was passed: *A Guide to Angling on the Kentish Rivers*.

Ah, the country gentleman's pursuits, Matthew thought.

'Well, well,' murmured Ned, pulling out some linen-backed OS maps.

Maps. Maps of the Sussex coast, the Kent coast, and a chart of the Essex coast. Swin Deep off Clacton-on-Sea, from where the fleet was to sail to Zeebrugge between March the fourteenth and the nineteenth.

31

Claire woke from the recurring nightmare of Emil's bloody eye, the fears of the night returning as a wave of sudden terror. She looked up to see Giselle looking down at her. Her expression was unreadable in the shadow of the oil lamp which she'd brought to the bedside table. Claire's heart turned over. She hadn't heard her come in.

'You're frightened. What's happened?' Giselle sat down on the end of the bed. Her face, now lit, was as it had been when she'd left, entirely composed, and her voice was calm. 'Tell me.'

Claire found her voice. 'I was dreaming — of Emil —and—'

'I'm sorry, but I had to do it. You're shocked, aren't you? You thought I was callous.'

'I was, I admit. I didn't expect that. It was so sudden.'

'I'll tell you about him and about me. I expect you're wondering how I could be so ruthless.'

'Yes, I am. I've seen terrible things at the front. I was an ambulance driver before they sent me here, but I wasn't prepared for that.'

'I went to the Belle Vue this morning. If I tell you about it, you'll understand. I saw your Greta Lang in her furs and that colonel in his clean uniform. Such luxury, such plenty — it sickens me. Most of us ordinary people have so little; rents have doubled and food is too dear, but the rich are making money from this war. The armaments men, the bankers, the foreigners, the spies, the colonels, all profiteering. Did you know that the general of the Swiss army is pro-German? Many of the military leaders are pro-German. Yet our men, who loathe the Germans, our conscripts, are sent to guard the border for hundreds of days with little pay. I hate the Germans, but there are many who do not.'

'I understand.'

'My brother was a worker in a porcelain factory in Nyon. He was sent to the border. He hated it and ran away. He came back to Geneva. He's in hiding. Emil knew — you can guess what he wanted for keeping my secret. It wasn't just money. He would have done it to you — before he killed you.'

'Oh, God.'

'There were food riots in 1916 — mostly women. I was arrested because I wanted bread. There is an anti-militarist movement. We have political meetings in our association to fight for better pay and conditions, but the government loathes the radicals, and the bourgeoisie call us Bolsheviks —' Giselle laughed — 'I would have fought with the Bolsheviks in their revolution. Some of our friends went to Russia. I don't care what the rich call us. We want justice. So you see I have to be careful, and there's my brother. It's complicated. He has a daughter — his wife is dead. They are living with one of our political friends. That's why I don't want the police here.'

'But why do you work at a place like Café Martin?'

Giselle gave her a cynical smile. 'I need to eat. And it's a good cover. I can find out what the Germans are up to. Emil was spying on me and on people I know. I have fought in the streets, so I'm not scared. If your Greta held a gun to my head, I would fight her with my bare hands. She would lose.'

'I'd have been dead without you. Thank you, and thank you for telling me all this.'

'Now, we must sleep. I must work tomorrow, and then we will get you out of here.'

Claire dozed for most of the next two days, aided by Giselle's brandy. Physically, she felt better, but she couldn't help fretting about Mr Sutton. He might be looking for her. Guy Pelham might know she was missing. Matthew might know — it was agony to think of that. And they needed to know about this Admiral König operation and about Colonel Raulin and Greta, and Agnes White's death.

On the third day, she was woken by a tapping on the door. She waited for Giselle's whisper. Nothing. Then it came again. Three long taps and then two short. She froze where she lay, her heart thumping so loudly that she thought it must be heard beyond the door. In the silence, she thought she could hear someone breathing hoarsely. A man, she was sure. She heard the rattle of the door handle and then the breathing again and a shuffling of feet. 'Giselle, for God's sake,' the hoarse voice whispered in German. She felt terror then and pulled the covers over her head, holding her breath. She heard a woman's voice calling in French that Giselle was at work. The heavy footsteps retreated down the stairs.

Claire didn't move until Giselle came back. 'Someone came,' she said as soon as Giselle was in the room. 'A man, I'm sure.'

'Did he speak?'

'He asked for you, in German, and he knocked and rattled the door handle. I heard a woman's voice say that you were at work.'

'That would be Annette. She lives downstairs.'

'The German, though. Someone about Emil? Someone who's after you?'

'Maybe. Someone may have seen me with him — so many come and go. He was always pestering me, but it doesn't matter. I can handle those people at the café, and I have plenty of friends. More important is that I need to get you out. Someone was asking about you at the café. An Englishman.'

Mr Sutton, Claire hoped. 'What did he look like?'

'A priest in a black hat and a soutane — you say a —'

'Cassock, but I don't know any —'

'He knew you. He said he was concerned about you. Some friends had told him you were missing and that you had been seen at the café.'

'I can't think who —' Then she remembered the clergyman at the cathedral who had seemed to materialise behind her. *Trust no one.* What a fool she had been. And a clergyman had got off the steamer — on the top deck, perhaps. The someone that Colonel Raulin had been looking at? And Mr Sutton had been on that deck, too.

'You know him?' asked Giselle.

'No, but I've seen him. I think it was he who followed me the other night. What did you say?'

'I had no idea what he was talking about. I told him that I don't know any English ladies. English ladies do not come to the Café Martin.'

'Oh, Giselle, you make a better spy than I do. Look what a mess I've made so far.'

'No, you have done very well. You got rid of that lady, and you fought Emil like a tigress. Now, we must go tomorrow.'

'You had better not come to Thonon — you mustn't be seen there.'

'I won't be. Here are our disguises.' Giselle unwrapped a brown paper parcel and unrolled the clothes inside. 'Monsieur Mallory,' she said.

Claire burst out laughing. She forgot the German at the door.

32

'Missing?'

'I'm afraid so, Captain Riviere. We haven't heard anything from our man in Thonon, who was keeping an eye on Miss Mallory, and nothing from her or about her from anyone at the hotel. I sent a man from the consulate to the Belle Vue. He reported back about a death in the hotel which has been hushed up.'

After a long and stormy sea crossing on the hospital ship, *Aberdonian*, the day after they had met Anna Cresswell, Matthew and Ned had arrived at Montreuil, where Guy Pelham broke the news about Claire and Mr Sutton. The colour drained from Matthew's face.

'Oh God, Claire.'

'We can't be sure. One of the chambermaids told our man. She knew only that a woman was found dead in Mrs Lang's suite. He's trying to find out more, but he'll have to be discreet. The consulate's not supposed to be involved in spying. I'm sorry. It's —'

'I know — it's war, and we both knew it was dangerous. Claire knew. But did they know or guess about her?'

'Hold on, it could be Mrs Lang herself or Mrs White. They're in a dangerous game, too. Got greedy or careless, maybe. Miss Mallory might have found out about the death and thought it prudent to make herself scarce,' Ned offered. 'From what you've told me, your Miss Mallory is a resourceful lady.'

Pelham picked up on the word "your". He looked regretful. 'I am so sorry, Riviere, I didn't realise, but Ned has a point.

She stayed at a pension run by one of our people before she went to the Belle Vue —'

'She was at Greta's hotel?'

Guy Pelham explained that the man from Thonon — Mr Sutton — had met Claire to tell her about the names 'Raulin' and 'Rudi' and that Claire had seen Agnes White at the Belle Vue. Sutton had told Claire to take a room and make herself known — convalescing and all that. It was entirely possible that Claire was lying low at the pension and Sutton was waiting to hear from her.

'When did you last hear from Sutton?' Matthew asked.

'Four days ago. Admittedly, that is unusual, but he and Miss Mallory could be on the train by now. He'd given her instructions to telegraph him in an emergency, and she'd know to get to Thonon. That's easy enough — plenty of ferries. I'm afraid we can only wait for news from the consulate or from Sutton. In the meantime, you have news of Rudolph Schmidt?'

Ned explained everything and Pelham looked grave at the news of Schmidt's knowledge of the proposed Zeebrugge raid. 'Bloody hell, that's a disaster. All the preparations — the fleet on the move and we're guessing. Where is the bastard?'

'He was supposed to be at the British Military Mission in Paris, but that was a week ago,' said Ned. 'MI5 know about him now. They've men in Hull — that's the quickest route to Zeebrugge if he's gone that way. Harwich to Hook of Holland is being watched, too, but he was on that train to London from Lancaster.'

'Unless he doubled back — but what the devil would he be coming to France for? The raid is in Belgium.'

'Cover — he's got time to take the long way round. No one saw him at Folkestone, worse luck. He could be in Calais, Dunkirk, Holland — sailed to Vlissingen from Folkestone.

Remember that Kestein company? A cover for that fellow Dierks receiving reports from Britain. Schmidt could be posing as an innocent shipping man, his alias Smythe left behind in France.'

'I remember Dierks — we got him.'

'Dierks,' Matthew said, wrenching his thoughts from Claire and picking up the name, 'that oil man arrested in 1914 — his name was Dierks. He was at Treasonfield. Could have met Schmidt there.'

'I remember. Peter Dierks. The fellow in Vlissingen was Florian Dierks. Swiss as well — connected, maybe.'

'More than likely,' Ned said. 'And have a look at this.' He handed Pelham the photograph of Rudolph Schmidt outside the French café.

Pelham looked. 'That's Paris-Plage. I know that tower and the café. Just a minute —' he plucked a magnifying glass from his desk and peered closely — 'and I know that waiter. Madame Foulon, the owner, is one of our correspondence addresses. Maybe she or the waiter will remember him.'

'A little holiday before the fun started,' Ned said.

The telephone rang and Pelham answered. Ned and Matthew listened to his end of the conversation. 'Old one? Von Ende, that is interesting… Thomet… Austrian, very interesting… Nyon, right. Not much we can do about them… Miss Mallory… I see… Ask about, would you? And there's an English clergyman of interest in Lausanne, name of von Rahn Nicholl… Yes, English… See what you can fish out up there. Good man. Grateful. Anything else, let me know.' Pelham put down the phone and turned back to Ned and Matthew. 'My consulate man. It's not Miss Mallory, thank God. The dead woman is a Mrs von Ende — the older one, according to his source, the chambermaid. Heart attack, the hotel manager is saying.'

'Agnes White?' Matthew asked.

'Sounds like it. If it's a heart attack, why hush it up, I wonder? Something fishy there, and the hotel manager is in on it. German, maybe. Thomet by name. Has an Austrian mistress, a singer. The consulate man tells me that Mrs Lang has decamped to Nyon with Colonel Raulin. Sutton gave his name to Miss Mallory as one to listen out for.'

'But where is Claire?'

'Vanished. All her stuff is still at the hotel. I'm sorry. You heard. My man will continue enquiries about her. She's a British citizen so he has the right to do that, and he'll contact Lausanne about von Rahn Nicholl — might be something in it.'

Ned changed the subject. 'Enquiries at Paris-Plage?'

Pelham thought. 'Captain Riviere, you remember Miss Lemmon, one of the WAAC girls?' Matthew nodded. 'She can go with you to the café. She knows Madame Foulon. She can ask for her while you take a casual coffee. Madame Foulon will know it's important and ask for the waiter, the one who seemed to be speaking to Schmidt in the photograph.'

'And us?' Ned asked.

'The French Military Embassy across the road first — see if they know him, and then a call to the British Mission at French HQ in Paris. He might have gone there — still operating as one of Strange's men. Train from Paris up to Nieuport, just our side of the line, official business, all his papers in order. I'll get Miss Lemmon on the phone now.'

Guy and Ned tactfully left Matthew alone to wait for May. He stared out of the window, not seeing the buildings below, the uniforms passing to and fro, the heavily guarded gates or the church spires. He only saw the empty sky at which he and Claire had looked on the day they had met May Lemmon and set in motion the hunt for Greta Lang. Claire could be dead. His thoughts spun in a hopeless circle. He shouldn't have let her — but he couldn't have stopped her, just as he couldn't have stopped her driving an ambulance. But still, to let her go on her own to Geneva. He should have told Pelham that they would go together. Pelham could have sent Ned to Treasonfield, where he had been so pleased about finding those photographs — so caught up in the chase — oh, God — why hadn't he…

He heard the knock at the door. May Lemmon came in. 'I'm so sorry, Matthew, Major Pelham has just told me.'

33

Claire tried not to flinch as Giselle held up the scissors. 'I am sorry, Claire, but it is necessary.'

Claire took the pins out of her hair and unravelled her bun. 'They say short hair is coming into fashion.'

Giselle laughed. 'Not the way I do it.'

Claire watched the clumps of hair drop to the floor. Her crowning glory — well, not exactly; mousy, she admitted to herself, looking at Giselle's silvery curls. Giselle's scissors chopped remorselessly. The metallic sound set her teeth on edge.

'You want to see?' Giselle pointed to the mirror on the wall. Claire went to look. 'Well, it's true. My own mother wouldn't know me.' Giselle had hacked at the hair so that it fell in a jagged fringe over one eye and stuck out in sharp points over her ears. She put her hand to her neck and felt the roughened ends.

'Your cap, monsieur,' Giselle said, grinning. 'Gamin is the word, I think.'

'Labourer's chic, maybe.'

Then Claire was getting dressed — a yellowing, collarless cotton shirt, slightly worn at the cuffs, a cheap woollen muffler, a corduroy waistcoat, and baggy brown woollen trousers held up by a leather belt. Clumsy boots and the cap completed the look. Everything was clean, if rather shabby. There was a rough tweed coat on the bed with an old canvas knapsack, in which her handbag and her own clothes were packed. Her money, passport and the papers were tucked into her camisole next to her skin.

Claire Mallory, sometime ambulance driver on the Western Front, plain English miss at the Belle Vue, had vanished, and here was a young man of the labouring class. No one would notice him.

'Respectable working class,' Giselle told her. 'We're not criminals. Boyfriend and girlfriend out for the day on the steamer.'

Giselle put on a plain black dress, darned here and there, a brown coat with a bit of fur at the neck, her own buttoned boots, and a simple black felt hat.

She picked up the scattered hair and threw it on the fire. 'Just in case anyone comes in. Now, my friend Robert will come in a minute or so. He will take you to the jetty on the Quai du Mont-Blanc across the bridge. I will not be far behind and will meet you there. You might need this.' Giselle handed Claire her gun. She'd cleaned Emil's blood from it. Claire put it in her pocket.

There was a knock at the door. Claire felt for the package under her camisole. Safe and sound. She put on the coat, wound the muffler about her neck, put on the wire spectacles Giselle had provided and pulled down the cap over her brow. Giselle put on her own coat and hat. 'Ready?'

As I'll ever be, thought Claire, nodding. Giselle opened the door and a young man came in, a young man almost the mirror image of the shabby young man who stepped forward to meet him.

Two hours later, Claire and Giselle stood in a quiet side street near another Madeleine church, its clock striking the half hour and leaving a Sunday silence behind. They were looking at the brass plaque which told them that the Mochat Import/Export Company resided on the first floor. However, there was no sign of life upstairs, where the window shutters were closed. The ground floor housed what must have been a shop, but it was firmly closed and shuttered, a notice advising that the business had closed down. *In the last century*, Claire thought. There was a door at the side which must lead up to the Mochat Company, but that was locked. The key which Mr Sutton had given Claire obviously didn't fit the lock. Hearing the sound of a door opening and closing somewhere behind them and then slow footsteps and a walking stick tapping along, they stayed looking at the shop window until the footsteps passed. Claire sneaked a glance and saw an elderly woman going towards the church.

Round the back? she wondered, looking at the narrow passage next to the shop. At the end of the passage, they found a door which opened into a yard, across which they saw another door which Claire's key opened, revealing a tiny lobby and a flight of stairs.

'You go up. I'll find somewhere to hide in the alley — just in case someone comes,' Giselle whispered. 'If he's not there, come quickly. Can you whistle?'

'I can.'

'Signal me when you're back at the yard door.'

Giselle vanished and Claire crept slowly up the stairs. One creaked and she froze, waiting, uneasy at the silence which congealed about her. The air was stale. It smelt of cabbage and coffee, and something else which she recognised and feared, a faint metallic something. The hairs on the back of her neck prickled. There was something wrong up those stairs.

The door at the top of the stairs was ajar and she pushed it very slowly. It made no sound. The room was a small kitchen with a sink and a gas-cooking stove on which a coffee pot stood, one of those little metal pots you found all over France.

On the little wooden table was a cup, some sugar, a plate, and a piece of bread fallen from it. There was a broken saucer on the floor and a knife with butter smeared on its blade. The stool next to the table was turned over. *Breakfast interrupted*, thought Claire. She stood still, listening, afraid to go into the next room.

She took a deep breath and stepped through the open door. Mr Sutton lay on the floor, his eyes open to the ceiling, a black hole in his forehead, his green scarf spattered with blood. She'd known, really, the moment that she had stood on the stair. She'd smelt blood then. Someone had searched the room. Drawers had been ransacked and thrown on the floor with blood-stained papers, bearing the legend, *Mochat Company*. Mr Sutton's cover had been blown. They had taken his secrets, but it wouldn't matter to him now. She should get out.

Claire heard the creak of the stair and turned to go back into the kitchen. 'Giselle?' she whispered. No answer but footsteps, light and hurried. Hand in her pocket. The cold metal of her gun against her fingers.

The clergyman appeared at the kitchen door. He took off his black fedora and bowed, his smile mocking, his grey eyes cold as ice, his gun trained on her.

'Miss Mallory, we meet again, though I was very nearly fooled. Congratulations to you. I didn't realise when two young men came out. I prayed for you to come, but it was Miss Giselle who gave you away — those silver curls just showing underneath the simple hat. I was on the steamer, but you were so busy congratulating yourselves that you didn't notice me. Tut, tut, not as clever as you think you are. Where is your girlfriend?'

'She's gone back to the ferry — she's on her way back to Geneva.'

The grey eyes narrowed. Claire could see that he was debating whether to believe her, but with a contemptuous sneer, he made up his mind. 'It doesn't matter where she is. My friends will find her. We know all about her treachery. I knew she was lying about not knowing you. I saw you go into that grubby little café — you remember me, the nice English clergyman who pointed the way into sanctuary. And poor Emil — not that he matters, but your girlfriend killed him. A knife in the eye. It wasn't you. Not British, of course. A pistol for you, but don't think of using it now. I have the advantage. You'll be dead before your hand is out of your pocket.'

Buy time, she thought, her fingers on the muzzle of her pistol. He hadn't seen Giselle. She'd know something was wrong. She might even have seen the clergyman walk into the yard. Giselle would come. 'Who are you?'

'Reverend Conrad von Rahn Nicholl, late of Fernhall School in Lancashire. An English public school. A tinpot place in a miserable, flat landscape. It looked like a factory. They had no idea who we were. So complacent in their superiority, and so naïve. I was just a foreigner, a half-German schoolmaster, grateful for my humble station in their oh-so-English common room, but my favourite pupils knew better. You know them, I think; Stephen von Ende and his cousin, Rudolph Schmidt, whose mother you murdered, Mrs Agnes White.'

'It was an accident. I didn't mean to kill her.'

'No matter. She is dead, a martyr to our cause. A fact of war, Miss Mallory, as is Mr Sutton here — and as you will be in a few moments. A fine thing, to die for your country — you'll no doubt be a heroine, albeit a dead one. A useless sacrifice of your young life. *Einsatz Admiral König* will happen.'

'I don't understand. What is *Einsatz Admiral König*?'

That sneer again. 'Ah, I could tell you, but it is better that you go to your grave guessing. Such a cataclysm and Great Britain will lose this war. So, my dear Miss Mallory, my blessing upon you.'

He raised the gun just as the bell of the Madeleine church began to ring. 'For whom the bell tolls, my dear.'

The bell struck again, a deep, resounding note. A shot rang out simultaneously, and the Reverend Conrad von Rahn Nicholl dropped like a stone onto the floor. As it continued to strike, there was Giselle with Emil's gun.

'I'm sorry I kept you waiting. I was waiting for the hour to strike and cover the noise of the shot.'

'Mr Sutton is dead,' Claire said.

'There is nothing we can do for him. We must go. I've left the knapsack downstairs, and my shoes. You should change into your own clothes. They're downstairs, in the lobby. There's an outbuilding in the yard. Throw those clothes in there. I'll go on to the ferry station. There's a café. Meet me there. Be quick, I beg you.'

Claire turned back into the other room and stood for a moment to bid farewell to Mr Sutton. She didn't touch him, but she remembered the coffee they'd had, his wry smile as he had held her hand, and that touch of vulnerability in the gap between his teeth. Her eyes pricked. She hoped there wasn't a Mrs Sutton in Manchester.

As the twelfth stroke of the Madeleine bell died away, she was putting on her own clothes, fixing on her beret with a hat pin, exchanging the wire spectacles for the ones Charlotte Payne had given her in Paris, checking her money and passport. She locked the door, threw the clothes into the shed, took a deep breath to quiet her thumping heart, and walked back along the quiet street at an even pace. She didn't look back. Giselle was standing outside the café by the jetty, where a steamer was waiting to depart.

'We must split up now. Lausanne will be best for you. You can take the train to Paris.'

'Come with me — we'll look after you.'

'I wish I could, but I can't — my brother. Now go. Later — afterwards, when there is peace, write to me.'

'I will. But if you need anything, write to the address I gave you. Write to Sir Roland Riviere. And you must have this.' Claire took a handful of notes from her pocket. 'I didn't pay my hotel bill. They can afford it.'

'Thank you. Now go, please — we don't know who might be after us.' Giselle looked over her shoulder and back to Claire, who saw a fleeting expression of fear which made her heart flutter.

'Come with me.'

'Go — just go.'

Claire watched her as the ferry pulled away to take her to safety on the train from Lausanne to France, if all went well. Giselle was already walking away — *into what danger?* Claire wondered.

34

No news is good news, so his old nanny used to say. *Not in intelligence work*, thought Guy Pelham. No news meant that someone was missing. An agent was lost or dead. Like Claire Mallory and Sutton. The consulate man had used his position to make enquiries about Miss Mallory, the English lady missing from her hotel, and gained permission to look at her luggage. Her passport and money were gone — which could mean that she had them, or that they had been stolen. A British passport — gold to the other side. And money was money.

He'd sent word to an agent in Lausanne to get to Thonon — he couldn't use the consulate man for the Thonon angle. It wasn't the done thing to involve diplomats in the work of agents. A diplomat might be discovered doing covert work and that would offend the Swiss, and be an embarrassment to the Foreign Office, but Guy needed to know what had happened to Sutton. Despite Uncle Ned's theories, he knew in his heart that something had gone wrong for him. Probably for Miss Mallory, too. The only hope was Madame Grenier at the pension, but she had not been in contact. Nothing from the French about Rudolph Schmidt. Of course, he hadn't turned up at the French Military Embassy as Lieutenant Ashton Hamilton Smythe.

Somewhere several telephones were ringing. London, Paris, Brussels, Antwerp, anywhere and nowhere; telegraph messages were coming in, the web of wires thrumming across Europe, and not a word about a young woman who had vanished in Geneva.

Dejected, he lit a cigarette and looked at the papers and telegrams on his desk. A memo about a visit from the king — unofficial. He was crossing the Channel in a destroyer, accompanied by his private secretary, Lord Stamfordham, and Colonel Wigram. It was not unusual for the British press to find out about a visit until His Majesty was already on French soil. Well, the visit was his chief's worry. In any case, the king would be staying at Haig's Château de Beaurepaire, a couple of miles from Montreuil from where Haig would accompany him on a tour of the troops. The king wanted to see the fighting men and visit the wounded, and to show support for Haig, who had his difficulties with the Prime Minister, Lloyd George.

Guy turned his attention to the other stuff, aerial photographs from behind the German lines, news of interrogated prisoners, information about German bombardments, raids and patrols on both sides, news from the 'pigeon post' — pigeons dropped behind the lines in baskets with messages for patriotic French people to report on troop movements in their area. But if the Germans found the baskets, then they'd send false information. And the British still didn't know when or where the attack would come, even though German divisions were on the move. The German Army was at its strongest, which was a chilling thought, and the British were short of arms and men, and not enough American troops had arrived. There were secret memos about the possibility of evacuation at an hour's notice if the worst happened. A lorry was parked in the yard day and night, ready to carry away maps and papers — the lorry's purpose was only known to a few, of course. There were plans to blow up every harbour, canal, and road. They might be secret plans, but no one was unaware of the consequences if the Germans broke through.

And now this Zeebrugge business. Guy felt a quickening in his chest. Should he advise that it be called off, on the grounds that a spy might have information? A spy they couldn't find, and whose superior, Captain Strange, didn't actually know what he'd got. Yes, Schmidt had a chart showing Swin Deep, but was it enough? He'd sent word to Ostend that B9, their man there, should listen out for a whisper that the Germans knew about the raid. It was B9 who had reported in 1917 that the Germans had constructed new concrete shelters along the sea wall at Zeebrugge — he was a Belgian, posing as a neutral Dutchman, who worked as a marine engineer based in a ferry port off Vlissingen; he knew the docks and the coast. The British colonel running La Dame Blanche in Belgium reported by telegraph to the British Mission at French GHQ, and they knew Guy was after a man who called himself Smythe. The colonel might hear a whisper on the wind.

Guy lit another cigarette and blew out the smoke on a sigh. He'd done what he could for now. March the fourteenth — two weeks away. He'd give it a day or two more, just in case they found him.

May knocked on the open door and came in. 'Madame Foulon at the Paris-Plage café remembered Schmidt because of the Englishwoman with him — red hair and freckles. You know Madame Foulon; she doesn't miss much. She's always on the watch for something unusual. The woman obviously adored him, but Madame didn't think the feeling was mutual. The woman wanted the waiter to take a photograph of the two of them — she had a little snapshot camera with a leather case, but Schmidt wouldn't let the waiter take the photograph. He was quite bad-tempered about it and even when he let her take a photograph, he wouldn't look at the camera. She saw them last year but not since.'

'What about the waiter who was talking to Schmidt in the photograph?'

'Fed up of waitering and gone to work in Étaples for the British — more money, Madame Foulon said. Not that she cared — she has someone else now.'

'Schmidt was using his girlfriend as cover, I think. They probably came into Boulogne. She'd assume he'd have secret work on hand. I'd like to know where he went from Paris-Plage. Up the coast, I suppose. Plenty of intelligence to gather at the ports. Where is Riviere, by the way?'

'Gone for a walk. He's shattered by this. He's so afraid that Claire is dead — blames himself. Thinks he should have gone to Geneva with her.'

'Maybe he should have. Ned could have handled Treasonfield. I thought it would be good for Riviere — I know he wouldn't have been happy to hang about doing nothing, and he knows the ground.'

'Claire understood what she was getting into and she's no fool. If there's a way out of Geneva, she'll find it.'

'I hope so. And then there's Sutton. I have a bad feeling about him. He's usually so punctual — I thought he'd look after Miss Mallory —'

'I'm sorry, Guy, but I've got to go. I'm on night shift. I daren't be late.'

'Telephone me if anything comes in that's pertinent to all this.'

'I will.'

As May went out, Guy's telephone rang. Ned came in as he answered it and waited.

Guy put down the receiver with a frown. 'Geneva — queer things afoot. Some low-life German agent was found dead in a lavatory in Café Martin. The café is known to us. This chap was stabbed in the eye. However, the local police aren't much interested in a low-life from Café Martin. Neither am I, except that the place is a nest of all sorts of sweepings from the gutter who'll spy on anyone for money — or drugs, or women. The German spies deal in drugs. The really bad news is that my man, Sutton, is dead and there's no sign of Miss Mallory in Thonon.'

'No reason for Miss Mallory to be at this café, or Sutton?'

'I hope to God she wasn't. Sutton could have been there, of course, if he'd had a tip-off about somebody at the Belle Vue which led him to Café Martin.'

'How was Sutton killed?'

'Shot in the head, and the queer thing is that the clergyman, von Rahn Nicholl, was also found shot dead in Sutton's flat.'

'Good God, so he was in it all with Schmidt.'

'And Mrs Lang and Mrs White — he was in Lausanne; he must have been in contact with them. They were onto Sutton, somehow.'

Ned looked at him bleakly. 'And Miss Mallory.'

'It's stranger still. Sutton shot in one room, von Rahn shot in the back in the kitchen. It's all a bit murky. Sutton had been dead for days, my chap thinks.'

'Which is why you hadn't heard from him.'

'Four days, I said to Riviere.'

'So, he hasn't been in contact with Miss Mallory for more than four days. It looks bad for her.'

'I know. I shouldn't have waited — I should have —'

'It's the game we're in, old son,' Ned cut in. 'Impossible to predict everything.'

'Thanks, Ned, I know it, really, but to think of Miss Mallory in the wrong hands…'

'I still think she could have got away, you know. Sutton would have told her what to do. Who shot von Rahn, though, if he was working for them?'

'It's damned odd. Von Rahn's gun was found with him, but someone else shot him from behind. Someone who came up the staircase. And, odder still, the door was locked.'

'Anyone see anything?'

'My man asked around the nearby houses. Said he was looking for Mr Sutton from the import/export company. A neighbour on her way to church saw a young couple outside the building — nothing to remark about them, and she only saw their backs. Just an impression of rather shabby clothes. Not much help, except he's wondering if there were two different killers, as Sutton's been dead for a few days and von Rahn Nicholl only a matter of hours.'

'It doesn't make much sense, but two people outside the building on a quiet Sunday morning — makes you think.'

'It does. My man's wondering if the killer or killers went away on the ferry. Anyway, he's following it up.'

A knock came at the door and Matthew entered. Guy thought he looked strained, and now they'd have to tell him about the deaths of Sutton and the clergyman. Riviere would know exactly what the implications were for Miss Mallory.

Guy told him. 'We can only wait, I'm afraid.'

Matthew didn't answer. The chances were that Miss Mallory had been caught and they all knew it, but Matthew's words came as a complete surprise.

'I saw him — Schmidt. He's here in Montreuil.'

225

35

Claire stood at the stern of the second-class promenade deck and kept her eyes on Giselle until she vanished into the crowd. She would be taking the boat to Geneva. Claire could only hope that von Rahn Nicholl had worked alone and that no one else had been waiting for him in Thonon. Giselle had looked afraid for the first time. The danger was real because Giselle had killed von Rahn Nicholl. His body would be found. Claire was filled with anguish. She had put Giselle in danger. *Oh, God,* she prayed, *keep her safe.*

Now she had an hour or so on the ferry. Claire kept to the promenade deck, sitting on one of the wooden benches so that she could watch for anyone who might be watching her. Not that it was possible to tell. She remembered looking at the passengers on the train to Geneva and wondering what secrets they carried in their luggage. Who would have thought that an English clergyman was really a spy for the Germans?

She sat, thoroughly miserable, chilled to the bone, worrying about Giselle and the friends von Rahn had said would find her. Friends of Greta and Colonel Raulin. People like Emil. Claire looked at her watch. The crossing seemed interminable. Her mouth was dry; it was hours since she had had a drink or anything to eat, but she didn't dare go into the salon for coffee. She decided that she must take the train from Lausanne immediately. She would feel safer on the train, and she could telegraph Major Pelham from Lyon. What should she say? How could she warn them about *Einsatz Admiral König Vulkan?*

A woman sat down beside her. Claire's instinct was to get up and walk away, but she knew she ought not to draw attention to herself. She turned up her coat collar and tightened her scarf. A young man came to speak to the woman. '*Maman*,' he said, smiling, and they walked away together, arm in arm. Her relief was fleeting. Mothers could be killers. And sons. Emil must have had a mother. Von Rahn, too. He had seemed so kind at the cathedral — as kind as that young man who had linked arms with his mother. Claire thought of the gun in her handbag.

At last, she was aware of people moving. She went to the rail, from where she could see the terracotta roofs and grey spires of Lausanne. A few more minutes and she would be making her way to the station.

She waited in line to disembark, her nerves taut as other passengers came behind her. She half expected a hand on her arm and the voice of Colonel Raulin to bid her good day and steer her off the boat. It seemed to take an age for the ropes to be flung out and tied up, for the gangway to be lowered, and for the queue to start moving. She needed directions to the railway station. She mustn't hover uncertainly on the pier. There was a woman in a fur coat in front of her, holding a handsome little boy by the hand. Safe, surely. She asked the way to the railway station. The woman turned, smiling, and told her it was a long walk up the hill — twenty minutes, perhaps. Claire followed her down the gangway and onto the jetty. Where now? The smiling woman pointed.

It was indeed a long walk, and Claire felt her heart hammering as she paused to glance briefly behind her to check if she were being followed. She saw the woman who had sat beside her on the boat. Ah, *maman* and her son. Were they following her? She hurried on. Then she was crossing the road, landing breathless in front of the grand station, hurrying through one of the great arches, and then among the crowds inside the vast departure hall. She queued at the ticket office and at the counter, her money in her hand, she asked for a ticket to Paris. The man smiled at her, gave her the ticket, and pointed her to the correct platform. All well, so far.

The train, its locomotive hissing out steam, whistles blowing and doors slamming, was making ready to depart. Uniformed porters were unloading trunks and suitcases into the luggage van. Guards waited at the first-class compartments where silk-hatted and fur-coated travellers were boarding. Claire had chosen second class, where she thought she might be anonymous. There was always a danger that someone in first class might want to strike up a conversation, and she hadn't a newspaper to hide behind. Not even a book to read — not that she would be able to concentrate on anything but the rattling of the iron wheels on the track going towards France.

An open door presented itself. The large man in front was fully laden with a large basket, a leather hat box, a walking stick, and assorted travelling rugs. A travelling rug dropped at her feet and the stick caught in the door. *Hurry up*, she thought to herself as she waited for him to disentangle himself. *Hurry up*. She just wanted to be on the train. The guard's whistle blew; several doors clunked shut further along the platform. She held up the rug, and her foot was on the step when she felt a tug on the strap of her handbag, which she'd looped over her shoulder. Her foot missed the step, and she tottered backwards.

'Miss Mallory,' a voice hissed in her ear.

She only felt terror. Instinct made her kick out backwards; she heard a yelp and lurched forward, grabbing for the carriage door. A warm hand seized hers and dragged her into the carriage, where she found herself sprawled on the basket. The door was slammed shut, the wheels of the train already grinding. A genial red face looked down at her.

'Ah, mademoiselle, you nearly missed the train, as did that man who was behind you. Ah, well, there will be another. But not for my rug, alas.'

Claire was speechless. Who was it who knew her name? She struggled to her feet and looked out of the window. Her heart stopped when she saw the black fedora lying on the platform, but her assailant had vanished. Or had he managed to get on the train? She turned and saw that her saviour was looking at her curiously. 'That man — you are afraid of him?'

Trust no one. She thought of Giselle walking away from the ferry. *Sometimes you had to.* The man spoke French, not German. 'He wanted to stop me. I have to reach France.'

'Ah, you are English.' He beamed at her and spoke in English. 'On the run, as you say.' His smile faded as he looked at her. 'You think he may have boarded the train?'

'He wasn't there when I looked out.'

'I am French, mademoiselle; we like the English. We do not like the Germans. The Allies must win this war. I do not ask what you are escaping from, but you must not worry. He cannot get in here now, and if he should try when we stop at a station, I will be at the window. The carriage is full. That is what I shall tell him.' He patted his stomach. 'He will not get past me. Where do you go?'

'To Paris.'

'Ah, yes, change at Lyon where I am going. I will see you onto the Paris train. You will come to no harm. There will be a policeman at the Lyon station and if that man tries anything, he will be arrested. I shall tell them he is a German spy.' The man grinned.

Whistles blew. The wheels moved again. The train lurched forward and faltered. Claire held her breath. She heard the metallic groan of wheels as the train made up its mind. They were really on the way now. She looked back through the window. The platform was empty. She turned to her smiling saviour.

'And now you must sit down and rest. I have some very good things in my basket. A little luncheon, perhaps?'

Lunch on a train with a stranger. As if she were on a day trip. Claire banished thoughts of the clergyman and Mr Sutton. And Giselle. And the man who had followed her from Thonon. She dared not think about all that now, nor of the telegraph to Guy Pelham, and every other thing that made her heart race with dread. She looked up at the twinkling eyes of her new friend, dismissed the idea that he might be an enemy, and said, 'Thank you. Lunch would be delightful.' She could smell sausage and cheese. Half-ashamed, she realised she was famished.

36

Guy and Ned stared at Matthew. 'Are you sure?' Guy asked.

'Of course I can't be sure, but you both know as well as I do that we have an instinct about these things. You don't spend a night in No Man's Land without sensing that someone's there. You know when you're being watched.'

'Or when you're on surveillance,' Ned said. 'You can't see him, but you damn well know he's there.'

'You saw him, though?' asked Guy.

'I was on the ramparts — just looking and thinking. The prickling at the back of my neck told me, just as it did when I saw that red glow of a cigarette at Treasonfield. I didn't know it was Schmidt then, but I knew someone was there, even though the light had gone. Same thing on those ramparts and when I turned, I caught a glimpse of his face. I looked, of course, but I couldn't find him.'

A face, Guy Pelham thought, remembering Matthew's story of seeing Stephen von Ende in the raid. Riviere had been right then.

'Now you see him, now you don't. What the hell is he doing here?' Ned asked.

'Has he a contact? Think about it. A population of five thousand military personnel here. Three hundred and fifty officers plus NCOs, Military Police, guards, privates, clerks, grooms, batmen, medics, nurses, WAACs, cooks, waiters, labourers — Chinese, Indian, Egyptian and the rest. The Army Embassies — French, Belgian, Portuguese, American. German prisoners in the workshops. Another two hundred and fifty officers scattered about in Paris-Plage and Le Touquet, the forest of Crécy — and their support staff. And there are the local residents, houses, cafés, restaurants, shops. People coming and going all the time, lorries, motor cars, motorcycles on the move — and not always stopped by the Military Police. Supplies in and out every day. Horses taken out for rides. Barges on the river. Security is good, but it's not perfect.'

'Hiding in plain sight,' Ned observed. 'Was he in uniform?'

Matthew closed his eyes. 'The coat — I'm sure I had an impression of a military coat.'

'One man amongst many in an officer's uniform. Green tabs for Intelligence, I daresay. Well, we must assume he knows you're here, and maybe he knows that we've got the information on Zeebrugge. He could be on his way now. I'll get onto Major Ferrars,' Pelham said, picking up the telephone.

Ned nodded. He remembered Ferrars from Special Branch in London, one of the earliest recruits to the Intelligence Corps, nominally a major in the Royal Fusiliers.

'Intelligence Police,' he whispered to Matthew. 'Security Duties Section — passes, permits, prisoners, and spies, of course. Contacts with the civilian population which could be useful.'

They listened while Pelham explained about Schmidt and his alias, Ashton Hamilton Smythe, wanted for spying activities in England, formerly in Folkestone under Cameron and Strange. Captain Riviere knew him and was sure he had seen him. Yes, there was a photograph. They'd bring it downstairs.

Messages were sent to the Military Police at the outlying offices, including Crécy Forest, Paris-Plage, Le Touquet and Étaples, and the villages near Montreuil, as far as Haig's Château de Beaurepaire, to the other châteaux which were used as billeting accommodation. Lieutenant Ashton Hamilton

Smythe was to be detained. The matter was urgent, and Major Pelham would come to fetch him.

Questions were asked at the town houses of the French families who provided accommodation for the military personnel and at the cafés and restaurants. Men were sent to scour the web of narrow streets, the churches, and even the underground tunnels and dugouts, constructed in case of attack by air. There were passages to these from points in the ramparts. Anyone might know of their existence, Pelham thought. Major Ferrars himself started with motorcycle transport, on the reasonable assumption that having caught sight of Captain Riviere, Schmidt would have gone north, perhaps, towards Nieuport on the coast. A motorcycle was the fastest mode of transport.

Every day, every hour, despatch riders on their motorcycles scorched away from GHQ, north to Boulogne, Calais, and Dunkirk, north-west to Ypres, south towards the Somme, taking their messages to General Horne's First Army at Ranchicourt, to General Byng's Third Army at Beauquesne, and to Rawlinson's Fifth Army at Villers-Bretonneux, and as far as Paris to the French Army GHQ. Major Ferrars looked aghast at the sergeant who inspected the transport passes, signed by the Director of Motor Transport. The sergeant had supplied the motorcycle for Lieutenant Ashton Hamilton Smythe, who was on a special mission for the Intelligence Section for Major Pelham.

'Green tabs on his collar,' said the sergeant. 'Army coat — rode off about thirty minutes ago. Didn't say where he was going. Not my place to ask.' He looked warily at Ferrars's red face.

Major Ferrars's moustache bristled. He was about to speak when Major Pelham cut in smoothly, 'No matter, Sergeant. I'll catch up with him by telegraph.'

'Disappeared into one of those underground passages from the ramparts after he saw you, I'll bet. That's how he got off so quickly,' Pelham said to Ned and Matthew after he had told them about the motorcycle. 'If he's on any of the roads, we'll get him. The Military Police are out in force, as are Ferrars's chaps.'

37

Matthew looked out at a grey, misty landscape flat as a billiard table, except for the poplar trees waving in the breeze. Ypres was not far away to the north — and Passchendaele. Memories of rain, great sloughs of mud and gas shells, sheets of flame and smoke. And a thousand silent graves. The German plan for the Third Battle of Ypres had been to push forward to attack the ports of Ostend and Zeebrugge. That name again. Matthew shook his head and leaned forward in the passenger seat as if it would make the car go faster. Ned's eyes were fixed on the road. They didn't speak.

The familiar names echoed in Matthew's head: Hazebrouck, Bailleul, Armentieres, Frelinghien, where battles had been won and lost. It was a long journey from Montreuil, but at last they turned off the road from Armentieres into the narrower road which led to Le Touquet — not the Le Touquet on the coast, but the village in Belgium, which was just inside the British line, about a hundred miles north-east from Montreuil. However, it had been from an officer billeted in the coastal Le Touquet that news had come which had sent them racing away in Guy Pelham's car.

Enquiries had been made at the intelligence headquarters in the more famous Le Touquet, where an officer told them that he had talked to Lieutenant Hamilton Smythe earlier in the month. He was on his way to Belgium. The officer had met him before; he knew that he had a billet somewhere on the road beyond Le Touquet — a farm, he believed. Smythe had told him it was a very good billet. Plenty of grub. Decent wine.

Dairy farm supplying to the British. Smythe was keeping an eye on German activity across the river at Frelinghien.

'Well, he would be,' Ned had snorted.

The geography made sense. The British had taken the Belgian Le Touquet in 1917. Schmidt as a British Intelligence Officer had every reason to be there now that the Germans were digging in at Frelinghien. Schmidt only had to dump the motorcycle in some bushes and sneak across the river to safety. He knew the lie of the land, by the sound of it. He'd probably have his German uniform at the farm and, hey presto, Leutnant Rudolph Schmidt would be reporting for duty.

The question was, could they catch him on his motorcycle? Or rather, the British Army's motorcycle, Pelham observed bitterly. It was more than a three-hour trip. Schmidt might well have a head start. He could be long gone.

'It's worth a look at the farm, though,' Matthew said, anxious to be doing something, anything that would stop him thinking about Claire.

Pelham understood. 'Take my car,' he said. 'It's fast. You might make it.'

They made it to Le Touquet, the village almost entirely given over to the British Army preparing for the spring offensive, though most of the locals had stayed. There was a bakery and café still run by a French family, and a couple of shops, but the church was being set up as an advanced dressing station, the cottages, barns and stables used for billeting. It was full of troops who were there to dig trenches and dugouts, repair roads, and build gun emplacements. The schoolhouse served as headquarters. They went in search of an officer.

Matthew and Lieutenant Cropper stared at each other in astonishment. Matthew remembered Claire telling him that

Cropper's company had gone north. 'I thought you'd be in England, sir,' Cropper said.

'I was. Transferred to Military Intelligence. This is Superintendent Turner, Special Branch. We want to make contact with a Lieutenant Ashton Hamilton Smythe.'

'Oh, the Folkestone man — he has been here from time to time. Goes into Belgium.'

'We'd better have a word with the major.'

'Right, yes, he's in his office. I'll just —' Cropper paused and gave Matthew an anguished look. 'You'll come back to us, sir, won't you?'

Before Matthew could answer, the major came out with a sheaf of papers in his hand. Matthew didn't recognise the major — new, he presumed. He dismissed Lieutenant Cropper and the papers with a curt order and took the newcomers into his office.

'Something new to tell me about what's going on over there?'

The major's mouth tightened in anger when they told him who they were looking for and why. He knew Smythe slightly. The Folkestone man. Yes, he'd been at the farm in early February. Couldn't remember exactly when. Came and went as he pleased — hush-hush and all that. Going into Belgium, apparently. Didn't come back their way. He told them that the dairy farm was about half a mile outside the village. There was a gate on the right and the track led to the farmhouse.

The isolated farmhouse with its steep mossy red roof and pale green shutters seemed untouched by the war. No doubt when the Germans had occupied the village, they had commandeered the farmhouse and the dairy and its milk. Ned knocked at the door. A stout, middle-aged, white-aproned farmer's wife answered. She looked at their uniforms, at Ned's genial face, and smiled a welcome. They asked about

Lieutenant Hamilton Smythe with whom they were keen to make contact on a military matter. In a mixture of French and halting English, she told them that she hadn't seen him for a while — oh, not since the beginning of the month, but that was not unexpected. Sometimes she didn't see him for weeks. He had told her he was attached to the Intelligence Section, a liaison officer, so he travelled about a lot, but she kept his room. He paid well and was always so polite. An English gentleman.

They looked at the room — nothing to see but a single bed, a table, and a chest of drawers. He'd left no trace this time. Not even a cigarette end. Matthew didn't bother to look under the bed for the chamber pot. Madame would have emptied that. The room was spotlessly clean. There was no way of knowing if he were coming back.

Ned drove back to the village to see the major and to tell him to make sure the farmhouse was guarded. Matthew waited in the farmhouse kitchen for a few minutes and then, restless, strolled into the garden where Madame was taking her washing off the line. Matthew watched in a kind of frozen fascination. Towels, sheets, men's shirts and undergarments swayed on the line, dried by the wind, and, staggeringly, a uniform — field grey. A German uniform.

Madame unpegged the washing and came to Matthew, smiling guilelessly. 'I took his things to wash. I hope it is all right. I thought it would be nice for him to have everything clean when he comes back.'

'The uniform,' Matthew managed to say.

'Oh, it was in the drawer. I wanted to make it fresh for him.'

'Yes, of course, very thoughtful, Madame.'

She smiled conspiratorially. 'It is his disguise. He does not tell me, but I know, of course, that he must go into enemy territory.'

Ned came back, having impressed upon the major that Schmidt must not get away. 'A bloody regiment'll guard the place and every road in and out,' the major had said, furious that he had had a spy in his midst. He felt it as a personal slight.

Ned gazed at the uniform in Madame's arms. Matthew said quickly, 'Lieutenant Smythe's disguise. Madame has guessed that he uses it when he goes across the border.'

'A brave man,' Madame said. 'I am fond of him.'

Ned smiled at her. 'Ah well, we must take it, I'm afraid, Madame. Must keep it secret. You understand, of course.'

They bade farewell to Madame, promising that they would return the uniform when they met Lieutenant Smythe again, and raced back to Montreuil to report to Guy Pelham.

'He won't get out of that village,' Ned said.

'He seems to have vanished, though,' Pelham responded. 'Not a thing from any of the patrols. I suppose he could have slipped across the river to Frelinghien. He knows the terrain.'

'A wild goose chase.'

'I'm afraid so. I'd better see the chief.'

A clerk knocked and came in with a telegram. Pelham read it. 'Nothing much, I'm afraid. An odd report from the man I sent from Lausanne. He found some men's clothing abandoned in a shed at Sutton's place in Thonon. A disguise, I suppose. So, now our killer in Thonon looks like somebody else altogether.'

38

Matthew and Ned dined at the English Teashop where they were billeted. Madame Roche gave them coq au vin, some very good cheese, and a glass of wine. Not that Matthew tasted much of anything. They'd turned down Pelham's offer of dinner at the Officers' Club; they'd wanted to get out of Pelham's office for a while. Ned thought they should eat something. Pelham was snatching a sandwich at his desk. He wanted to stay by the telephone.

'How about a walk on the ramparts?' Ned suggested, looking at Matthew's half-eaten food. 'And then we'll call in on Pelham. He'll be there all night.'

They wandered aimlessly about the town. The streets were quiet now, the gates heavily guarded, but lights were on in the various offices. Telephones would still ring. Telegrams would come in throughout the night. The hush-hush girls on the night shift would be deciphering the German codes. To the east of Montreuil on the front line, a raid might be in progress, or a patrol listening in the darkness of No Man's Land. An ambulance might be trundling its way to a casualty clearing station. A ship might be ploughing its way through the dark and fathomless sea to Boulogne or Calais or Le Havre, bringing troops and supplies. A motorcycle might be roaring to the coast of Belgium, its headlamp cutting through the shadows, its rider a man with treachery in his heart. Somewhere a train would be rattling along a line, a train coming from Belgium or Holland, bringing news, or from Germany, bringing arms and men. Maybe from Paris, bringing an exhausted woman, dreaming of a man in a green scarf lying dead in an empty apartment.

'Where is he?' Matthew asked, as they climbed up the ramparts. He knew it was a pointless question, but he didn't want to talk about Claire. She could be dead. The news about Sutton had shaken him. If an experienced agent could be killed in his own lodgings, then what chance had Claire, alone in Geneva? May Lemmon had said that Claire would find a way out, but he knew she was trying to cheer him up. Claire had left her things at the Hotel Belle Vue. Her passport and money were missing. Pelham hadn't said so, but Matthew knew that they could have been stolen. Claire could have been taken in the street if she'd been out at night, like the doctor's sister from Luxembourg. Or she could have been killed in broad daylight, pushed under a tram. An unfortunate accident.

Ned didn't answer the question. He only said, 'If they don't find him, they'll have to call off Zeebrugge. Of course, the Germans might know already.'

'Unless he's keeping it to himself until he gets there and meets his handler. No chance of any letters intercepted, or codes broken. He's arrogant enough to think he can do it all on his own and get away with it.'

'At least we know what they might be up to, and disaster will be averted — God, if the raid happened and the Germans were expecting the ships, think of the losses.'

They were silent for a while, staring out into the dark night. It was quiet up on the ramparts and the air was crisp. Extraordinary to see the infinite stars glittering above like points of ice, but the war was present like a waiting beast, breathing its foul breath in the dark. It was so close. They could sense it in their bones, in their blood, in their hearts.

'Let's go,' Matthew said, feeling a shudder go through him.

Ned flung his cigarette end into the blackness. They watched its dying fall. Its light went out and they walked away, back to Guy Pelham's office.

'They've found the motorcycle in the Wailly woods, a couple of miles away. No sign of Schmidt,' Guy told them wearily. 'Meeting place, I wonder. Maybe someone picked him up.'

'That's it then,' Ned said, seeing the flat hopelessness in Guy's eyes.

'I don't think we can risk any more time. It'll be dawn in a few hours. It's two o'clock now. At six tomorrow my chief will tell Haig about Zeebrugge. Haig will get in touch with the War Office. I'll wait here. You two might as well turn in for a few hours.'

Ned and Matthew turned to go and were stopped by a knock at the door, which opened to reveal a private who said, 'Miss Mallory, sir.'

Guy Pelham stood up too, but no one spoke. They just looked at the exhausted, pale-looking woman who came in.

Guy recovered first. 'Where on earth —?'

'I've been on several trains for about thirteen hours,' Claire stuttered. 'I didn't dare telegraph from Lyon — a Frenchman escorted me, so I couldn't —'

'Sit down while we arrange tea and sandwiches,' Guy said, hustling Ned out of the room. 'Back in five minutes.'

Before the door closed, Claire was in Matthew's arms. 'I thought you were dead,' he said, not quite believing his eyes.

'Alive, but not kicking, I'm afraid. I could sleep for a week.'

'Can you stay awake long enough to tell your story?'

'When I've had that tea. Oh, Matthew, I was never more frightened in my life. Not even driving the ambulance. I thought I'd never see you again. I kept wondering where you were, and when I heard about Willy Lang's death at Treasonfield, I was terrified for you.'

'Same here, when we had news you were missing. Better not tell me now — Pelham will want to know all.'

'Good of them to leave us for a few minutes. Who's the other chap?'

'They call him Uncle Ned. Superintendent Turner, Special Branch, from London. We've a lot to tell you, too.'

'Honestly, it's like a dream. I can't believe that yesterday morning I was in Thonon — Mr Sutton is dead. It was dreadful — I liked him. He was so ordinary in a way. Oh, I saw him just lying there —'

Matthew held her until she stopped shaking. 'Oh, darling.'

'I'm all right. It's just remembering his poor face, and there was another man, a clergyman called —'

'Von Rahn. We know all about him, too, but Pelham will explain. Let me look at you so I'm sure you're here.'

'I'm surprised you recognised me.' Claire took off her hat to reveal her jagged hair.

'Good God. Who did that to you?'

'Another long story.'

Guy came back with the sandwiches. The private brought in a tray of tea. Ned was last with a bottle of brandy and three glasses. 'I think we might all need this.'

They let Claire drink two cups of tea and eat a corned beef sandwich before Pelham asked what had happened. She told them about Mr Sutton and von Rahn Nicholl and Giselle who killed him and saved her, and the man who had tried to get her on the station platform. She didn't know who he was. The Frenchman on the train was all right, but she didn't dare trust him enough to telegraph.

'And I didn't know if the man who tried to grab me was on the train. It was safer to get here as fast as I could.'

'Very sensible,' Guy said.

'But I think there's something more important than all that just now.' Claire scrabbled in her bag. 'I've got a letter to Agnes White from —'

'She's dead. We heard.'

'I know. It was an accident. She found me searching her room. She had a gun, and I threw a paperweight at her. She fell and cracked her head on the parquet floor, I'm afraid. I scooped up her papers — she had invisible ink and crystals. This is a letter from Rudolph Schmidt, which I held to the fire. It's about something called *Einsatz Admiral König Vulkan*, and Greta was writing to von Ende. You can make out the name on the blotting paper.'

Guy scanned the letter. 'Good Lord — "*Einsatz*" — an operation of some kind,' he said, 'in February. We've not had any intelligence.'

'I thought "Admiral König" might be a ship, because I remembered what you said about Zeebrugge. Agnes White told me that England would be rocked to her foundations and that Germany would win the war. Von Rahn Nicholl also knew about it. He said it would be a cataclysm.'

Guy shot to his feet and left the office. They heard him shouting to someone, 'Get me a list of German shipping and be quick about it!'

He came back as Ned was explaining about Rudolph Schmidt and that he had masqueraded as Ashton Hamilton Smythe and was thought to have had access to papers about the raid. They had thought he was on his way to Belgium, but his motorcycle had been found in some woods. Maybe he had been picked up by a contact.

'Though what he was doing here, we can't work out, only that he somehow knew that Ned and I had found him out. It's a puzzle,' Matthew said.

'It damn well is,' Guy said. 'The raid is scheduled for March. The letter says February. I don't understand it. And now we've lost Schmidt, but we might be able to work out what he's up to if we can find something about *Admiral König Vulkan*.'

'*Vulkan* is volcano — I wondered if they were planning something in London,' Claire put in.

'Sabotage?' Ned said. 'There have been attempts before. There was a plot to attack the main telephone and cable centre in Westminster, explosions at ammunitions factories — explosion — volcano — it might —'

'But Schmidt was here,' Matthew cut in.

'It sounds like a ship to me,' Guy said.

The private came in with a buff folder. 'Right,' said Guy, 'let's see. It won't be a U-boat — they don't have names. Neither do destroyers. Just numbers — hundreds of the beggars. Battleship, maybe, Kaiser class. Here we are — a lot of Kaisers, *Wilhelm II*, of course.' They watched his finger move down the list. 'König class — SMS *König*, *König Albert*, *Kronprinz*... Dreadnoughts — no ... cruisers ... minelayers ... gunboats...' Guy looked at them. 'Not an Admiral to be found, let alone a King.'

'One of ours, maybe?' Ned suggested. 'He's using German as code. It's been done. Explosives smuggled onto ships bound for England. King George V class — HMS *King George V* —'

'In the North Sea. It doesn't make sense — nothing to do with Folkestone —' Guy stared at the list. 'Oh, good God! George the Fifth —'

'What is it?' Ned asked.

'Admiral King — King Admiral — not a ship, not Zeebrugge — but *the* King Admiral.'

Ned caught on. 'The king? Our King George?'

'An Admiral of the Fleet.'

'Then Claire's right — something in London,' Matthew said.

'No, Schmidt's here. You saw him. That motorcycle in the woods. He's still here and the king is in France now at the Château de Beaurepaire. He came across this afternoon with Stamfordham, his private secretary. No one knows yet. I mean it's not in the English papers. An informal visit — no ceremony... A cataclysm, von Rahn said — something which would rock England to her foundations...'

They all gaped at Guy and Ned said, 'My God, assassination—'

'It's been done before,' Guy said drily. 'The Archduke comes to mind.'

'Dear Lord, volcano — the château blown up. But how would Schmidt have known?'

'Someone talked. His private office, the War Office, the war cabinet, they'll know that the king is there. It doesn't matter. I have to get on the phone before the place is blown —'

Major Ferrars barged into the room. 'We've got someone. A waiter who used to work at Madame Foulon's café in Paris-Plage — found him hiding in the Wailly woods with a broken leg. Couple of my men brought him in. He's in a cell and the MO's seeing to him. He knows Schmidt — took him a Mauser Gewehr 98 rifle.'

'Sniper's rifle,' Matthew said.

'Good God, not a bomb,' Ned said.

'What the devil do you mean?' Ferrars asked.

Guy told him succinctly what they had deduced. 'We can deal with the waiter afterwards. Now, we assume that Schmidt is on foot to the château.'

It took a moment for Major Ferrars to recover from his shock. 'The Wailly woods are being searched now. He'll cut across to Beaurepaire. Haig's plan is to come out of the château with the king after breakfast — eight o'clock sharp.'

'But he won't be coming out. We'll make sure of that. However, we have to find Schmidt. Get some of your men who know the château and its grounds, Major Ferrars. Not a word about the king — just a German agent after secrets. Superintendent Turner will be with you. Captain Riviere — your arm?'

'I can search with one arm, Major Pelham. I know his face.'

'Good man. I'll have to raise my chief and tell him. He'll contact Haig's ADC, so I suggest you all get on your way. I'll follow in a car.'

Claire didn't say anything. She simply followed them out of the room. When Uncle Ned turned a raised eyebrow on her, she said, 'I can drive.'

39

Somewhere across the woods and fields, a church clock chimed the hour. A sleep-laced enchantment seemed to lie on the quiet Château de Beaurepaire in the misty darkness of the night. The white swans slept, their heads under their wings. The lake slept, drifts of vapour rising from its surface, smooth and motionless as black velvet. Even the poplar trees which surrounded the château were still. The black outline of the tall chimneys was etched against the deep blue-black of the sky. Camelot, some people called it, but sometimes they meant it bitterly, resenting the luxury of the staff officers' accommodation — while they were in the mud and the stench of the front line. And it might have been a fairy-tale castle, for a king lay there in a canopied bed, dreaming of his cousin in a blue uniform encrusted with gold braid, with a jewelled cross on his breast, a man with a withered arm, a man whose grandmother was his, too, a man whose blue eyes burned as he gazed across a wasted land where the long lines of his grey army gathered. In the dream, the king saw scarred and mud-filled fields and his men in khaki, huddled under sweeping rain, waiting for the battle, preparing for victory, or the death of all hope.

The king stirred uneasily on his pillow, but he didn't wake, even to the sound of vehicles coming up the drive, or the hurried footstep on the stairs. The watchers in the woods saw a faint light through a chink in the shutters in an upstairs room. The king's Field Marshal woke from his dream of a fleshless hand clutching a rusty rifle, his blue eyes widening in alarm, for someone was touching his shoulder and whispering urgent words. The Field Marshal rose, put on his dressing gown, and followed the messenger down the unlit staircase to meet his unwelcome visitor, Major Guy Pelham of Military Intelligence.

Outside the gate, an army lorry was parked, its engine still warm from the journey. A single figure was in the driver's seat. And one cork-blackened face watched it. In the motionless woods, other men with blackened faces and woollen hats wove through the trees on silent feet. A beam of light shone up from time to time into pine branches thick with dark green needles, and a bird flew out, sending out an alarm call. Trees and men held their breath until the sound died away.

The men circled the black lake, but the swans didn't wake. Round the back of the château in the courtyard, men searched the outbuildings, climbed up to haylofts and wriggled out onto sloping roofs where they stayed, eyes trained on the opposite roofs, rifles pointing. Others dropped down noiselessly and climbed up again to another roof. Two men lay on the flat roof of the annexe at the side of the château, staring into the trees, alert for any breath of sound or movement.

Matthew and Ned watched the front door, their eyes on the steps where Field Marshal Haig had greeted King George on his last visit to the front line in 1917. Major Pelham didn't come out.

'Sticky for him,' Ned murmured. 'Haig will be grilling him, but the king won't be coming out in the morning and that's a relief. Let's melt away into those trees.'

They slipped through the trees, stopping to listen every few seconds, ears and eyes straining in the unearthly quiet. The grasses and the trees breathed lightly in the dark, but there was no human sound. Were they wrong? Was Schmidt somewhere else? They worked their way deeper into the woods until they reached the far side of the lake, where they stood looking at its mist-wreathed stillness and the occasional flashes of light in the distance. They thought about the men searching the railway station at Montreuil where Haig's train waited. Did Schmidt know where the king would be tomorrow? Was he already waiting in some church tower with his sniper's rifle trained on a railway carriage?

As they turned, Matthew's torch picked out the sliver of metal gleaming under a pile of leaves and pine needles. 'A bloody German rifle,' Ned whispered as Matthew knelt to shift the leaves. 'He knows we're here. He's gone.'

They stared at the Mauser Gewehr. Into the silence came the sudden, shocking sound of an engine starting up.

40

Claire sat in the lorry, staring into the darkness. The word "cataclysm" echoed in her head, and she saw in her mind's eye the cold, sneering face of von Rahn Nicholl. A plot to kill the king. It was beyond comprehension. She thought of the images she had seen of the king with his heavy moustaches, dressed in his army uniform, the soldiers standing to attention. The King of England. Indomitable, surely. They must find Schmidt.

She was so lost in thought that she didn't realise soon enough that someone was climbing into the passenger seat and holding a gun to her head. She knew who it was.

'Start the engine, Miss Mallory, and put your foot down. Straight on. No looking back.' The cold ring of steel pressed into her temple.

She glanced at him. He seemed to have no face. There was an impression of eyes, fathomless pools of black. It was like looking at a mask — as emotionless as his voice. Claire could smell earth and damp leaves, and something else, something bitter, as if the sweat he exuded were tainted with hatred. He knew her and he didn't care. He was ruthless, she thought, and mad. And therefore terrifying. It would be pointless to try to buy time. The clergyman, von Rahn Nicholl, had been human in his vanity and he hadn't been able to resist talking about his own cleverness. He hadn't known that Giselle was creeping up the stairs. This man wouldn't waste words.

Claire started the engine, selected first gear and the lorry lurched forward. She felt the increased pressure of the gun and put her foot down.

He didn't speak except to give directions. 'Faster,' he said. Claire's knuckles shone white in the dark, her hands felt rigid on the wheel, her right foot was practically on the floor, but she had no idea of her speed or of where she was going. Sometimes there was a light in a window, sometimes a huddle of buildings, sometimes a church tower, but they flew past. There were never any lights behind. No one knew where she was.

'Slow down.' That inhuman voice again. She was just a thing to him, useful only for as long as he needed her to drive.

Claire eased her foot off the accelerator. She didn't know how slowly he wanted her to go.

'Slower. We turn in a few yards.'

And then they were on a narrow, bumpy road. Claire thought of her ambulance, of crawling along to Hermies to find Matthew. She had been afraid then, afraid of crashing or breaking down, afraid of being shelled, afraid for her patient, but this was different. He could order her to stop at any time, his farewell a bullet in the brain.

They could be anywhere, going north, south, east or west, and she had neither star nor light to guide her, only the steely commands. *The coast?* she wondered. Major Pelham had mentioned that.

Her eyes seemed to be full of sand as she stared into the darkness. The night seemed an eternity. Her back ached, and she felt the pain in her arm where Emil had wrenched it. She wouldn't last, she thought, as they entered a tunnel of trees. She'd simply stop, her hands frozen to the wheel, and she'd be too numb to know anything.

They were on a smoother, wider road. Claire thought she saw a pointing fingerpost. *Saint-Aub...* Then it was gone. Aubrey, Auberge, Aubin, perhaps. She felt light-headed, the words jumbling in her brain. Not that it made any difference... She felt her eyes closing.

'Faster,' the voice said. The pistol jabbed at her temple. Claire's eyes flew open. She put her foot down.

41

Matthew and Ned blundered through the trees and sprinted down the drive to the front gates. Of course, they were too late. The lorry had gone. They could hear it in the distance, racing away.

'South-west,' Ned gasped, 'away from Montreuil. A motorcycle — back at the house. There must be one. We might catch him.'

'He'll see us, and he'll kill her.'

Running steps came up behind. It was Guy. 'One of the men said they heard the lorry —'

'He's gone and taken Claire. I thought a motorcycle, but Riviere says he'll see us.'

'And kill her,' Matthew repeated.

'Which way?'

'South-west.'

'Towards Hesdin. We'll get Ferrars to set up roadblocks.'

'He'll keep off the main roads,' Ned said. 'He won't go back Montreuil way.'

'No, you're right, but he'll make for the coast, I reckon — we need a map. My car.'

Time, time, time, thought Matthew as they ran back up the drive and huddled into Pelham's car, their torches illuminating the map.

'Étaples,' Guy said. 'That's where Miss Lemmon said the waiter had gone to work — some job with the British, Madame Foulon told her. Schmidt doesn't know we've got his waiter. It'd make sense for him to go back there. Camps, hospitals, barracks — it's vast. He can lose himself there and he'll reckon no one'll stop him — he's got his papers. Le Touquet possibly, just across the river. That chap who knew him. He knows we want him as Smythe.'

They studied the map, following Guy's forefinger along the by-roads back to Étaples. 'He's gone south — let's say he doubles back on that road to Campigneulles and north again. We can get blocks at these crossroads — see — at Sorrus on that minor road, then just above Saint-Josse. That bit of coast road at Merlimont. Just above Cucq, due north in case he tries a quick way. At Bellevue on the road to Le Touquet, and any road north of Étaples. I'll get Ferrars onto transport and to Étaples and Le Touquet, and he and his men can be on their way, too — I won't be long.'

'It looks all right,' Ned said, his eyes on the map.

'If only we could get going — all the time he's getting further away.'

Guy was back within minutes. He took up the map again. 'Ferrars is on the phone now. His men will be on their way from here in a trice. It'll happen, Riviere, and fast. Ned, I've got you a motorcycle — take the road to Montreuil. Cross over at that junction and you're on the road to Sorrus. Try the left fork to Saint-Aubin. All back roads there. Riviere and I will take the car to Campigneulles —' his forefinger jabbed the map — 'and we'll join the Saint-Aubin road at that junction.'

As Guy turned his car, Ned was on his way to Montreuil, covering the two miles in minutes. He didn't look back to see if the others were behind. At the junction he crossed to take the road to Sorrus, which was narrow, pitch dark, and deserted. He ached to scorch along, but he kept his speed down. No point in warning every farm and cottage that he was coming in a hurry, and indeed, there was no use warning a lorry that might be ahead. He kept close to the side of the road and had angled the headlamp as best he could so that the road surface, the grass edges, and any ditches were illumined. But there was nothing ahead and no sound of anything behind him.

He came to a crossroads. Left to Saint-Aubin, Pelham had said. He looked down the turn. It didn't look as if it went anywhere, but he went on until he found a right turn. Where the hell did that lead? A farm, he thought, seeing a dot of yellow light through a gap in the hedge and making out a low building and what looked like barns. He stopped to look at his compass. North — well, that was something. He cursed himself for an idiot. A wrong turn. No use turning back. He carried on, cursing the furrowed lane, cursing the potholes, cursing the eyes that shone briefly and vanished into a hedge — damn-fool cat — peering at every possible opening in the hedges. A gate, a farm track, another pinprick of light in the distance, and then without warning what seemed like a better, wider road. Thank God. He was about to turn when he heard it. The grumble of an engine. The rattle of wheels. Too fast. Damn. Slowing now. A flash of headlamps at a bend. He turned off his own headlamp but not his engine. They'd not hear him. Whoever they were.

Ned listened and inched forward. He dared not be seen, but he had to be sure it was an army truck. He listened intently again. Sounded like a one-tonner clattering along. Like the Pierce-Arrow truck in which they'd arrived at the château. No doors to the cab. That would make it easier.

The lorry was coming nearer, the engine getting louder. The opening of the lane was on the passenger side. Was Miss Mallory driving? Must be. She had been in the driving seat when they had left her. Schmidt would keep her there. She'd be dangerous as a passenger. He'd have a pistol aimed at her as she drove. The lorry seemed to speed up. Headlamps cut through the dark. His heart raced. It was a hell of a risk. It might not be them and he'd lose the bike. And if it were, the pistol might go off. The shock would jolt Schmidt, though, wrench his arm. He'd fire wide. He might not even have time to fire.

He could think of nothing else to do. If he waited to be sure, then it would be too late. He had to jam the cab. If he just followed or tried to stop the lorry by overtaking, Schmidt would kill her. Ned gripped the handlebars and lifted his right foot from the ground.

42

A deafening crash. The crunch of metal on metal. The lorry jolted and bucked, shunting Claire sideways half out of the cab. Ned heard a gun go off, and as the lorry bucked again he saw Claire fall, her head meeting rough stone, her arm cracking like another pistol shot.

Ned was off his mangled bike in seconds, grabbing the passenger by the arm, dragging him out of the cab, wrestling him to the ground, and punching him in the face. He felt a fist against his own jaw, but seizing the lapel of the man's coat he punched again until the body went limp. Dragging him to the bike, Ned used his scarf to tie the man to the wreckage.

Miss Mallory? Ned shot round to the driver's side and there she was. Her hat had fallen off, revealing the jagged hair, her face an oval of white like a fallen moon. *Oh God, please don't be dead.* He dragged his torch from his pocket and knelt beside her. She was breathing shallowly. He saw that her face was scratched from the stones. There was a water flask on the bike. He was all fingers and thumbs untying it. Then he was moistening her lips, and she moaned slightly. Her eyes opened. 'Arm,' she said. 'It hurts.' Her eyes closed again.

He couldn't really tell the condition of her arm under her coat. He'd keep her warm at any rate. He took off his coat and rolled her gently onto it, wrapped her up, and took off his sweater to make a pillow. He needed to keep her awake until he was sure that he'd be able to leave her, for he'd have to get help. There was a farm track back down the lane he'd ridden along. He looked at his watch. Five o'clock, which meant that it would be dawn soon — the farmer might be about by then.

In the meantime, he could only make sure that his prisoner didn't escape. Rope, he thought, in the cab. Bound to be some. He'd truss the rotter up like a piece of pork. And a gag would keep him quiet. He could manage without his coat, too. If he froze to death, too bad. Claire Mallory's life was worth more than his.

Having swiftly disposed of his prisoner, Ned went back to Claire, covered her with the other coat, slipped his arm under her to raise her slightly, and moistened her lips again. 'Claire,' he said, 'wake up. You're safe now. I've got him. He's tied up. Matthew's coming.'

At Matthew's name, she opened her eyes again. 'Matthew?'

'It's Ned Turner, Claire. I've got you. I need you to stay awake. Take a sip of water. Just a sip.'

She opened her mouth, and he poured a little water into it. Ned let her rest again. Time went on. She sipped and rested, and he told her again that she was safe, and that help would come. He watched the sky begin to lighten in the east, watched the ghosts of trees and hedges appear, and sensed a change in her as she opened her eyes and seemed to take him in.

'Mr Turner — what happened?'

'I crashed the motorcycle into the lorry. I had to stop him. I'm sorry you were injured.'

'He would have killed me.' She closed her eyes again, then opened them to ask, 'Is he dead?'

'No, I just knocked him for six. He'll feel like hell when he wakes up.'

Claire managed a grin. 'Serves him right. But where's —'

A roaring engine. Lights came round the bend in the road. A speeding car. 'The cavalry,' Ned said. 'I hope.'

43

The morning after her operation, Claire woke up in her hospital bed to find Matthew looking down on her. She was propped up on several pillows, her arm in splints, her head fuzzy from the morphine she'd been given.

'You're a sight for sore eyes,' she said.

He took her good hand and smiled. 'Same scene several weeks later. Roles reversed.'

'Weeks? It feels like years. I still can't believe I'm here.'

'Does it hurt?'

'Does yours?'

Matthew laughed. 'What a pair we make — I think we may be suited.'

'No one else will have me in this state. Oh, Matthew, I'm so glad to see you.'

'I wasn't going anywhere until I saw your eyes open. You've been through it, all right, and here you are, blooded but unbowed. How you managed in Geneva, I don't know, and then that crash. Ned is beside himself. Thinks he could have killed you.'

'Well, he didn't. He kept me alive, but Schmidt would have killed me. I could tell. When we reached wherever it was he wanted me to take him, he'd have shot me without any compunction. What's happened to him?'

'Patched up and in a cell. Nothing to say, of course. Ned stayed with him while Guy and I raced here with you.'

'I remember the car screeching to a halt and then lying in the back with you. You gave me morphine. I remember the operating theatre and not much else.'

'There was a field medical kit in the lorry. Guy sent a lorry back to pick up Ned and Schmidt. Ned has a couple of black eyes and a split lip, but he's all right.'

'What happens now?'

'You rest. I go to see if I can get something out of Schmidt.'

'What about Geneva? Greta and Colonel Raulin?'

'Guy's been on the phone to Geneva. He sent his man to Nyon, so we'll wait and see. The weasel's been picked up, by the way. A few days ago in Basel.'

'So that's what sent Greta and Colonel Raulin to Nyon. Doctor Wesel. They were expecting him to come to Geneva. When Greta asked me to go with them, I thought something was wrong. She was uncharacteristically edgy, and she insisted I stay in bed. She said she'd tell the manager to look after me. She wanted to make sure I stayed in my room. Raulin had already questioned me about you — he wanted to know where you were, and he knew that you were serving with the West Lancashires. He asked about Willy Lang as well. They knew he was dead and that I was lying.'

'Pelham thinks the hotel manager was in on it. He had an Austrian mistress, some singer.'

'Regine Diane. The manager told me she was French. She was very friendly with Colonel Raulin. I think they were all in on it. There was a Doctor Brahms and his wife, too. And I think a man called Mannheim. Major Pelham mentioned him.'

'His name was in a letter I found from Greta to Willy — a money man.'

'They were all moneyed, so well groomed, so polished-looking, so self-satisfied. When I thought of the things I'd seen at the front, I was so angry. But they must have been worried when they heard about Doctor Wesel. Certainly worried about me. I was followed the night before Greta invited me to Nyon.

I said I was too tired to go. Agnes White came back and found me in their suite — I caused her — oh, Matthew, it was horrible.'

Matthew squeezed her good hand. 'Think of the alternative. And think of what we prevented last night because of you. I'm so proud of you, and Ned thinks the world of you. Brave girl, he kept saying. Guy's been complimentary, too. And May says she knew all along that you'd find your way out. Now, get some rest, my darling, and I'll come back later.'

'I will, but tell Major Pelham about Doctor Brahms and his wife. I didn't get a chance before —'

'*Einsatz Admiral König* — they'll know it failed soon enough. That'll wipe the smile off Greta's face. Now sleep.'

Claire obediently closed her eyes. Then her eyelids flew open. *Giselle*, she thought, walking away for the ferry to Geneva. Too late, Matthew had gone.

Ned was grateful that the brandy he'd picked up the night before was still in Guy Pelham's office. He gulped it down and looked across the desk at Guy, who was gazing anxiously at his bruised face.

'Claire will be all right. They've put her arm in a splint. It'll heal, they say — she's young and strong, thank the Lord.'

Pelham raised his glass. 'Seconded.'

'I honestly thought I'd killed her. I was a bloody fool to go in so hard.'

'You got him, though. It was a damned clever trick.'

'It wouldn't have been so clever if Miss Mallory had copped it. Just as well you came when you did. God, I was never so pleased to see anything as much as you two scorching along. What have you done with Schmidt?'

'The doc's patched him up, but he looks pretty battered. Worse than you.'

Ned winced as the brandy stung his lip. 'Good. I hope he's in a lot of pain.'

'He's cooling off in a cell. Nothing to say, of course. I've asked Riviere to question him when he gets back. He knew the beggar.'

'And His Majesty?'

'Slept through it all. He need never know. Hush-hush and all that. Ferrars's men know only that the German was after papers and maps, that sort of thing. And speaking of maps, I've had a long think about Rudolph Schmidt, alias Ashton Hamilton Smythe, working out of Folkestone.'

'You mean those maps of the coast? He wanted anyone who found them to believe that the Zeebrugge raid was the target.'

'Agreed, but he still knew about it, and he'd been in Belgium after the order went out to raise the battalion in Deal.'

'You mean, why waste all that information?'

'Precisely. My agent in Belgium has sent word. A couple of German battalions are moving to the coast when they should be moving to the front line. A lot of activity in Zeebrugge.'

'So they know.'

'All in hand. Cameron's onto it. There won't be a raid between the fourteenth and nineteenth of March.'

Ned raised his glass. 'Two birds with one stone, so to speak.'

'Thanks to you and Riviere.'

'And Miss Mallory.'

'Lord, yes. Riviere's a lucky man.'

'Anything from Geneva?'

'Mrs Lang and Colonel Raulin are not to be found in Nyon. We've had a quiet word with our Swiss friends about the hotel manager and his Austrian songstress. They'll be deported, probably. Miss Mallory may have some other names we can pass on.'

'And what about the Lang chappie I moved from Treasonfield — what's in a name, eh?'

'I had a good look at the letter from Schmidt to Agnes White. Schmidt killed Willy Lang all right. He calls him a coward in the letter. I wonder if the murder of the king was too much for him.'

'Frightened him off, maybe. He didn't mind helping the Germans to win and dictate the terms of a peace treaty. England's nose out of joint, but relations with the cousins restored. Cousin Wilhelm top dog, but no matter to Lang and his cronies. Plenty of money still to be made. But assassination — phew, that was a step too far.'

'Peace treaty is about right. I think Lang was part of a consortium of international financiers who met in secret late in 1917 in Geneva to consider the effects of war on international finance. They wanted a peace deal. Our government didn't know of any British businessmen who attended, but Lang was the sort to have been involved. And he and his friends would know that the assassination of the king wouldn't bring any sort of peace. It was more likely to have prolonged the war. Think of the outrage against anyone of German extraction. Lang would have reasoned all that.'

'Schmidt's not the type to listen to reason. Miss Mallory said she thought he was mad. Completely ruthless. But Lang's wife didn't sound the fanatical sort.'

'Greta Lang liked the high life. Bored with Westmorland and the country bumpkins. Riviere said the neighbours didn't like her. Life at the Belle Vue with the colonel would have seemed a better bet. Think of the aristos in Geneva. And there was the von Ende connection. The baron, Ludwig von Ende, was her cousin.'

'Germany — that's where they'll have gone — to the bosom of the family.'

'I'll bet you're right. Lang was connected to von Bohlen, the Krupp man. Riviere said that von Bohlen and Mrs Lang were thick as thieves at some lunch do.'

'Pal of the Kaiser's, von Bohlen. They'll be all right then.'

'Not if we win.'

Ned raised his glass. 'When we win.'

Matthew came in to tell them that Claire was awake and seemed to be much restored. 'I told her to get some rest, but she insisted on my telling you a couple more names, Doctor and Mrs Brahms. The doctor seemed to take a great deal of interest in Claire — he asked where she had been and all about Oxford.'

'Interesting — we picked up a German agent in Oxford a couple of years back,' Ned told them. 'I suppose they wondered if Miss Mallory knew anything.'

'They were onto her. She was followed the night before she left — by von Rahn, she thinks. She didn't suspect an English clergyman who gave her directions, and then Greta Lang wanted to take her to Nyon. Claire thinks they'd heard about Doctor Wesel by then.'

'They've got nothing out of him in Basel, but, still, it frightened Mrs Lang and the others into moving on. I'll pass on the Brahms name. The Swiss will find a way to let them know they're under suspicion. They can't arrest them without concrete evidence. We'll have to be satisfied that we've broken them up. And without Miss Mallory we'd not have known about the plot to assassinate the king. I'm sorry about Sutton. Just as much a casualty as if he'd been shot in the trenches.

And the Zeebrugge raid is off, thanks to you and Ned. I had word from Belgium that German troops were being moved there.'

'Has Schmidt said anything?'

'Not a dicky bird. You might have a go.'

'Maybe I'll ask about his schooldays.'

Matthew watched Schmidt through the spy hole. He had his muddy British coat back and he was sitting on the iron bed, smoking and staring up at the barred window through which he could see the grey sky. *Wondering how he can escape*, Matthew thought. That wouldn't happen. He'd be transferred to a British prison. And then what? Tried and shot at dawn in the Tower like the other spies. He would be the twelfth.

The bruised face turned. He looked nothing like the boy in the photograph who had sat so erect and confident in his youthful strength, his future before him. An open book with blank pages. Well, so had all their futures been unwritten. The words on Rudolph Schmidt's page now would be *spy* and *murderer*. The war had done that. He should have joined the German Army and fought his enemy face to face. At least Stephen had done that, and Lieutenant-General von Ende, and all the other German soldiers who had died for their country.

Shot at dawn, though. The phrase was chilling enough without remembering Private Billy Stevenson, shot at dawn for desertion from Cambrai. A pipsqueak of a man with bad teeth and vacant eyes, whose letters home might have been written by a child — *were* written by a child who cried about his blisters. Matthew remembered his terrified face when they went forward on the first day. There were others shot for desertion. Murder, in some cases. He'd seen a sergeant shoot a German officer who had surrendered. The sergeant was killed by a shell later that night. It was hard to blame the deserters or the sergeant. It was war, that was all you knew. You dared not think about them too much, or the pity of it. The shame. The waste.

Was being shot at dawn a kind of murder? An eye for an eye.

Matthew looked at the battered man again. Perhaps they'd give him a very long sentence and send him back to Germany when the war was over. No one would be waiting for him — certainly not Greta Lang or Lieutenant-General von Ende. He thought of his grandfather waiting for him at Hawthorn Park and Claire alive. They had a home to go to.

He went into the cell and put down the German uniform he'd been carrying. Two cold eyes turned on him, and the sneer that he had seen in the school photograph. There was no point in asking Schmidt why. His face set in iron told Matthew the answer to that question. He would have shot Claire at dawn on an empty road near Saint-Aubin. All pity dissolved.

'Captain Riviere, what do you want?'

'Treasonfield,' Matthew said. 'You were there.'

'I was often there. So what?'

'I found Willy Lang there — dead.'

Schmidt's eyes blazed now. 'He was a fool and a coward. All to save his money and his country house. He was soft — too like an Englishman. He would have betrayed us.'

'You were in Larch Cottage.'

'I was visiting Mrs White. If you recall, I am related to her.'

'Were. Agnes von Ende is dead. She was your mother.'

Schmidt blinked at that, but his face didn't change, and he made no reply.

'Where are Greta Lang and Colonel Raulin?'

267

'Ah, the lovers. Who knows? They won't be caught. Anyway, I have had enough of you. I disliked you then. I dislike you now. I have nothing else to say.'

'*Einsatz Admiral König*. The King Admiral. We worked it out.'

'Your German king of the House of Saxe-Coburg-Gotha. The House of Windsor — a made-up name to appease the English. He is the coward and the traitor, and he will know it when his cousin, our Kaiser Wilhelm, meets him face to face. Your German king will sue for mercy then.'

'You failed.'

'You think I'm the only one? You think my death will matter to the cause or to me? This spring offensive will sweep your armies away into the sea, and at Zeebrugge —'

'We know about that, too,' Matthew cut in. 'We were at Ivy House and spoke to Miss Cresswell. You left traces.'

Schmidt blew out a stream of smoke and stubbed out his cigarette. Was that the slightest tremor in his hand?

Matthew pressed home his point. 'There will be no victory at Zeebrugge.'

Schmidt's mouth twisted in contempt. 'There will be others. You don't know it all. I was at Folkestone where your weakling traitor, Captain Strange, let me into his office. I have seen so many things. We know so much about you British. You haven't enough in arms or men. We have our *Sturmtruppen*. Operation Michael will finish you. The French will be no use to you.'

Stormtroopers. Schmidt was right. The British did not have enough arms and men, but he wasn't going to admit that. He tried a different ploy. 'A pity you won't live to see it.'

'Maybe I will, maybe I won't. I don't care. I have played my part just as you have played yours, but yours will make no difference. Yours is the failure, Captain Riviere. We will not meet again, I hope.'

Matthew pointed to the uniform. 'You'll need that for your trial.'

Schmidt turned away. Matthew knew he would get no more out of him. But he had learned that the German stormtroopers were moving — lightly armed, fast-moving, highly skilled, hardened soldiers. And there was Operation Michael to come.

He went to open the door. Schmidt had one more word for him. '*Vernichtungsschlacht.*' War of annihilation. Matthew closed the door.

Guy Pelham had been trying to untangle the skein of connections which linked England to Switzerland and to France. Now he was pointing to the photograph of Rudolph Schmidt and the waiter at the café in Paris-Plage, where he had spent a profitable hour with its owner, Madame Foulon, who, alas, had not seen what her waiter was up to.

'I looked at it again under a magnifying glass. Just wanted to see if I could make anything out between the waiter and Schmidt. The waiter was certainly speaking to him. Anyhow, I took myself there. Madame told me he's Swiss — French-speaking, been with her a few years. She was surprised that he went, but if the pay was better, which he assured her it was, she wasn't much interested. She remembered his waiting on Schmidt and his girlfriend, and she remembered that although Schmidt was bad-tempered about the photograph, he was very polite to the waiter.'

'What's he got to say for himself?' Ned asked.

'Sang like a bird. His brother is a waiter in a café at Nyon, much frequented by Colonel Raulin. Our waiter sent information from Schmidt to his brother in Nyon.'

'And the brother passed it on to Raulin. So, Schmidt had been at the café pretty often?'

'Not according to Madame Foulon. They must have met elsewhere when Schmidt was doing his Hamilton Smythe turn along the coast.'

'Did the waiter believe Schmidt was English and working for the Allies?'

'Hard to say. He insists he was taken in by Schmidt and knew him only as Smythe, and his brother in Nyon assured him that Colonel Raulin was in cahoots with the British in Geneva.'

'And the German rifle we found in the middle of the wood?'

'Said he didn't know what kind it was. Schmidt told him he was on a secret mission, and he paid well, of course.'

'Where did he get the rifle?'

'Says Schmidt left it with him. I couldn't shift him on that.'

'Possible, I suppose. It might have looked fishy for a British Intelligence officer to be strolling about Montreuil with a German sniper rifle under his coat.'

'He was a fool to come here. He should have stayed in Étaples. Couldn't resist swanning around GHQ — arrogant bastard.'

'And was the waiter working for the British in Étaples?'

'I've set inquiries in motion — I couldn't spare the time to investigate every damned nook and cranny he might have crawled into. It would be interesting to know if there are any other rotten eggs.'

'What'll you do with him?'

'Keep him in suspense for a bit and then a prisoner labour company. Something filthy. Sanitary work — or rather insanitary. Something he can't escape from — not that he's likely to. Too scared the Germans might come for him. Ah, news from Mr Schmidt?' Guy asked as Matthew came in.

'Not much, I'm afraid. Spouted about the House of Saxe-Coburg-Gotha and our German king's treachery. Insists on German victory because he knows things we don't. Two things stood out: Operation Michael and stormtroopers.'

'Did he say when?'

'No, I could tell he was not going to say any more. He doesn't care what we do to him.'

'We don't hang them now — long prison sentence in England and eventual release. Plenty of evidence of his spying. Right, I'd best go and talk to the chief about Operation Michael.'

The telephone rang as Guy stood up. He listened and said, 'I understand. Yes, they'll come.' Putting the telephone down, he turned to Matthew and Ned. 'May Lemmon's at the hospital. Miss Mallory wants to speak to us about the woman, Giselle, who helped her. You two go while I see the chief.'

Matthew and Ned listened open-mouthed as Claire told them about Giselle, the death of Emil, the disguises, and the details of the death of Conrad von Rahn Nicholl. 'Both of them would have killed me if she hadn't been there — I owe her my life. Conrad von Rahn Nicholl said his friends would find her. I wondered if Major Pelham could find out if she is all right.'

Ned offered to go immediately and tell Guy. He would surely be able to find out about Giselle. 'She sounds like a woman who can take care of herself,' he said.

'She is, but when I think of the kind of man Emil was, I can't help worrying. I asked her to come with me, but, of course, she has her brother to consider. He deserted his post, but Giselle has been protecting him and his daughter. They are in Geneva, but I don't know where. Emil knew about her brother. He blackmailed her — and not just for money. But if he knew, then others will too — and I put her in more danger.'

'I'll get onto it,' Ned said.

After he'd gone, Matthew and Claire held hands in silence, until Claire said, 'Giselle was so brave. I doubted her sometimes. Major Pelham had said that we shouldn't trust anyone, and when she stabbed Emil, I wondered. She was so cool, but I had to trust someone, and when she told me about her political feelings, and what Emil had done to her, I understood why she was so ruthless. And there was the man who pulled me onto the train. I trusted him. It's so difficult when you are in the thick of it —'

'I know — we don't really belong in the spying world. I felt the same about Grandfather — not that I didn't trust him, but the lying was so uncomfortable. I told Todd some of it, but the people you met were strangers. How is one to know which risks to take?'

'Instinct, I suppose, and the circumstances we were in. I distrusted Colonel Raulin's charm from the beginning, and when he took me on the steamer to Nyon, I knew.'

'Rudolph Schmidt took in his girlfriend, and his landlady at the farm. They trusted him, but they had no reason not to. But even he had to trust someone. He had to trust that waiter, but then he had money to pay.'

'Oh, the one found hiding in the woods. What's happened to him?'

Matthew told her about the waiter's brother in Nyon and his connection with Colonel Raulin.

'I remember him. I didn't think anything of it at the time, but he invited Colonel Raulin to the counter to choose the wine, and it wasn't long after that when Raulin said he must take me to the ferry. Some message, I suppose, and then I think von

Rahn Nicholl was on the ferry.' Claire shuddered. 'I'm glad to be out of it. Looking back, you can almost see a net closing about you — all those people watching. I don't know if I could do it again.'

'I think I prefer the front line. At least you know where the enemy is.'

'You'll go back?'

Matthew thought of Lieutenant Cropper's anguished face in the schoolhouse in Belgian Le Touquet. 'When I can. You?'

'When I can.'

44

Major Pelham's new man in Thonon had made the anonymous telephone call to the police about the bodies at the Mochat Import/Export Company and watched as the police came to investigate. He had lost track of the young couple who had been standing outside the building, but Pelham told him about the disguised Claire and Giselle. He asked the agent to see if he could trace the woman, Giselle, at the Café Martin. She was to be protected. But the news came back that she had not been seen for several days.

In the days that followed, the agent, masquerading as a Swiss-French cousin of Giselle, spent his evenings buying drinks for a very pretty woman, a prostitute living in the Rue Belle Filles. She willingly spilt the beans about Giselle's neighbours, in particular a French woman named Annette Roquine, another habitué of the Café Martin, who was living with a deserter from the French Army, one Raymond Barroz, a man who dealt in drugs and who was friendly with the Germans. '*Traître*,' she spat.

The agent went to Giselle's lodgings to ask about his cousin. They had not seen her, so Annette Roquine told him, but the agent was not convinced by her. She looked used-up, dreadfully thin with a gaunt face and hooded eyes which brooded on him. He didn't trust the French deserter either, a shifty type with a narrow face, darting eyes and bitten nails. Whose side were they on? The agent told Annette that he had a key to Giselle's rooms. He would see if she had left a note for him. He took himself upstairs, where he opened the door with his skeleton key. There was nothing to see. It was obvious that Giselle had cleared out. Everything was tidy. There were no clothes, no papers, and nothing to indicate any violence. He thought, hoped, that she had left Geneva.

He told Annette that he would stay upstairs for a few days in case she came back. He couldn't understand it, he told her. His cousin knew he was coming. He was looking for work in Geneva. She'd said he could stay. Sent him a key. Had Annette no idea where she might be? Annette didn't know. Giselle didn't talk much. She had a brother who lived in Nyon. Giselle might be there. The agent nodded. Of course, he knew Giselle's brother. Yes, she might be there. He would go across to see him. He asked his questions of Annette, but he could tell that she was reluctant to answer. Everyone had something to hide, he knew. He kept his eye on the Frenchman, a sullen-faced character. The man might be shifty because he was a deserter or because he was thick with the Germans, but he determined to keep an eye on him at the Café Martin, where he used his money to keep the very pretty woman sweet. Not that he could trust her entirely. When he had arrived at the café one night, he had seen her in a booth deep in conversation with a young man whom he knew to be German. Money changed hands — but that was her job, he reflected. Life was too precarious to be choosy.

He heard a whisper about Giselle's brother, whom his pretty woman also thought was living in Nyon. Miss Mallory had said Geneva to Pelham. Odd, but whichever it was, he felt he was in a bind about that. Pelham had told him the brother was a deserter from the Swiss Army. If he asked too many questions, then he might put the brother and Giselle in danger, and there was a child, apparently. He'd best ask Pelham how far he should go. If Giselle had vanished with the brother and the child, then it was probably best to leave them. They'd survived so far.

But he did hear that the deserter, Raymond Barroz, was leaving for France — on business. Dirty business on behalf of the Germans, the agent concluded. It was time for another tip-off to the police. Barroz was arrested with his cocaine and a number of forged travel permits. Annette was arrested, too, and told all she knew about Barroz and others at the Café Martin. She thought Giselle had a Swiss lover, an army man, high up, but she didn't know his name. Barroz had said that the lover was a German officer. Impossible to know whom to believe.

'Barroz will be deported to France,' Guy told Ned. 'He'll be shot for desertion and treason. The French don't show mercy about such things.'

'What about Giselle?'

'She must have known the danger she was in; she seems to have gone back to see her brother and the child, it looks like they all left town. According to Miss Mallory, Giselle had friends in the socialist movement. Maybe they looked after her and the brother.'

'What about the German lover? Army man. Someone known to Raulin. It makes it all a bit murky.'

'Could be true, hard to say. Barroz was a liar. He wanted to take the heat off himself, maybe, by suggesting that Giselle was the traitor. Equally Annette Roquine could have lied for the same reason. Neither is very trustworthy, but given the reputation of the Café Martin, it wouldn't be surprising if Giselle had some unsavoury entanglements. After all, to put it politely, a woman like Giselle won't have led a sheltered life. All sorts gathered in that café —'

'And on all sides,' Ned said. 'Matter of survival.'

Pelham took his meaning. 'She saved Claire's life, and that's all we know. The Zeebrugge raid's off and the king is alive. If Giselle has gone away with a lover, then let's hope he'll keep her safe. Better to leave it. If it's all moonshine, we don't want to risk putting her and the brother and his child into any more danger. It's the least we can do for her.'

'That's true, and no sign of violence at the lodgings suggests that Giselle went of her own accord. Giselle seems to be able to look after herself.'

'I agree. Let's keep any doubts between us. We'll tell Miss Mallory and Riviere that we think she's safely gone. She'll know that there's always a doubt, but it's the best construction we can put on it for now. There are always loose ends.'

One end came suddenly and shockingly. Major Pelham was called to the cells urgently. He and Ned stood at the open door of the cell in which the prisoner had hanged himself with the tie that had been neatly folded in the pocket of his uniform jacket, where Madame, his Belgian landlady, had thoughtfully left it for him. He was wearing his German uniform.

They stood for a while, not speaking. They'd seen too much for the shock to be more than fleeting. It was war, and they thought of what Rudolph Schmidt had done and what he had intended to do.

'Just as well,' Guy Pelham said, letting out a deep breath after they had closed the door. 'It saves a deal of awkward questions.'

'Case closed,' said Uncle Ned of Special Branch.

Leutnant Rudolph Schmidt of the *Nachrichten-Abteilung im Admiralstab* — just N to those in German Intelligence who knew — would not be reporting to his masters. He had disappeared on a secret mission. Such things happened in war. The von Ende family knew that. Greta shrugged. She wept a few tears when the news came that her own son, Stephan was dead, but as the lieutenant-general told her, she should be proud. Stephan von Ende was a hero of the fatherland. They toasted him with champagne.

Anna Cresswell wept when she heard that Lieutenant Ashton Hamilton Smythe had also disappeared in France. There was no one else to care. Such things happened in war. There was never a plot to assassinate King George V of the House of Windsor. And the Zeebrugge raid was cancelled because of predicted bad weather.

45

The bad weather came in March as foretold, with squally showers and sleet and a bitterly cold east wind which sailed down the fells and rattled the slates on the church roof. Inside the church was very cold, too, but Claire, swathed in the fur coat that belonged to the former Lady Riviere and smelt slightly of moth balls, was warm enough as she stepped out of the car. Matthew in his uniform looked a bit pinched but his smile was broad as Sir Roland escorted Claire up the aisle. Ned fiddled in his waistcoat pocket for the ring.

They had waited while the bishop granted a common licence for the marriage to take place. Matthew's arm was stiff, but there was no lasting damage and the bruise on his forehead had faded. At least they had one good arm each, Claire had said. Her broken arm was still in a sling, but she could take it off for the ceremony. What was a little pain amid so much joy? And her left hand was all right. The ring would go on. Her hair had grown a little and the hairdresser had done what she could with her sharp scissors and curling tongs. Claire had looked in the mirror and thought she didn't look half bad, really, certainly better than the shabby young man who'd gone to Thonon. She'd thought of Giselle, too, of whom nothing had been heard. She must have got away, as Major Pelham had told her. Giselle was clever and resourceful enough. *Don't think about that now*, she told herself. They would find her eventually. Matthew was sure of it.

A light touch of powder finished her toilette. She adjusted the little velvet hat and its veil so that it sat neatly on her curls. She couldn't help smiling into the mirror. What would come, would come, but now, she and Matthew could be happy for a few weeks at least. She managed to put on the fur coat and went down to meet Sir Roland.

Mr and Mrs Todd and the servants from Hawthorn Park were the only other guests. Claire's mother was too ill with a bad cold to travel all the way to Westmorland and Aunt Margaret too busy with her refugees, but Claire and Matthew would visit them in Oxford.

The ceremony didn't take long. No one came forward to object. Claire and Matthew spoke their lines with confidence. Ned produced the ring on cue. Sir Roland smiled broadly — he'd always known. Mrs Todd felt satisfied — she had foreseen it, too, as she had told Mr Todd, who kept his own counsel about many things. Treasonfield was shut up. All Mrs Todd knew was that Mr and Mrs Lang would not be coming back to England and that Mrs White had died of a heart attack in Geneva. Matthew had told Mr Todd the truth.

The clouds dispersed as they left the church, and a weak sun shone down as they stood for Ned's photographs. They went back to Hawthorn Park for lunch, read the telegrams from Major Pelham and May Lemmon, and escorted Ned to the front door. He was going back to his flat in Westminster — he had important business to complete.

'Hush-hush, of course,' Ned said, 'but as it's to do with our recent high jinks, I'll give you the juicy details. You remember that chap in government, the one with the Austrian housekeeper, pal of Frau Greta's?'

'Yes, a loose end,' Matthew said.

'Ah well, all tied up with a neat little bow. We got Schmidt, of course, but Pelham wondered about the leak. Who told Schmidt that the king was to visit France? It was imperative to find out. It had to be someone from the War Office or

Stamfordham's office. Someone high up. Pelham remembered your tale about the government man with the Austrian housekeeper who lived in St James's Square, and whose wife was Greta's particular friend.'

'A Swiss friend, I'm guessing,' Claire said.

'Exactly. Nothing came back about him when Pelham first enquired, but the Swiss wife stuck in his mind, so he sent me to do a bit of digging. Lo and behold — a man with an office in Whitehall Gardens, where the War Cabinet secretariat is to be found. Assistant to an assistant secretary to the War Cabinet. The secretariat records proceedings therein, circulates documents, prepares agendas — an assistant with access to very secret dealings. Naturally, I wanted a look at St James's Square. Very smart house, all white stucco. I watched him — servants, a butler, even, wife in diamonds. A Swiss wife in diamonds.'

'An assistant to an assistant and diamonds?' Matthew asked.

'Fascinating, ain't it? I looked him up in *Who's Who*. Very interesting. Father a vicar in Cheshire, quite a pedigree, though. Grandfather a country squire — Linden Court near Chester; mother a daughter of Lord somebody or other. Public school, naturally —' Ned's eyes twinkled mischievously.

'You don't mean —'

'In the north, of course. Scholarships for the sons of the clergy on the bracing Lancashire coast.'

'Fernhall,' Matthew said.

'The very same. A different generation from our gymnastic German lads, but the connection is there.'

'Knew von Rahn Nicholl, maybe.'

'Very possible. And speaking of coasts, our assistant to the assistant has a very nice little country house not far from Folkestone, from which he returns tomorrow morning. One of my ladies from Westminster is touring the Kent countryside as we speak. If he's thinking of taking ship anytime soon, he won't get on board.'

'What about the Swiss wife?' asked Claire.

'That's where the money is. Swiss-German, of course, well-connected and father in the arms business. She'll slip away, no doubt, when we've got him.'

'The War Cabinet,' Matthew said. 'He must have had access to all sorts of information.'

'That's why it's crucial. Think of all communications from Haig to the War Cabinet about the present situation — shortage of troops, differences of opinion between Haig and the government, the PM's doubts about a German attack. All guaranteed to boost the confidence of the Germans if they know.' Ned's eyes hardened. 'When I think of what he's been up to — well, I'd better get going. See you in France, maybe.'

Matthew and Claire listened to the sound of Ned's car until it faded away.

'A walk, I think,' Claire said. 'I need some fresh air after hearing all that. It's frightening to think what damage may have been done.'

They walked to the fell above Treasonfield and stood looking down at the silent house where all that they had endured had begun. The river gleamed occasionally under the dying sun. Treasonfield was a black silhouette, the window blinds down, and the front door firmly closed. It was as dark and inimical as it had looked when Matthew had stood there on that snowy evening, thinking about Stephen and Rudolph Schmidt, and how he had thought when he had entered the house that no one would live there again. It was a house of ill-omen. The father he had never known had died there; his mother's heart had been broken there; Lang had been murdered there; betrayal had been its theme. Perhaps he'd sense it in the very walls if he ever had to go in there again.

Claire felt him shiver. 'I don't think I want to go into that house ever again,' she said, echoing his thoughts. 'We don't belong there.'

'Just what I feel. Grandfather tells me to leave it — at least until after the war. I don't know what to do about it. I can't sell it. I can't bear to think of telling new people about the Langs — people are bound to ask. It's bad enough having to lie to Mrs Todd and others — one day, I'll have to say that Willy Lang is dead in Switzerland, and that Greta isn't coming back—'

'Because she's got away with it. In Germany with her wealthy family.'

'But the king is alive, Schmidt and Stepen are dead, and —'

'You have to face what's to come —'

'The dreaded hour. Odd, isn't it, how one can feel dread and longing at the same time, as if the war commands — no, calls, even as it did at the beginning, when we knew nothing, when we thought it was what every man of honour should do. Now we know all its brutalities and horror, and yet still I have to go. Duty, I suppose. Loyalty, too. I keep thinking of Lieutenant Cropper at Le Touquet. He saved my life. I can't let him down.'

Claire nodded, remembering Cropper's sensitive face and very blue eyes, his ambition to be a poet, and she thought of Padre Henry Evans. And a little flame in an immense darkness. 'I know,' she said, and then she smiled. 'I don't know what welcome I'll get from my commandant, but I'll risk it — when my arm's fit for driving.'

Matthew put his arm around her, and they stood for a few moments longer, looking down at the house. A last flare of sunset touched the windows as if they were suddenly on fire. Fire and flame to come. Then they turned away and walked together into their uncertain future.

PART THREE: 1952

46

In the quiet churchyard, among the shivering trees where the wind from the hills moaned, Uncle Ned and Marie shivered, too, as they stood by the new grave with its mound of freshly turned earth. There was a single wreath of greenery and winter-flowering honeysuckle woven by Mrs Punch. Ned had asked her to do it. He hardly liked to leave the grave unadorned, though he thought Giselle would not have cared.

They walked away to look at another grave at a distance from the first. Ned read the inscriptions, one for Claire Riviere, beloved wife of Matthew Riviere, 1895–1918, killed in action, April 1918, the one beneath for Captain Matthew Riviere, MC, 1895–1930. Ned had come up for the laying of Claire's stone. Matthew had been shattered by what had happened. A twist of malignant fate.

It was heartbreaking. Claire had been twenty-three. So young and so brave. Her work as an ambulance driver had been harrowing and her mission to Geneva — how had she borne all that? And then to die in 1918 — after she and Matthew had returned to France. That was brave, too. They had only just married, and duty had called them back. Matthew had returned and married Giselle. It was to do with Claire — and a mistake, it seemed.

'What happened to Claire?' Marie asked. She was waiting for the last chapter. Ned looked pained as he turned to face her.

'A bloody tragedy,' he said. 'Apologies, my dear, but it was. A monumental waste. She was coming back because she was expecting a child. Matthew knew, but he couldn't wangle any leave — Operation Michael was in full swing. The Germans began the spring offensive on the twenty-first of March with a massive blitz by eight thousand heavy and medium artillery and large trench mortars. At nine o'clock in the morning, the German infantry swept across No Man's Land — sorry, you don't need to know all that. You'll understand that by April, Matthew was in the thick of it at Givenchy, where he got his MC —' Ned looked down at the grave again — 'for conspicuous gallantry and devotion to duty.' Marie heard the gruffness in his voice and waited for him to continue. 'Sorry, my dear, when I think of what came after — anyway, he led ten men to capture seven machine guns and forty prisoners.'

'Brave man.' Marie thought of that silent, distant man with his limp and his scarred face. She had hardly known her uncle, and she felt sorry. 'What happened to him?'

'Another time, he was leading a storming party against the German trenches when he was wounded — his kneecap was shot away. He was gassed as well. They say that the British defence of Givenchy was the turning point for the Allies, but the cost... Where was I?'

'Claire.'

'Yes, Claire. She was on a hospital train from Doullens where her casualty clearing station had been moved — she was going to Abbeville, then back to Montreuil. May Lemmon was to meet her and get her to Boulogne and a ship. The train was shelled, and Claire was killed. After all she had done — all she had been through. If she hadn't been on that train... She wouldn't have been on it if it hadn't been for the child. Matthew couldn't get over that. It seemed so cruel.' Ned looked at the grave again. 'She's not there, but Matthew was determined that she should have a memorial — as his wife.'

Marie looked over to Giselle's grave. 'What will it say on that one? Not "beloved wife", I suppose. That's sad, too. What happened to her and Matthew?'

47

Ned put a match to the wood in the grate and when the fire had caught, he stood and waited for Marie to come down. It had been too cold in the graveyard to tell more. Not in front of those graves. Too painful, but he'd gone too far to retreat into platitudes about the marriage being a mistake. He had not wanted to come to Hawthorn Park or to look at Treasonfield ever again, but Giselle had no one else. It was a duty, and now here was another one. Giselle had commanded that Marie should know the truth, though the truth was never simple, he reflected, especially at a distance.

Looking back after thirty years, you understood more about the complexity of people's actions, which were influenced by so many things: danger and its companions, terror, and pride, and hatred. He thought about Rudolph's Schmidt's suicide. Pride in it, certainly, shame, perhaps, and hatred of the enemy. And honour — no doubt, he thought he was doing what he did for Germany. Prepared to murder, but just a lad, really, when you were looking at him from the age of seventy-odd. Cowardice, some would say, but looked at another way, he had been brave to take that way out. He remembered Matthew telling him about the terrified lad shot at dawn for cowardice. Of course he ran away — he was mad with fear and horror. And he wasn't the only one. Who would not be a coward before that terrible spectre, death? Ned felt the fire warming his chilled hands. So easy to rush to judgement, to condemn from the safety of hearth and home.

There was one simple truth, though, which he had learned from experience. No one could say what he or she would have done in the extreme exigencies of war when seconds might mean life or death. Him or you. The instinct for self-preservation was a force in every life — unless you were a saint, of course. And betrayal, that most heinous of acts, even that wasn't simple. The treachery of Greta Lang was simple enough to condemn. She had not been in the firing line. Motivated by greed, she had wriggled out of danger into the luxury of a Geneva hotel and then back to her well-connected friends in Germany — Germany had lost the war, but Greta Lang had survived because she had no loyalties. Willy Lang had paid with his life. Too bad — he had liked his money too much, and Agnes White had probably murdered her husband and would have killed Claire. But Giselle — she was not the same at all, a young woman, hardened by poverty and betrayal, too. And in grave peril. It was hard to judge what she had done, though Matthew had judged her. And himself.

Ned looked into the flames. Golden lads and girls — that thing of Shakespeare's — come to dust. Claire and Matthew had been so young, so damaged, and yet hopeful near the end. There was to be a child. There was a child. A woman, now, of course, with children of her own, but he must make her see them all through his eyes down that long perspective of years.

'Come and get warm,' he said as Marie came in. 'Let me give you a sherry.'

'I can't understand her. Why has she left me this house?' Marie asked. She took a gulp of her sherry. 'No one else to leave it to, I suppose.'

'It's true that there is no one else, but that wasn't the only reason. I think Giselle regretted many things, but she hoped that your children would benefit —'

'She never gave them a thought before. I sent her photographs, but she never commented on them.'

'She kept them in her desk — all of them.' Ned saw her dumbfounded face. 'Let me tell you about her.'

'And Matthew. How on earth did they get together?'

'Giselle couldn't stay in Geneva after von Rahn Nicholl's death. She escaped to France and made her way to Belgium as a refugee, from where she wrote to Sir Roland asking for help. Of course, Matthew was keen to help. He reached out to Claire's Aunt Margaret, who was working with Belgian refugees, and Margaret used her contacts to get Giselle to London. She should have stayed there.'

'Why didn't she?'

'It was Matthew — Claire had insisted they must try to find Giselle. I think he married her for Claire's sake, and Giselle needed a home.'

'I can understand that — I never had a home until I married Geoffrey, but they seemed not to even like each other. Something must have gone badly wrong. I mean, they had Claire in common — that might have been a bond.'

'Giselle had led a very different life — they were strangers, really. Matthew didn't know her at all, and he couldn't forget Claire and the child they might have had. The marriage was a mistake. He kept trying to persuade Giselle to live apart from him, but she refused. She wasn't to be cast aside for a dead woman, a woman whose life she had saved, and in her bitterness and anger, she told him about the life she had lived. At the beginning of the war, she had a lover, a German who was an officer in the Swiss Army.He abandoned her and her—'

'That's why she hated them.'

'Not exactly. She took money from him — in exchange for information.'

'A spy for the Germans? All that political stuff was a lie?'

'I don't know for certain. She told me that her work at the Café Martin was information-gathering, sniffing out double agents — plenty worked for both sides, any side for the money. It kept her safe — and, probably, her political friends. The poverty was true, too — she had to support her brother. Keep food on the table. And the fear under which people lived was all too real — never knowing whom you could trust. It's so hard now to condemn. Think of it as a matter of survival for her.'

'But why did she help Claire if she was working for the Germans?'

'I'm not sure that she was on any side, really. Giselle knew what the likes of Emil were capable of, and she did hate Emil, who was a nasty piece of work. He knew about her brother. It was her instinct to protect Claire from him. I think Giselle liked Claire — she liked her courage. It was impossible not to admire Claire. We all did. And Giselle thought it would be easy enough to get Claire out, but she hadn't reckoned on von Rahn Nicholl. He was more important than Emil — friends in high places. Giselle had to leave. But in saving Claire she put her brother and the child in danger, which is why I think he was shot — the Swiss Army man must have known about him. Someone had to pay for von Rahn Nicholl's death.'

'I still don't understand her attitude towards me. What had I done? I was just a child.'

Ned looked at the fire for a few moments, but when he looked up and she saw the sadness in his eyes, she knew.

'The child,' she said, 'the German officer who abandoned her, but from whom she took money. You were going to say "her and her child" — she was my mother, wasn't she?'

'She was.'

Marie was stung into bitterness. 'She didn't want me — a reminder of her sins. What other lovers had she had? Oh, there was Emil, who was supposed to have forced her, and the Rue Belle Filles. Claire knew what that place was. Giselle was a prostitute — my mother. God, I never suspected. My father could have been anyone — any low-life visitor to the Café Martin.'

Ned tried to soften the matter. 'We don't know that, Marie — she only told me about the German officer.'

'But it's why Matthew loathed her. He must have realised what she was — pretending to be the lady of this house when all the while she was a traitor and a prostitute who abandoned her own child.'

The bald, angry words hung in the air. Ned understood Marie's anger and shock. He remembered his and Guy's conversation about the missing Giselle and her life at the Café Martin. They had not known who she really was. Ned had tried to dissuade Matthew without touching on the rumours he and Guy had discussed. It wouldn't have been fair on Giselle. The rumours might not have been true. But whatever Giselle's life had been, Matthew had been at fault, too. He had married her out of a sense of duty.

His grandfather had cautioned him against the marriage, but Matthew was so changed by Claire's death and what he had experienced at Givenchy, he had not listened to reason, and when his grandfather had died suddenly, that had made things worse. Matthew knew he had been wrong, and he had not really reconciled with his grandfather. More guilt was added to the grief and loss and sense of betrayal. But it was the child, he thought. He had been robbed of his, and Giselle had given hers away. She had never told him until the last frightful row which precipitated his suicide. Then it was too late. Marie had already been sent away.

'It wasn't just her fault, you know. Matthew wasn't fit to marry. He knew it was a mistake. He couldn't love her because she wasn't Claire, and Giselle told him about you to punish him. She had left her child for Claire's sake. She told him it was Claire's fault, and Matthew's, and Major Pelham's, and it was, in a way.'

'How can you defend her? She blamed everyone else, but I was her child, *hers*. She killed two men in cold blood, and she drove Matthew to suicide.'

Ned looked at her sadly. 'No, the war did that. The war ruined him, just as it ruined Giselle — and so many others. There's this —' Ned handed Marie a letter — 'I'll leave you to read it.'

'From her? You know what's in it?'

'She dictated it to me. It might help.'

Marie sat with the letter in her hand. She finished her sherry and waited until her anger subsided. She felt ashamed of her words to Uncle Ned. She had felt a surge of anger at Giselle. She wanted to lash out and she'd shouted at Ned. He was a good man and a wise one. It was the war, he had said. That war thirty years ago which still blighted lives. She thought of her husband, Geoffrey. He had come back from the last war. Outwardly unchanged, but he had been different. Graver, somehow. Sometimes lost in thought, but he wouldn't speak about it. He would rouse himself and he would hold her tight. She never doubted his love for her and the children, but there was something hidden. A secret self, she thought now, with knowledge of unspeakable things. Like her. She had a secret self — the self that she had never shared with her children. Geoffrey knew about her childhood — his love had healed her, but her children were not to be touched by the icy finger of the past. The past — a wound that had been opened to bleed again. A secret self. Like Matthew Riviere. Like Giselle Favre.

Suddenly decisive, she opened the letter. It took very little time to read it, but Giselle had never wasted words.

You will know my story now. I am dying. It is too late to make amends for what I did to you. I cannot forgive myself. I do not expect that you can forgive me, but I hope you will accept this house and the money I have left you, and that it will do some good for your children who need only know that I was an old aunt you never saw. I have no right to call them grandchildren, but I have looked at your photographs very often and wished things could have been different. However, the past and our deeds there cannot be changed nor excused. I did what I did and have paid my price. I am sorry that you had to pay a price, too.

I wish you well, Marie.

Giselle Favre

How like her, Marie thought, looking at the neat, precise writing on the page. Black and white. No excuses, but there was that hint of regret. Giselle had looked at the photographs and wished that things had been different. Marie thought of those photographs — a happy family on the beach, a picnic in the sun, cricket in the back garden, a Christmas tree surrounded by presents, a child with silver-blonde hair sitting on a swing. Each child growing taller as the years went by.

The past. Her own childhood, bewildering and lonely, then Geoffrey and the children to fill up the spaces so that she could leave that emptiness behind. Suppose she had not met Geoffrey, suppose she had been alone in a loveless, childless marriage like Giselle. Suppose she had done unspeakable things that could not be changed.

The past and our deeds there cannot be changed nor excused. Such bleak words. Giselle's ruthless judgement on herself. There was an apology, too. The words were spare, but Giselle had meant them, not expecting forgiveness, and she had tried to atone by leaving her grandchildren this house. Marie felt the tears well up and let them come unchecked.

When she was calm, she folded the letter and put it in her pocket. She put on her coat and went out to find Uncle Ned smoking his pipe on the terrace. She put her arm through his. He saw that she was not ready to speak yet, and he led her down the steps and towards the woods.

When they were looking down at Treasonfield, Marie spoke at last. 'She wrote that the past cannot be changed or excused. She accepted what she had done and the price she paid. There's courage in that, and she didn't ask for anything — not for forgiveness. She didn't think she deserved it.'

'Did she?'

'From me? It's hard. I felt pity and terror when I listened to it all, and admiration for her, as if she were the heroine of a story, but I didn't know those last things — that last thing. She was my mother. I don't know how to feel about that, but if I think of her as she was then — just a girl, not much older than my daughter, who has been loved and protected and was too young to understand the last war, then I can understand that young Giselle. You've made me see it all. Such a vast, incomprehensible thing in which her actions were dictated by unseen forces. Unimaginable circumstances. And she saved Claire. But I remember her coldness, her rejection — I don't know, Uncle Ned…'

'It's too soon, I know. We can never know it all and we'll never understand it all — that's the lesson, I suppose, learning to accept that the past cannot be changed, and to reflect that we cannot know what we would have done then. It's what we do now that counts. You'll take your legacy for your children's future?'

'I will, and I'll remember what you have taught me, and what you did for me all those years ago when I was a child. We won't lose touch again.'

'Home,' Ned said, 'home to your husband and children. That's where you should be.'

Marie smiled at him. 'You're right. I don't belong here. I won't come back to Hawthorn Park. Let someone else have it.'

After Marie had gone, Ned packed his bag and bade farewell to Mrs Punch. He would never come back. The solicitor would handle the sale. A new family, he hoped, and a new life for Hawthorn Park. And, he reflected, Treasonfield would one day be gone, just a few stones lost in the encroaching woods, covered by those ferns where Rudolph Schmidt had hidden, watching Matthew Riviere and wondering if he should kill him. No one would remember the foreigners who were once tenants there decades ago. A stranger might stand in the wind-scoured churchyard and contemplate a moss-covered gravestone and wonder about Captain Matthew Riviere, MC, and his wife, Claire, killed in action in 1918, and the stranger might think for a moment about a long-ago war and the waste of it, the pity of it. Then they would pass on into their own future.

As Ned walked away, the past was with him, a dark companion of the shadows, walking with him always. Some words came back to him, something he'd read years ago by a soldier-poet. Cropper, that's who it was, a poet in the making. Matthew's devoted lieutenant, killed at Givenchy. Ned had felt those words to be true. They were true now. *For us there can be no real forgetting.*

HISTORICAL NOTES

The idea for this book came from an old wooden sign attached to a gate at the side of the road between Kirkby Lonsdale and Sedbergh. The sign indicated a place called 'Treasonfield'. Beyond the gate there is a path leading to some light industrial buildings. The sign has disappeared now, but it stayed in my mind. Naturally I wondered how this land had got its curious name. I wondered if there was a story there — a story of betrayal, star-crossed lovers, a family divided, or gunpowder, treason and plot. According to local history, one Antony Garnet, a catholic, who restored the Castle Dairy in Kendal, was a relative of the catholic priest Henry Garnet who was linked to the Gunpowder Plot. That was a possibility.

However, in the course of my research into World War I, I came across information about the Military Intelligence Branch at British General Headquarters in Montreuil. I abandoned the seventeenth century and stayed in World War I. The job of the Intelligence Branch was to collect and collate intelligence information from all over Europe, including the networks in France and Belgium such as La Dame Blanche in which served 278 women — housewives, nurse, midwives and teachers. This fascinating information led me to the book, *Women in Intelligence* by Helen Fry and gave me the idea of creating a female spy. And so my courageous ambulance driver, Claire Mallory, is drawn into the spying game with her fiancée, Matthew Riviere, who once lived at Treasonfield with his stepfather, a wealthy man of German descent whose Swiss wife has returned to Geneva. Claire is sent to Geneva and Matthew back to Treasonfield. Helen Fry's book pays tribute to the thousands of women who played a part in intelligence work, including the secretaries, the coders, and those in Europe who worked behind enemy lines in the greatest danger.

Switzerland was neutral in World War I and became a meeting place for secret agents of every nationality. The British Secret Service set up a network in Geneva and in Annemasse, and British GHQ set up their own networks, one including the author, Somerset Maugham, who recruited spies in Geneva. The British agents used roles as businessmen or commercial travellers as their cover, as does Mr Sutton in the novel. It is true that some of the spies recruited were double agents, as the Germans were active in Switzerland, too, and there were plenty of seedy cafes where the low-life spies did their deals.

The Secret History of MI6 by Keith Jefferey gave me enough information to write several books and led me into the labyrinth of the British Secret Service departments, many of which changed their titles as the war progressed. 'C', Commander Mansfield Smith-Cumming, was the first head of what was called the Secret Service Bureau in 1909. By 1913, the Bureau was recruiting agents in Europe, including women, and seeking out spies in Britain, including the astonishing von Gessler who could be recognised anywhere, as he had four rows of teeth — how he managed as a spy, I cannot imagine.

Cumming's Secret Service Bureau became MI1(c), part of MI1 section of the War Office, which included MI1b (cryptography) and many other Ms; another branch of the War Office, MO5, eventually became MI5. MI6 started as the Secret Intelligence Service dealing with overseas networks; MI5 was the home service and worked with the police in Special Branch. As far back as 1903, the head of Special Branch had been recruited by the Directorate of Military Operations to investigate German espionage in Britain. There were so many initials and sections in London and so many changes, and since I was concerned with military intelligence at GHQ in France, I have used the London Bureau as an umbrella term to make it easier for readers — and for me!

I also had to ask myself if there could have been German spies at Treasonfield. According to Sir John Lonsdale, M.P., in 1915, there was 'an extensive conspiracy carried out by German agents' in England. Was there, indeed? And, if so, were there any in Westmorland? I tried Westmorland newspapers, but no one was spying in the far reaches of Westmorland, though *The Lakes Herald* reported on the discovery of a blotter which would remove the traces of writing on blotting paper so that the would-be spy, heavily disguised as a hotel chambermaid, could not read what her target had written to the Allies. But there was a spy in Morecambe and that's not far away, I thought, and there was a spy ring in Sunderland early in the war and at least one in Manchester. They were coming closer.

An article in the *Sheffield Independent* observed sagely that 'the cleverest and most dangerous spies are likely to be the last detected'. I discovered the story of the spy William Brown, who had been born in Wales in 1870, whose parents had been German. Brown had been manager of the Krupp's Chemical Works in Shoreham. Krupp — a German company. William Brown had also worked as chief draughtsman for Macdonald Gibbs, Engineers to the War Office — what secrets did he obtain? And he wasn't the only spy of German descent found to have infiltrated munitions companies. Thus, I had a basis for the story of Willy Lang, who is of German descent and has financial interests in Germany and Switzerland.

The proposed raid on Zeebrugge is very well documented. The British intended to sink their observation ships at the entrance to the canal in order to prevent German vessels from leaving port. Zeebrugge was used by the German Navy as a base for U-boats and therefore a threat to Allied control of the North Sea and English Channel. The intention was to land one thousand troops on the breakwater. It was highly secret, but on 6th February, 1918, orders were issued for a battalion to be raised at Deal for one specific operation, and later in the month, an appeal went out for volunteers for a special operation. HMS *Vindictive* was equipped at Chatham, and submarines converted in Plymouth. It seemed possible that my German spy posing as a British Intelligence officer might get to know about it. The raid was intended for March, then April, but was called off because of bad weather. It eventually took place on 23rd April, but it was not a success.

King George V did visit Field Marshall Haig at Chateau de Beaurepaire and those visits were not always made public until the king was in France. However, there is no evidence of an assassination plot against the king. There might have been, but I doubt that it would have been publicised. In *The Secret History of MI6*, Keith Jeffery refers to missing papers and gaps in handwritten diaries. The historical novelist is at liberty to ponder what information may be missing or never recorded, and in those gaps create a story. This is what I have done.

A NOTE TO THE READER

Dear Reader,

One of the most fascinating aspects of the research for this novel was the discovery of the methods the spies used in their trade, some of which had not really changed since the days of Francis Walsingham and Queen Elizabeth I. Invisible ink comes to mind. Mary, Queen of Scots, no stranger to the spying game, had a recipe for secret ink. She advocated alum dissolved in water, the solution to be made twenty-four hours before the writing was needed. The recipient should dip the paper into water and the message would be revealed. Walsingham favoured coal dust to uncover secret writing in milk. He recruited an expert in secret writing to decipher letters between the gunpowder plotters. That information might have been useful if I had stuck to the seventeenth century.

I'll bet many of you have tried the lemon juice method, scorching the paper before the fire when trying to reveal the secret message. This method of secret writing is not new; lemon juice was first used in Italy in the sixteenth century. During WWI, Commander Mansfield Smith-Cumming, first head of what was called the Secret service Bureau enlisted scientists to try to come up with the perfect secret ink. German agents made invisible ink by soaking a piece of clothing in the necessary chemicals. The Secret Service scientist, Thomas Merton, invented a method of secret writing on glass with a silver point. The writing would be invisible but could be made visible with a solution of chemicals — assuming that the spy had access to silver nitrate, citric acid, acetic acid and the recipe.

Walsingham used codebreakers, but cryptology dates back to the seventh century BC in the Arab world. The Romans used the most famous technique, which is the substitution alphabet where a substitute letter is chosen by moving along the alphabet by a certain number of degrees, so, for example, 'a' becomes 'd' if the coder uses a four-degree shift.

Somerset Maugham spent time as a secret agent, running a spy network in Geneva in World War I, and he wrote about his experiences in his short stories about the secret agent, Ashenden. Maugham's code was a numerical code in two parts, one contained in a book, and one given to him on a sheet of paper which he memorised. Ashenden receives secret messages from an old peasant woman who sells butter and eggs at a market. I included the story of the washerwoman who used her laundry on the line to send messages to the Germans. This is a true story, as is the story of codes worked into knitting. Numerical codes were part of the repertoire of the Tudors and Stuarts. James I's daughter Elizabeth was a skilled cryptographer and is known to have used a number code.

The washerwoman is astonishing enough, but there were all sorts of extraordinary people in the spying world — far too extraordinary to fit in my novel. I don't think you would have believed in the spy with four rows of teeth. There were those who had been actors in their previous lives — very useful training, I imagine. There was a man who had worked for *Tatler* before the war, writing about celebrities — useful contacts, I suppose. And there was the wealthy man who brought 'stage beauties' to parties, and the man who had been seduced by a friend of Oscar Wilde. The German spy, Otto Kruger, was a hairdresser in Wales. And it is true that one of the military intelligence men at Folkstone was married to a morphine addict. He had served a jail sentence for fraud, too

— something to do with a pearl necklace. Blackmail and drugs, both very juicy ingredients for a spy novel.

The cigar-smoking Lady Hambro was head of Room 40, the centre of Naval Intelligence operations during the war. Room 40 was staffed by women, including skilled cryptographers engaged in breaking enemy codes and cyphers. I came across Mata Hari, too, an erotic dancer and double agent, who was executed by the French in 1917, and in Geneva there was the so-called 'Lady of the Camellias', a beautiful American spy who passed information to the Germans.

Maugham's spying Baroness von Higgins — grandfather, a Yorkshire stable boy who married an arch-duchess — is not entirely fictitious. Geneva was full of aristocrats or pretend ones who had a living to make, and Maugham's 'Hairless Mexican' and his Indian spy who poisoned himself are no more incredible than von Gessler and his teeth. And neither is as colourful as the real-life Major HLB, who claimed that he had been Chief of Secret Police in Bolivia and that he had a Peruvian ring which contained an Indian poison that could fell a man in three seconds. Poison crops up in the history of spying and poison rings were not uncommon. The ring had a secret compartment meant for the hair of a loved one, but this was handy for secreting therein a piece of snakeskin soaked in the juice of deadly nightshade — though what the recipient was meant to do with the snakeskin, I didn't discover. Perhaps touching it was enough.

Referred to only as 'HLB', the major's name is not known. In World War I, the spies were known by their country of operation, so B for Belgium, D for Denmark and so on. However, there was a Scandinavian agent known — obviously — as 'Norseman'. Cumming had dealings with a spy, codename 'Ruffian'. Cumming's agent, Hector Bywater, was known facetiously as 'H2O', and there was a spy named 'Horse', based in Maastricht. Aliases were not new, of course. One of the spies belonging to Queen Elizabeth's Lord Burleigh was known as 'Fidelis'. He intercepted letters from a Lady Rich in which she referred to the Queen as 'Venus' and James VI as 'Victor'.

I think I might manage the substitution cipher, and I do rather like Leon Battista Alberti's fifteenth-century cipher wheel, an ingenious device where the substitute letter is chosen by the turn of two dials, each of which has letters inscribed on its circumference, but his polyalphabetic cipher looks a bit too complicated. Nevertheless, should MI5 or 6 come calling, I'm ready to join the spooks. I do now know the difference between a cipher and a code and could make use of both together if needed.

Reviews are very important to writers, so it would be great if you could spare the time to post a review on **Amazon** and **Goodreads**. Readers can connect with me online, on **Facebook (JCBriggsBooks)**, **Twitter (@JeanCBriggs)**, and you can find out more about the books and Charles Dickens via my website, **jcbriggsbooks.com**, where you will find Mr Dickens's A–Z of murder — all cases of murder to which I found a Dickens connection.

Thank you!

Jean Briggs

Sapere Books is an exciting new publisher of brilliant fiction and popular history.

To find out more about our latest releases and our monthly bargain books visit our website: **saperebooks.com**

Printed in Great Britain
by Amazon